I0645049

Man in the Woods

How could an old, faded, falling down, *For Sale* sign on a deserted country road in the western part of Maine create such havoc in my life? People disappeared, without a trace, and more interestingly, no one looked for them. People in the nearby small towns were totally spooked by the property. They wouldn't go there to investigate. The foreclosing banker, who posted it for sale, wouldn't show it. The more involved I became, the level of danger increased. The threat was not just to me personally, but involved many other innocent folks. If I'd gotten even a hint, or the slightest warning, of the percentage of danger I would eventually encounter, I would never have made that fateful inquiry. Hindsight is a good thing, but its timing stinks.

What They Are Saying About

Man in the Woods

If this is as exciting as your first book, *The Boat*, hurry up and get me a copy.

John Hardy

I couldn't put the first book you wrote down; now I can't wait for this one in print.

Lynn Finn

Please hurry with this publication. I need more excitement in my life.

Barb Fox

Man in the Woods

H. Wakefield

A Wings ePress, Inc.

Mystery Novel

Wings ePress, Inc.

Edited by: Jeanne Smith
Copy Edited by: Christie Kraemer
Executive Editor: Jeanne Smith
Cover Artist: Richard Stroud

All rights reserved

Names, characters and incidents depicted in this book are products of the author's imagination or are used fictitiously. Any resemblance to actual events, locales, organizations, or persons, living or dead, is entirely coincidental and beyond the intent of the author or the publisher.

No part of this book may be reproduced or transmitted in any form or by any means, electronic or mechanical, including photocopying, recording, or by any information storage and retrieval system, without permission in writing from the publisher.

Wings ePress Books
www.books-by-wings-epress.com

Copyright © 2017 by H. Wakefield
ISBN 978-1-61309-688-8

Published In the United States Of America

Wings ePress Inc.
3000 N. Rock Road
Newton, KS 67114

Dedication

To all the folks who assisted me with information while supporting me with their appreciation for my efforts, especially Wings and its great staff.

Prologue

How could an old, faded, falling down, *For Sale* sign on a deserted country road in the western part of Maine create such havoc in my life? People disappeared, without a trace, and more interestingly, no one looked for them. People in the nearby small towns were totally spooked by the property. They wouldn't go there to investigate. The foreclosing banker, who posted it for sale, wouldn't show it. The more involved I became, the level of danger increased. The threat was not just to me personally, but involved many other innocent folks. If I'd gotten even a hint, or the slightest warning, of the percentage of danger I would eventually encounter, I would never have made that fateful inquiry. Hindsight is a good thing, but its timing stinks.

One

At the end of a long, cold, very snowy, winter in Maine. I was anxious to find a cure for the cabin fever and associated blues that always come at that time of the year. I never dealt well with confinement for extended periods, with only shoveling and snow blowing for exercise. Miss Joy, my small Australian Shepherd, and I were ready for an adventure.

It had not only been a long dreary winter, but there was nothing but bad news upon bad news. It seemed like the whole country had gone from bad to worse with no end in sight.

Real and personal unrest began, for me, with the epidemic of the drug culture, which seemingly engulfed every aspect of our existence throughout the State of Maine and elsewhere. Recently, along with the seemingly ever present, home invasions committed by people searching for drugs or property to steal to sell for drugs, there were more situations of extreme violence. The deaths from overdoses were astronomical. The age range for these deaths ranged from very young to older people. It seemed there were no limits for age or behavior. I became increasingly distraught with the state of our society.

Point made with the rape and beating of a dear elderly neighbor woman. Most of these crimes were being committed against the elderly and mostly defenseless people. I found it abhorrent. That was my mind set at the end of winter when the melting snow began showing some bare ground.

I took my small motor home and headed north for the least inhabited part of our state. My thinking was, with fewer people, there would be less crime and more peace and quiet.

By way of introduction: I'm a short, but rugged, woman who enjoys outdoor work and sports. I'm bordering on getting older, but still spry enough to get into trouble, even when I don't go looking for it. I sometimes think I have a massive bull's-eye on my back. Admittedly, I most often am not where most folks my age should be, or engaging in some of the antics I choose to undertake. Being honest, I have three noticeable faults I admit to: I have an over-abundance of curiosity, I always drink creamer in my second cup of morning coffee, and I enjoy one glass of wine each evening before or with dinner.

I didn't know why, or what, I was looking for. Perhaps just some peace, and to find some sense of normalcy, or the reassurance it still existed. I realized most folks my age had come to the same conclusion at some time during their lives.

I'd lived in many communities within the state of Maine over the course of my years. It wasn't because I was a drifter; I always carried a heavy financial burden. Being a single woman, raising three children alone required me to remain out of the *low-need-achiever-group.* I'd been the sole supporter for my children, and I'd managed to accomplish that task adequately. It also required working more than one job at a time. Thankfully, God had given me an abundant supply of energy when He created me.

Having learned early in adulthood, my forte was home renovations and rejuvenating failing business ventures. I bought, renovated, and sold houses and, sometimes, a business or two while holding a full-time position. In our current era, folks talk often about 'flipping' houses; a term I find offensive and strange. I have renovated, removed, and rebuilt homes, but never turned one upside down.

My children are grown and no longer require my assistance financially. My only responsibility is Miss Joy, who shares my home and manages me.

I still enjoyed the lifestyle I'd known for so many years. I continued to buy and sell, enjoying the labor along with the end reward. I just wasn't as driven, so I could pick and choose which projects I really wanted to do.

We lived in a modest home close to a mid-sized city with no mortgage, allowing me the freedom to explore and roam.

~ * ~

The day began as any ordinary day when traveling with the camper. For most of my adult-life, which is pushing the over-sixty status, I'd owned some form of recreational vehicle. I was fortunate enough, at my age, to still be able to wander at will when, and if, I pleased. Lately, I wanted less to travel, being more interested in staying put in one area.

My ideal location would've been on a lake, a river, or the ocean. Then, I would park the camper, explore the area, or kayak whatever body of water I wanted. I liked to hunt and fish, both salt and fresh water, so any of those would be an added bonus.

I had often fantasized what the ideal location would look like. None being even remotely realistic, I was completely aware of my lack of reality regarding this matter.

Two

I was driving up through the state of Maine on a whim, thinking I would go toward Houlton in Aroostook County, and then make the loop down to the coast. I loved the Downeast coastal area.

Instead, I exited the interstate and wandered more westerly than planned. The country was pretty, remote, and sparsely populated. I had very little knowledge of the rivers, lakes, or roads up in the northwestern area of the state.

My parents had lived in this area when they birthed me. We'd moved to an island on the coast while I was a very young child during the beginning of the Second World War. I think this explained my love for the coast and the ocean.

Driving along a secondary road, following what I guessed to be a river, I spotted a faded, slightly askew, *For Sale* sign. It was stuck at the end of a dirt camp-road. Old, *For Sale* signs, are a tease to me because either someone had given up on ever selling, or it would be a foreclosed property. They are both my favorite types of projects.

The road looked wide enough to allow my rig to enter. However, many years of driving this type of vehicle taught me to be prudent and distrustful of *just the entrance*. If I drove in and couldn't find a space to turn around, I needed to be an excellent backer-upper.

I pulled ahead on the main road, found a wider spot to park, took my dog, Miss Joy, and walked back to the driveway displaying the sign. The sign had been there for a long time. It was faded, tilted back, and covered with dirt.

There wasn't any description of what was for sale, only a faded telephone number with a name, Jeff Smart. I jotted down the information.

I didn't have a pressing agenda, so I thought we'd take a stroll down the drive to see what was there. We walked in on a good section of dirt drive for a short distance. Then we encountered a boggy patch with alders growing up to the sides of the road. Water flowed across the road.

I could see ahead to what appeared to be a clearing. I was in that far, so I decided to continue. I picked up my dog and navigated the wet places on stones at the side of the road.

I managed to get across with only a small amount of water in my sneakers. I'm always up for an adventure… after all, no journey, no discovery. We walked on into the clearing.

The river was visible off to my right. It seemed fairly wide and calm. My guess was it would be deep as well.

On the left, there was an old field overgrown with brush. It was obvious nobody lived there.

I was interested to see what the shoreline looked like. We walked down the remainder of the drive; there hadn't been any repairs preformed on the drive for a long time as manifested by the growth of grass in the center.

The riverbank on the shore wasn't too steep; however, it appeared to be sufficient to stop any flooding during spring thaws. I saw no evidence of where debris had washed up onto the field.

As I walked farther, I noticed a section where the bank sloped down to the water. There was a very nice, sandy beach area with no rocks.

What a great place to launch the kayak and swim! Great, I liked that aspect of the property already. When I turned back from the shore, I spotted what looked to be an old out-building. I wanted a closer inspection, so we meandered up.

In the process, we spooked some partridges, setting them to flight, always a fun distraction. I loved to bird hunt.

As I neared the structure, it looked like perhaps it was a small barn with rough-cut board and batten siding. This was *not* an old building.

Beyond the barn a short distance off to the right, I spotted a small log cabin. It appeared to be in fair shape. It had a metal roof with a good pitch, a small, once screened-porch with large glass windows on the first floor and elongated triangle windows in what I guessed would be a loft space. What a nice setting for the cabin! The smell of pine and fir trees just added to the picture. I could imagine it with winter snow settling softly, creating a Currier and Ives scene.

I knew I shouldn't, but I did anyhow…I peeked in the windows. There was a large stone chimney with a Franklin-style stove attached for heat and ambiance and furniture in the room.

I looked into what I assumed was the kitchen. I could see an old cook stove and the partial end view of a sink-cabinet.

I checked for wires to see if there was electricity, but didn't notice any.

We walked around the cabin and realized it also was not old. It had been stick-built with the log siding applied to the exterior, giving it the appearance of a log home. The house sat on either a partial basement, or a substantial frost wall. It was larger than I first thought.

At one time, someone had cleared a nice back yard area with an outdoor fireplace built out of river stone. There was a very large propane tank at the back of the yard.

Three

I was impressed by what I'd seen.

Working with real estate was enjoyable for me; I'd bought and sold properties for years. It was worth the time it would take to make a call and gather the information.

We walked back to the camper where I tried the call on my cell phone. There wasn't much of a signal, so I waited until I was in a better reception area and placed the call again. It was a bank, and, yes, they could connect me to Mr. Smart… please hold.

When Mr. Smart answered, I introduced myself, "Good afternoon, Mr. Smart. This is Nettie Small. I'm calling about a small cabin in the woods by the river. I wonder if you could provide me with some information regarding the property, along with the asking price."

I received an immediate chuckle. His reply was simple, "The bank owns the property. What are you willing to offer for it?" The conversation was short-and-sweet to say the least.

"First of all, how much land is involved? Is the parcel of land leased or owned outright? Does the property have any systems in place? I noticed it doesn't appear to have electricity. Is there a well, septic system? Is it a foreclosure? What kind of deed will transfer the property? What is the amount of the taxes? Are there any liens against this parcel?"

There were no chuckles this time, just a dead silence. Finally, he spoke. "I would be happy to disclose to you any, and all, information I have. Can you come to my office?"

I assured him I could, providing he would supply me with directions from my present location. He did. The information I received regarding the office was that it belonged to a tiny bank in an adjacent town.

I figured it would be worth my time to talk with him about the property.

Mr. Smart wasn't what I anticipated for a banker in a very rural area. He was dressed in jeans, a plaid shirt open at the neck with the sleeves rolled up. He was about my age, give or take, but in his sixties. His hair and mustache were graying; he wore wire-rimmed glasses. When he stood, he was also taller than I'd expected, being well over six feet and muscular. He wasn't handsome, but pleasant looking, with a twinkle in his dark brown eyes.

He pulled out a folder from his file cabinet and placed it on top of his desk.

When he spoke, his voice was quiet and calm but with a lot of resonance. "Before we go into any depth regarding the property, I want to give you some history about it; as I know it. The previous owner was a man who came here from out of state somewhere. I can't recall just where, at the moment, or if I ever knew. From the title search, I know he bought the land outright, and built the structures there. He did this over a period of a few years. He was reclusive, so not well known here in town. Truthfully, I never met the man.

"Back three years ago a woman, I guessed also from out of state, came into the bank and told me she was his wife. She stated he'd deeded the property to her. She wanted to secure a mortgage on the property as they were going to make it into a year-round home.

"At that time, I went out to appraise the property. The value of the property by far exceeded the amount of the loan requested. I made her the loan and held the mortgage in-house because it's our policy on a seasonal place, or if the mortgage is below a certain dollar amount.

"Long story short, she took the money and never made any loan payments. The woman disappeared. Moreover, to my knowledge, nobody has ever seen her or him again. Beyond that, I can't tell you a thing.

"I did all the advertising and paper-work necessary to legally sell it as a foreclosure.

"As far as I know the property has been vacant for over three years. I have no idea of the present condition. If you would like you can go out, enter, and inspect the buildings, I do have keys."

My immediate impression was Mr. Smart seemed *very* reluctant to go out and show the property. Being honest, this fact intrigued me.

When I inquired if he didn't like the property or if there were other circumstances limiting his interest in the parcel, he merely shrugged.

Finally, he spoke. "To be honest with you, I'm not comfortable out there. I shouldn't tell you that, but it's true. I've been out there three times. Each time I left the property with a great feeling of unrest. I know it sounds ridiculous. I've lived here all my life. I also hunt, fish, snowshoe, and snowmobile without any reservations.

"Other folks who've gone out there came back and expressed the same feelings. At one point, I had the property sold and figured I'd never have to deal with it again. We were set to close the next day. When I came in to work on the day of the closing, the buyer was waiting. He came into my office, demanded the return of his deposit, and left in a huff without ever explaining the issue.

"If you would like, you are more than welcome to go out there with your camper and stay for a few days to see if the parcel will work for you"

I sat pondering the information. I've purchased many homes, open parcels of land, and camps over the years. I'd never encountered anything like this.

I know quite often, properties can and sometimes do, get hung up on local folk lore, such as it is. I've always been a calm person, looked for the *why*, more than the *what*, in any given set of circumstances; it would be no different with this.

My interest was in overdrive, not only for the property, but also for the folks who'd disappeared, seemingly without a trace. The fact nobody bothered to look for them was more than a little strange.

Before I went back out to the property, I would do some diligence in the little village. I was never a person who spooked easily. I believed in logic.

Mr. Smart was waiting for my answer. My reply was simple. "I will take the keys and the offer to park out there for a couple of days.

"Let's discuss the important information. I need to know the dollar amount the bank is hoping to recover from the sale. It may be so far out of my reach I wouldn't even be interested."

He studied me closely then consulted the folder, on his desk before answering. "The bank would like to, at least, get the amount of money we lent along with the taxes and cost of advertising paid."

I nodded. "I have no idea of the amount of the loan or the amount of the taxes, so sadly your answer has no relevance to me. Could you perhaps stop being a banker and let's talk buyer/seller language?"

I received a chuckle, "Fair enough. I loaned twenty-five thousand dollars and the total tax amount was twelve hundred. The bank will absorb the other costs.

"There is a fair amount of harvestable timber on the parcel. If my memory serves me correctly, there is also over twenty-five hundred feet of shore frontage. I think it is priced way below what it would appraise for."

My turn to chuckle. "Have you ever had anyone appraise it?"

He looked at me as if I'd just sworn at a lawn-party for old folks. "I couldn't get anyone to even go out there, let alone stay long enough to measure or photograph the place. The handyman I hired to go out and put the padlocks on the doors told me to never call him again if it involved going back out there."

"Can I ask what it is that spooks folks so much? Do you know? Did you ask?"

He could see the probability of the sale floating away. I could see it in his expression. However, he seemed to feel duty-bound to inform me of the situation. On the other hand, he wanted it off his books immediately. "No, I don't know. When I asked folks, they just told me it was an uncomfortable feeling, and they didn't like it. I understood what they meant. It was how I felt each time I was there. I never saw or heard anything out of the way, but something was not *right*.

"I hope I haven't spooked you to the extent you're no longer interested. I'd treat you right on the price and assist you in any way I could, if you decided to buy."

I took the keys with the promise I'd go investigate the property. I had already walked around the buildings and looked at some of the interior through the windows. I was interested. I needed to do a little investigative work before I drove back out to the land.

Four

I stopped at Nick's garage and introduced myself. "Hi, I'm Nettie Small. Mr. Smart told me you're the person who built the road into the parcel of land for sale out on the river. I wonder if you could give me some information regarding the job. I'd also appreciate any insight you might have regarding the person you worked for."

He stood watching me while I delivered the request without any change of expression showing on his face or in his eyes.

Nick was a man in his early forties, of average height, dark haired with hazel eyes and great laugh-lines. His welcoming smile invited honest conversation. When he answered, he spoke pleasantly. "I did build the road. You're right; it has been a long time. There were no callbacks for repairs, so I guessed it held up okay. The man I built it for came to see me one day, same as you're doing. He told me what he wanted. I gave him a price and told him how soon I could complete it. He gave me a nod, told me to do it, and he'd pay me when I was finished. I built the road. He paid me. End of the story."

Nick owned his own garage, which housed his equipment. He had an assortment of logging and utility trucks for servicing equipment. There were other pieces of equipment including a dozer, a couple of front-end loaders, and a skidder. His equipment appeared to be in good repair.

"Are you thinking about buying the place? You do understand nobody from this area will go out there. I hope Jeff Smart has given you the facts.

"I've no idea what happened out there. I met him the time he came here and again when I finished. We didn't exchange conversations other than for me to inquire if he was satisfied. He told me he was and paid me in cash.

"Otherwise I knew nothing about the man. You might check with the lumber company. He bought all his lumber from Brad Corey down at the mill. Is there anything else I can do for you?"

"Yes, there is, as a matter of fact. I'll need to have you come and repair the road. It seemed to be in good shape with the exception of the area in the alder swamp. Was there a culvert there? The water was over the road and I wasn't sure how deep it was. I parked the motor home and walked in. I'm going out there this afternoon and will be staying on the property for a couple of days. I'd like to know what you would charge to fix the road, and when you could do it. That is, if you're interested."

He smiled, "I don't have any problem going out to check the road. After checking it, I could give you an idea of what it would cost, along with the time frame to complete the work.

"When would you be out there? If I were you, I'd wait until I checked it out with my big truck before you drive in with the camper." He smiled then added, "I also tow vehicles."

"Are you going down to the lumber yard? If you are, I'll take a run out there right now. When you finish, stop back. I can tell you if you could drive in to the lot before I fix the road. Would that work for you?"

"Super. If I don't see your truck back here, I'll know the spook either sunk it or scared it to death." We both laughed.

My trip to the lumber store was interesting. I found Brad Corey, the owner. He was a man in his late sixties, rugged, somewhat portly with a scruffy beard and bright blue eyes. He was dressed in dungarees held up by suspenders resembling wide measuring tapes. He wore a plaid flannel shirt open at the neck with the sleeves rolled up. He was a worker.

I introduced myself and explained my intention to investigate purchasing the property on the river.

I asked him if he could, or would; give me any insight into the previous owner. As I spoke to him, nothing in his demeanor changed. Not until I asked for information about the owner. His expression became *very* guarded. Hummm. *I wonder what triggered the change.*

He answered my inquiries in what seemed a forthright, but somewhat stilted, manner. "The man who owned the property bought most, if not all, of his lumber and supplies from me. I didn't know him other than he came in with a list for me to fill. I'd gather the supplies, and he would return with his truck, load it, pay me, and leave. He always paid me in cash. Never ran a bill.

"He knew exactly what he wanted, including the quality and the quantity. I did quite a bit of custom sawing for him.

"I guessed he liked my work because he never discussed it one way or the other, and he kept coming back.

"I called him Pete because when he told me his name, it was something sounding like Peter, but different. Pete seemed to work for both of us. He was a man in his late fifties or early sixties, healthy, strong, polite, and very reserved. As I said, we *never* had a conversation.

"I also recall each time he came he had his dog with him. It was the largest dog I'd ever seen. The animal was fierce looking, and homely as a stick-fence. The dog never got out of the truck. It would sit there looking out through the open window. If that dog had gotten out of his vehicle, I wasn't going to be standing there. I can't recall what he called the dog. It wasn't a usual name for an animal.

"I hope you know what you're getting into out there. It's isolated; none of the locals would go out there if the place were on fire. I hope you understand that."

"I do; however, not one person can tell me why, or what the problem is.

"I find it peculiar nobody even bothered to make any inquiries as to what happened to the people involved. Didn't you find it odd?"

He shook his head. "Nope, not out here. When folks come from *away,* they don't want everyone knowing about his or her business. That's the reason they moved here. We respect those wishes even if we never understand them. We would do the same for you if you came here to live or vacation or whatever.

"Had you planned to drive the motor home into the property? If you are, you'd best call on Nick up at the garage to see if the road will take it. Be too bad to bury it in the swamp out there."

I thanked him for his assistance and concerns and assured him I had already checked with Nick regarding the road.

His answer was to smile and nod. "You might make this work. Good luck and feel free to call me if you need lumber or supplies."

I thanked him and headed back to the garage to see if Nick had returned from his inspection of the road.

I drove back to Nick's garage and spotted his truck sitting in the yard. I assumed he'd returned without any incidents.

When I drove in, he walked over to the camper with a big kid-like grin on his face. "I guess I was a better road-builder than I gave myself credit for. I drove in, turned the truck around, and drove back out. The base is still solid, but it does need to have the culvert replaced. When I installed it, I used a metal one; I would replace it with a fiber one. Then I'd redress the top of the roadbed with new gravel.

"You can get in there with the camper. Remember, if you get stuck, call me. I'll tow you out for free."

I drove away laughing after I told him I would let him know when, and if, I completed the sale. I liked him. I would enjoy doing business with both him and Brad Corey.

Five

I had everything I needed to go out to the lot and camp. It was time to go exploring. I was excited to begin a new adventure.

I was anxious to see what the inside of the house looked like. The barn would be a bonus building.

Miss Joy and I drove out to the driveway. I saw where Nick had driven in with his large ten-wheeler dump truck. It was a blessing for me because he had cleared out some of the low-hanging branches with his truck body. The branches would have brushed the sides of my camper. His truck had also been high enough I knew nothing would hit my air conditioner on the roof.

I drove slowly onto the drive and through the big puddle, coming out onto the other side into the field area. I planned to set the camper down by the beach so I could enjoy the water view and sunset.

With the camper parked, awning out, rug and chair in place, we were done. I would put the generator out later.

I started to walk up the slight incline to inspect the buildings. Then as an afterthought, I stepped back into the camper and pocketed my .38 Colt Detective Special. I always carry it with me when I'm on the road with the camper.

I'm not stupid enough to think a single woman, no matter the age, isn't a target for some idiot. I always try to err on the side of caution and, as jittery as these folks were about this place, I needed to pay attention. Most often, where there's smoke there *is* fire.

We walked up across the field to the cabin. I knew from my conversation with Brad, it had been hand-built by the owner. Knowing where the milled lumber came from gave it more personality. I enjoyed knowing the history of properties I bought.

I went to the back door where I'd seen the padlock on my first visit. The key fit; the lock turned easily. However, while unlocking the padlock I became acutely aware the hasp holding the padlock to the doorframe was too loose. I surmised there hadn't been any tampering with the hasp nor had anyone pried it loose. It had been unscrewed and left loose. I doubted anyone else would have given it a second thought.

My mind always gathers facts. It is a trait I appreciate and, at times, keeps me mostly out of harm's way.

When I bought either foreclosures or long abandoned properties, they always came with issues. I frequently encountered the old family still living there or perhaps even a squatter who had moved in. With the increase of homeless people, this was happening more often. They could be problematic, as they had no intention of leaving without a physical altercation with either a local law enforcement officer or me.

I was certain of one fact: no one ever left this home by his or her own free will. I was as certain as I was that God was still in Heaven.

If I moved here, even for summers, I would get myself a big dog. I loved Miss Joy, but she only weighed eighteen pounds, not much protection. I would say this: she was the best watchdog I ever owned. Her senses were so keen, I was never concerned someone could sneak up on me. After she alerted me to the danger, however, *I was on my own*.

We stepped into the kitchen. I stood quietly for a moment, listening and smelling. I'm a very sensory person with a nose like a bloodhound. The house didn't feel or smell as if it had been vacant for three years. It looked and smelled clean and fresh as if somebody had recently opened the windows and aired it out. It was a nice space with great cabinets. The woodworking, design, and artistry were outstanding. The stove was older, white enamel with wood burning on the front and three gas burners on the other end. It was clean and in great shape.

Wonders of wonders, there stood a copper hot water tank attached to the wood-fired portion of the stove. I couldn't understand why somebody hadn't stolen the tank. That, in itself, was a miracle and a mystery. Why they hadn't ransacked the place was beyond me. *Perhaps having an in-residence spook is a good thing.*

There was a small gas refrigerator. The counter tops were wooden. Perhaps they were maple, birch, or beech. Somebody had bleached and sanded them until they were nearly white. Then they sealed the wood with an acrylic gloss consisting of several layers. Truly, this was a labor of love.

As far as I could see, all the floors were wooden and sealed to perfection.

Off the kitchen was a bathroom. Interesting; there had to be a water source and septic system.

Beyond the bathroom was a large bedroom. The furniture appeared to have been handmade. It wasn't rough camp furniture, but hand crafted and quite lovely with intricate carvings on the headboard and drawer fronts. I was speechless.

I checked out the sliding door to the closet and found clothes hanging there. The clothing was all men's items, including a pair of dress shoes, slippers, and well-worn work boots. There wasn't any woman's clothing or shoes. Hummm...

Next, I explored the living room with the stone chimney. Other than the couch, a couple of leather chairs, and a large leather hassock, the room's furniture was also hand crafted with the same quality and artistic touch as the bedroom.

Wood was stacked in the carrier by the Franklin stove. A huge older oriental rug of good quality covered most of the floor.

I mounted the stairs to the loft area and found a bedroom set up there with another nice old oriental rug on the floor. The view from that space was panoramic, looking across the river to the mountains.

I re-locked the door, for what it was worth, with that lock. I would replace the locks as soon as I closed on the property.

I walked out behind the house to check the barn. From the exterior, it resembled the same craft and skills used with the building of the cabin.

Because it was getting late in the afternoon, I decided to delay exploring the interior of the barn until daylight the next day.

The dog and I returned to the camper to prepare dinner.

First, I would enjoy a glass of wine with a bit of cheese and crackers while watching the daylight fade behind the distant mountains. The reflection across the river was breathtaking as the sun was setting. It promised to be a beautiful sunset with the wispy clouds catching all the glorious colors.

We would have a nice moon and great star-shine being this far away from any artificial light. What a treat!

Early evening was always a special time of day for me, when the day-sounds cease, and the night-sounds begin.

Tonight, I didn't need to start the generator. I would just enjoy the quiet and fix dinner on the gas stove in the camper.

I'd never been a big outdoor fire person, unless there was a good safety zone around the blaze. I worried about stray sparks starting a fire in the woods or the camper awning.

I was smart and woods-savvy enough to know I needed to take some precautions for the first night's stay. I've enjoyed a lot of wilderness camping, so I'm not a stranger to securing my campsite.

I had parked the camper on a spot that was all sandy. Once it was dark, I would take a bush and rake the area to erase my footprints. In the morning, if there had been a visit by a snoop, I would know.

Our first night passed without incident.

We completed our morning chores, ate breakfast, and then I headed off to check out the barn.

I arrived at the barn with Miss Joy all but glued to my ankle. She only does that when she is scared, has been naughty or scolded. Her expression said it all: *do we really have to do this?*

I was interested enough after seeing the cabin to buy the property, so the barn would be just icing on the cake.

The building was well constructed, sturdy, and immaculate inside with a set of large sliding doors exiting to the back yard behind the house. There was a small door on the side facing the cottage. The small door had a padlock installed using the same sloppy manner as the one on the kitchen door. It was my point of entry.

The bottom floor was open with a loft area on the right-hand side with steps leading up with a substantial handrail.

Parked in the back of the building was an older, nondescript, Chevy pick-up truck. Along with the truck was an older model, small Kubota tractor with a mowing deck attached, while behind the tractor stood the bucket attachment, a snow blower, and a bush-hog. Although it was older equipment, everything appeared to be in good shape.

I wanted to check out the loft and see if there was any evidence of leaking from the roof, although it was a metal roof and didn't seem damaged from what I'd seen from my inspection on the ground. It was easier to assess it from inside the structure.

The loft was open with the exception of a section on the end closest to the sliding barn doors. I saw a small sliding door leading into the space. Carefully, I slid it open. There was a large metal tank filling the room. I guessed it to be either stainless steel or an alloy. It was covered. There was a gauge on the front.

After a careful inspection of the piping, I knew how the cabin got its water supplied.

Somewhere there was a pump, which filled this tank with water from the river. The water was then gravity fed into the cabin. This was pure genius in the design and simplicity!

Somewhere there had to be a source for power. I found the generator house buried into the hillside off to the side of the barn. I would not have guessed what was in there aside from the exhaust vent carefully installed behind a juniper. The access door was small with a padlock. This lock was not a recent install nor was it loose like the others. I would need to find the key.

Six

I was more resolved than ever to buy the property. I was off to see Mr. Smart. I didn't think he had been in the barn or understood the systems. Too bad…his loss, my gain; it had been his job to know the property and the equipment he was conveying.

I arrived at the bank with my game plan pretty well thought out in my mind. As an afterthought, I remembered to leave the revolver in the camper.

When I walked into the bank, Mr. Smart looked as if he were going to cry. He was so certain I was returning the keys and walking away. Good. That enhanced my advantage.

He did manage to greet me with a cheerful, "So did you enjoy camping out by the river?"

My retort was as upbeat. "Great, I wasn't eaten by a bear or anything."

Mr. Smart wasn't comfortable asking me if I was interested in a purchase.

I figured I would assist him with his discomfort. "I came to discuss the *probability* of purchasing the property. You're already aware of some monumental challenges.

"First one; no electricity and the cost associated with getting power to the cabin. I didn't find a well so that would need to be addressed if power could be brought in."

I was busy watching his expression change from defeat to hope. I was on the right track with my direction aimed at negotiations. "There is also the issue of nobody willing to set foot out there to do any work."

Mr. Smart's face again assumed the *defeated* look. This was good for me, but who was keeping score?

"Let's begin with the price...too high, considering the baggage included with the property. Cost of title and closing costs. The driveway will require some substantial work to make it useable."

I could see he was warming up to the idea he actually had a buyer. "Well Nettie, may I call you by your first name? I would also appreciate it if you call me Jeff. Mr. Smart seems way too formal when we're negotiating a complex deal."

He smiled a slight smile, and then got down to serious business. "When would you be thinking you'd want to close on the property?"

I just looked at him and offered no answer. He hadn't given me any indication of a compromise on anything. I waited, knowing I was exceptional at the game, having played it since I was eighteen.

When he realized I hadn't taken the bait, he changed his tactics. He shuffled papers on his desk, opened the folder for the property while appearing to study the contents. I was certain he knew them by heart and could quote book and verse.

I waited.

Jeff cleared his throat, nodded his head slightly, and then sat back in his chair, apparently trying to out-wait me.

I took the keys for the property he had given me out of my pocket and stood as if to pass them across the desk to him. I saw panic in his eyes. This man should never play serious poker. He was too easy to read.

He spoke, a little louder than he intended, "Now wait! I didn't say I wouldn't discuss this. Let me close the office door and we'll chat."

I remained standing.

Jeff closed the door then hastily sat down and indicated I should do the same. "I've given this some careful thought. I want this off the bank's books, as you well know. I could make you a deal. I took the time and effort yesterday to check your credit history. I know it wasn't kosher, but I did, and I've told you.

"I'm willing to sell you the property and take back a mortgage for the entire amount. I would of course, hold the mortgage in-house. I would pay for all legal fees including the title search along with paying for the transfer stamps. How does that sound?"

My answer was easy. "We never discussed the selling price of the property. I assumed the sale of the property was, 'as is', there would need to be a bill of sale for the contents of the house and barn.

"I didn't expect your bank to pay for the cost of road work or utilities. However, I felt it should be reflected in the asking price for the property."

Jeff looked sad. "Nettie, I have twenty-six thousand, two hundred dollars already sunk into the property."

I shrugged my shoulders and stood, as there seemed to be no middle ground here.

Jeff put out his hand in a halt signal. "If you were certain you wanted the property, I'd do everything I mentioned and settle at twenty-two thousand dollars if you closed immediately."

My guess had been we would have met on middle ground at twenty-five. This was even better.

"I'll close with those figures as soon as you have an update of title that is clear along with the rest of the necessary paper work needed. What do you think your time-frame would be?"

"Will day after tomorrow, at ten o'clock work for you?"

I nodded, "I don't want anyone going out there in the meantime. Is that understood?"

Jeff laughed. "I don't have enough money or influence to force anybody to go. Don't be concerned; if anyone shows up out there, they won't be from around here."

"See you in two days."

I left the bank feeling I'd made a good purchase. Having the bank keep the mortgage in-house meant I would have funds to repair the road and install a gate at the end of the drive so I could lock it.

My first stop was to see Nick about getting the roadwork done. I ventured he could direct me to someone who could install the gate.

He assured me he could do the roadwork after I closed with the bank. He could also install the gate but it would take about a week to get one shipped to him. We agreed on price.

I wanted to return to my home to pick up my tools and a couple of things I felt I needed to occupy the cabin. I would return with my camper in case I needed to use it for sleeping and showering.

On my way home, I made a quick decision to call the broker I often used. She would be happy to list my house. We set a time for the next morning to meet and sign the listing agreement. We had worked together on several properties, so she knew and respected my wants and needs. I was feeling more alive and invested in living than I had been for some time.

I was back at the bank with fifteen minutes to spare. I was ready to close the deal and get to work on the property. I also needed to get it insured.

Jeff was ready and *more* than willing to get the deal closed. He assisted me with the insurance for the property.

He was happy. I was happy. Let's hope it stayed that way.

Seven

My next move was to call in at the lumberyard to purchase screening for the repair of the porch. Being on the river I was certain bugs would be rampant as soon as it got a little warmer and leaves sprouted on the trees. I wanted to be ready.

When I returned to the property, Nick was busy unloading equipment. I was certain once I drove into the driveway, I wouldn't be able to drive out until he completed his work. I had plenty to do.

I again parked the camper down by the river. It was getting late in the afternoon, and I was tired. I would begin work on the cottage tomorrow.

Nick worked for a while then left.

Miss Joy and I sat out with a glass of wine and munchies for a short time before dinner. When I was ready to close the camper for the evening, I again brushed the sand. There was just something uncomfortable about the state of the property that made me edgy. I hadn't put my mental finger on it yet. I would continue to remain vigilant.

We had slept well. However, when I stepped out of the camper in the early morning, I found footprints of someone and something that had walked around the camper then back onto the grassy area of the field.

I had a man-sized print along with the biggest dog's paw print I had ever seen. At least I hoped it was a dog's paw print. This was interesting, but definitely not in a *good* way.

Damn certain I was wearing my revolver.

We drove up to the barn as if we had no idea of our nighttime visitor. Remember the expression; *never let them see you sweat*? I'd encountered other times when there was perceived danger, so this wouldn't be my first big rodeo.

I parked the camper beside the doors on the barn so I could unload things into the house and put tools into the barn.

My first job was to replace the locks on both buildings. I set my tool bucket on the ground and began the task. There would be no more loose hasps with people or peoples having access to the buildings by just shaking the locks loose.

I'd made certain all the battery-operated power tools had full charges before leaving my own garage. I knew I could recharge them with the camper generator if necessary.

Once the locks were changed, I began to go through the cabin, cleaning with a bucket of warm soapy water heated on the camper's stove. The place was already clean. The property hadn't been empty or unattended for very long.

This thought became more obvious when I wiped out the cupboard and found an opened box of crackers. The date-stamp told me I was correct. Whoever had been staying or using the cabin had cleaned out the food closet, overlooking the box of crackers.

I made the bed with the fresh linens brought from home. It looked comfortable and homey. With the windows all open, the breeze was softly blowing through the rooms making them smell fresh.

I walked down to the driveway to check on Nick's progress. He called to me to come and check out the work he'd completed. He had progressed much faster than I'd anticipated. He informed me he would be finished in about a half hour. I offered him a check for the project, which he declined. He wanted to wait until after he installed the gate. Then he would top-dress the length of the drive with new gravel.

I returned to the house to close up and lock the buildings, and then drove toward the village for more supplies from the lumberyard. I wanted to install some deadbolts on the doors of the house.

Eight

My cell phone rang. Not having coverage at the property had been a blessing. I was free to work without having to interact with anyone.

The call was from my broker; she had a buyer. I pulled over to the side of the road and dug out pencil and paper for details. They wanted to buy the house, cash, and wanted the furnishings. The catch was they wanted to close in a week, sooner if possible.

I chuckled… here we go again. My last two houses sold for cash with only short periods to pack and move. Why not, I can do this if I only have to move the personal things. The cabin was furnished, so I didn't need any more stuff, and I wouldn't want to store it. That was the blessing of getting older and moving to a smaller house each time. Each time I downsized, I had given all of my children my extra furniture and household items I no longer needed.

The broker assured me they had the cash necessary for the purchase because they'd just sold their home out of state. The funds would remain in escrow until our closing.

Changing my plans was easy. I turned the camper around, returning to the cabin to secure anything I'd overlooked and went back to my home to pack. The packing was finished in two days of real diligent work. I hired a small U-Haul truck with a car dolly to transport the household goods, and to tow my Ford Sport Trac to the cabin.

When I returned, everything was as I left it. I unloaded the truck, placing the entire contents into the barn, then parked the Sport Trac, and returned the U-Haul. It was good to be back in the camper again, much more comfortable than a rented truck. Miss Joy was happy to have her plush seat back.

We held the closing the next morning early, with donuts and coffee. They gave me a check, and I gave them the keys.

The sale transpired so quickly, and I was so busy with the moving I hadn't any time to consider seller's remorse until I was driving back to the cabin. I thought perhaps I needed to rethink the designation, because it was now not *the cabin,* but my *home.* I was good with the decision.

Returning to the cabin, I pulled the camper close to the side door of the barn to finish moving things in. I unlocked and opened the big sliding doors then walked outside and unlocked the side door to enter. As I entered the barn, a movement inside caught my eye. I knew it wasn't Miss Joy because she was standing by my foot.

I walked leisurely back to the camper, put her inside, and picked up my shotgun. I'd brought my rifle and shotgun with me in the camper this trip. I quietly loaded the breech, and walked into the barn through the small side door.

I was done with foolishness. I knew there wasn't a back door on the barn, and the windows were too high to use as an exit. I also knew each window had a lock and a brace.

I touched my pocket where my cell phone was, being acutely aware there was next to *no* service here.

I stood on the right side of the small barn door with my back to the wall by the corner under the stairs leading up to the loft. I listened, holding my breath. Total silence; I trust my skills along with my gut. Someone was in there. I could feel it in my bones. I stood stock-still and continued to listen. I was good at the *waiting game.*

About fifteen minutes passed; still I waited, then, I heard the creak of a board. Whoever was there moved. I waited. Another slight creak;

they were trying to get into a different position. The noise came from the direction of the parked truck.

I had the advantage of sight. With those big barn doors open, the sun was streaming in, flooding the floor with light. Because I was standing in the corner, I was in the shadow. I could see clearly into the depths of the barn. They, whoever they were, couldn't see me.

I stood quietly watching and waiting. I detected movement in the area behind the truck. I squatted, without moving my feet, to change my sightline. I clearly saw legs standing just behind the vehicle.

I didn't want to shoot holes in the truck or risk a fire or explosion in the building. I also didn't want to give up my advantage of being in the shadows and hidden from whoever was there. I waited.

My reward came sooner than expected. A movement at the big door drew my attention away from the person. A huge, ugly head came into view, and then quickly retreated.

I hadn't fully taken my eyes off the person. I could see he, or it, had shifted their position to the side of the truck closest to me. My impression was they were going to try to walk along the wall I was leaning on and slip out of the building.

That was a big mistake in their strategy. When he cleared the front of the truck, he was about twelve feet, or less, from me. Because he was looking at the open door and into the sunlight, he never saw me.

I stood, while jacking a shell into the chamber and spoke calmly. "Halt right where you are. This is number six birdshot. I will shoot you with no regrets. Put your hands on top of your head and walk slowly forward."

I gave him credit. When he heard me work the pump-action on the shotgun, I had his full attention. He put his hands on top of his head and walked slowly toward the big door.

"Who are you? What are you doing here? I want answers, and I want them fast. Start talking."

He knew, whatever his game had been, it was over. I read the defeat on his face and in the slump of his shoulders.

I stood with the gun aimed and ready as he surveyed me while trying to gauge my response to his presence. I'm a good poker player, having lived through many bad situations in my lifetime. I don't often give anything away in a staring contest. The slightest loss of concentration could and would get you harmed, sometimes badly.

When he spoke, I knew he wasn't from this area of the country. He had an accent, although I couldn't identify it. Perhaps it was a combination of areas blended together through the years.

His voice remained calm while he spoke softly, "I was the owner of the property until recently. I built it over the last few years. You've caught and captured me so what are you going to do with me?"

I thought he'd asked an honest question. I didn't know at that moment, nor did I have enough facts to know what I was going to do. "I need answers to questions before I make any decision."

He sounded a tad apologetic. "Could I please put my hands down?"

"First, I want to know if you're carrying any weapons. If so, put them on the floor; carefully."

He smiled, "My weapon of choice, if I had one, is sitting in the bushes over there. I'm not a violent person."

I knew anything he might say wouldn't surprise me, or be something I hadn't heard before, in one form or another. I'd heard too many tales, too many times. I lost count long ago. Now I believed nothing without solid proof. I patted him down while he continued to smile. "You may put your hands down, but don't make any sudden or stupid moves."

I stepped back and took a long look at my invader. He was a bit over six feet tall, weighed about one hundred and eighty, blond, or gray haired with greenish hazel eyes. He had a muscular physique, which only comes from eating well and doing physical labor. He had the persona of a man who'd spent a lot of time outdoors. His pants were a twill fabric similar to the Carhart brand working men wear, and the shirt was a faded cotton plaid with the sleeves rolled up.

When I patted him down, his scent was clean smelling, like the river and fresh air with the total absence of artificial products.

I wanted to get this done. "By the way, my name is Nettie Small. I bought the property under a foreclosure from the bank. Is your dog friendly? How does he take to strangers, small dogs? What's his name?"

"He's okay with strangers as long as he doesn't perceive they're any threat to me. I don't know about other dogs; he's never been around them. I call him Luce… its short for Lucifer. I got him as a puppy. I said he looked like the devil. I rescued him from a mean old farmer with a very muddy pig-yard. He was born on the farm but he kept wandering away from the litter. He ended up in the mud and couldn't get out. The farmer was going to leave him there to teach him a lesson. The farmer figured if his pigs didn't eat him that would make him a smarter dog. He was so small; being only a month old… he couldn't get himself unstuck from the mire. I went into the pen, picked him out, gave the farmer fifty dollars, washed him with a hose, and he's been with me ever since. He *does not* like pigs."

We sat on the barn floor near the door to talk. I wasn't ready to invite him into the house.

"Alright, let me hear your story. I warn you right now I'm not easily conned. If you lie to me, you're done. I'll call the law and have you arrested for trespassing in a heartbeat.

"First, I want to know what happened to your wife who took out the mortgage at the bank and never made a payment. The fact she was never seen again requires *some* clarification."

He shook his head, "She *wasn't* my wife. She worked for the Federal Government. When I explain why I'm here, perhaps you'll understand... perhaps not. Maybe nobody will ever understand.

"You can put the shotgun down. I'm truly not a violent man. Other than, to kill something to eat, if I'm desperate, I wouldn't harm anything or anyone. The situation you've found me in will be a testament to the fact I'm not a fighter.

"I was an accountant by profession. I worked for many, many years for a firm enjoying every bit of my time there. The owner was an older man with a stellar reputation and a pillar of the community.

"I worked my way up until I was one of the top CPAs in the firm and was well compensated.

"I was married with a family of two children. We enjoyed a good life, had a nice home, the kids went to college. It was all good. We were truly living the 'American Dream,' or so I thought.

"The man who owned the firm died from a heart attack very suddenly. He was older, apparently healthy, and his death came as a terrible shock. His son had worked with the firm for a couple of years. He didn't seem to have the same affinity for it his father had, and he never bothered to acquire his CPA. After his father died, he assumed the management end of the business.

"He brought in a couple of new people, neither of whom were CPAs. He called them *partners* and the three of them began to make all the decisions for the firm. I anticipated changes after the death of the founder. He'd been a man of vision, knowing how to accomplish the goals he'd set for the firm.

"I thought perhaps I'd apply at another agency because I didn't like the direction his son was taking the firm. When I mentioned the idea to my wife, she panicked. She never liked change and wanted nothing to interfere with her present situation. When I tried to explain my concerns to her, she laughed and told me I was an old fuddy-duddy. She told me to get over it.

"Dutifully, I never broached the subject again.

"That became my downfall. I don't want to indicate it was her fault. She had no clue about anything outside her world, which included the house, children, her friends, and volunteer work.

"The firm began to work with some unsavory clients. They told me to complete an audit and write a report to support a very large bank loan.

"I don't know what your background is, or if you'll even understand what I'm going to tell you. Do you want me to continue or do you just want to call the police?"

I understood he was distressed. Not by the content of what he was revealing, but the fact he might not be making any sense to me. I assured him I understood everything he was relating, and to continue. Perhaps the statement of my understanding gave him the courage to proceed.

"When I began the audit, I was told I could only look at certain aspects of the business in question. My job was to put together the figures with an adequate report to secure *that* loan. End of the story. I'd always enjoyed an excellent reputation, which garnered respect within the business community. The banks would never question the integrity of my report. The son's bottom-line was, '*make it happen.*'

"I hadn't even gotten into the company's paperwork before I realized it was dealing in black-market drugs and weapons. They were also into gambling, prostitution, child pornography, as well as child trafficking.

"I called the son and asked for a meeting at once. His father would *never* have entertained working with a client of that caliber. My thought was perhaps the son was unaware of the scope of criminal activities or the involvement of that firm.

"Again, I'd made another major mistake. The son immediately informed me to shut my mouth, do my work, or pack up my office and leave. He would blackball me. Another agency would never hire me. Like the dull and unassuming man I was, I believed he could and would.

"On the drive home that evening, I thought I'd talk to my wife regarding a minor portion of what I knew was going on. It was my second mistake. She told me I was an idiot. If I wanted to throw away our lifestyle over my stupid fetishes about always being honest and everything balancing to the penny, she would divorce me.

"We'd never had an outstanding relationship to begin with. She thought of me as a boxy, boring kind of guy who made a good living for her and the kids. As she explained the situation, she could '*do one hell of a lot better and not die of boredom.*'

"Somewhere in the night I knew exactly what was going to happen. I arrived at work the next day and took up my duties as always without causing a ripple. I worked for weeks getting what they thought were reports ready for the great loan presentation.

"Long story short, I became a whistle-blower. Not just on the original client, but with the three other entities involved and intertwined with the primary business. They were all involved in similar circumstances and backgrounds.

"By the time the dust settled, after the court hearing and indictments came down, I was unemployed, divorced, disowned and anything else that could possibly happen.

"Because of the scope of the investigation, other companies besides the original ones I worked on were taken down. It was huge. I received a substantial whistle blower's settlement. The Feds put me into the witness protection program.

"The beginning of my end was entering the program. There were several options offered. The option I chose was to change my identity, and not have them relocate me. I was on my own.

"I drifted from place-to-place doing odd jobs and living in different situations. It didn't work for me.

"I bought this parcel of land years ago on a whim. I never came to look at it. One day I packed up the truck and Luce, and came to see if I could make a life again.

"During my drifting, the woman, who claimed to be my wife at the bank, would pop into my life. She would show up and demand money to keep quiet about where I was. She was a clerk in the office of the witness protection unit. She processed my paperwork, and thus she knew all of the changes to my identity.

"My first mistake was I panicked and paid her the twenty-five thousand dollars she demanded. She told me if I called the office and reported her, she would kill my family. Sadly, I believed she would. She caught up with me again in Nevada… same situation.

"When I came here, I was more careful about my dealings. I was learning how to be undercover and invisible. I obviously didn't do a very good job; she found me again.

"She didn't see me here; I stayed hidden, but she jimmied the lock and searched the house. She must have found the deed in my papers and forged my name. I knew how far she'd gone when I watched the banker out here looking over the property. I knew my cover was blown. It was time to move on. I liked it here and didn't want to move, so I stayed hidden."

My turn now, for questions. "Where are you staying? How do you keep the dog quiet so he doesn't give you away? How are you getting supplies without someone seeing you? You must have known once she found an easy mark to shakedown, she would never leave you alone as long as you're alive? Do you have a photo of the person? Do you have any contacts with the office where this was set up? Did you take a one-time payout or is there an annual payment? By the way, what's your name? The man at the lumber store said he called you Pete."

The man, understandably, seemed overwhelmed with my inquiries and sat quietly as if sifting his mind for answers. Finally, he spoke. "Pete is close enough for a name. My real last name used to be Petersen, so Pete worked for me.

"I don't have a photo of the woman, but I can sketch her. She walked with an odd gait, sort of a hitch in her step. She's taller than you are and a bit heavier, very muscular, not in an attractive way. Her hair is short and dark. She's quite masculine in her appearance. She once told me she worked in the stockade after her military service. I believed her; she looked the part.

"I was too worried about retribution to contact the office. I don't want any harm to come to my family, even though they disowned me.

"I took a single payout, but with her taking funds, it's nearly gone. I worked most of the time to support Luce and myself. I became so paranoid when I came here, about her finding me; I built a tree house way back in the woods. When she arrived, I retreated there.

"In the beginning, I would go to the lumberyard for building supplies and drive a couple of towns away for groceries. I have an old canoe I keep hidden in the creek, so after she showed up, when I needed supplies, I paddled up river going to a campground store to stock up. There were so many visitors they didn't pay any attention to me. I didn't go often, living mostly on what I fished and foraged.

"Luce is well trained. Not because I was a good trainer, but he always seemed grateful I saved him from the pigs. He's very loyal to me. However, he hasn't had much socialization, so I don't know how he would be with people or other animals."

Pete's story stunned me. It meant several things: the foreclosure, and thus, the sale to me were not legal. The fraud at the bank was Federal. I had just sold my home, making me homeless. Well, wasn't this one hell of a mess? I was going to have to puzzle it out in a hurry.

I felt it was only fair to share those thoughts with Pete. He'd lost his home through fraud. However, while I was trying to state my concerns, his face paled. Why, what was going on in his mind to cause such a level of concern?

When he found his voice, his concern was evident. "No. This property is yours now. I'll leave. I can't go to the bank… she would find out and kill my family. Let her think I just moved on. I'm terrified of what she would do."

"Pete, calm down and let me think this through. We're both in a jam. Getting all in a dither won't solve anything. We're both here and involved, so we need to figure it out.

"Do you know if she ever contacted your family? Have you ever contacted them? Have you checked the internet to see where they are, or anything?

"For the moment, all anyone knows is that I bought the property from the bank, and you're gone. We'll leave it that way. Can you continue to live in your tree house? If you can, we're going to pretend we don't know anything else is going on. It would buy me some time to figure out a solution. I won't do anything without telling you prior to executing a plan."

Pete looked as if he had just escaped a death sentence. I could somewhat understand his relief although I wasn't quite sure how I was going to fix this situation.

I thought for the hundredth time, *how on earth, can I manage to get myself into these situations? I must have a sign on my back.*

The new burst of information put my plans of moving into the cabin on hold. I would have to reside here, as I didn't have any other place to live other than my camper.

Nine

Could the situation get any worse? I knew better than to even think the thought… certainly it could, and it did.

I shared with Pete the fact I was having Nick install a gate at the end of the driveway we could lock. I would also install cameras and an alarm system down there. I had purchased one that was a solar system with battery backup. He liked the idea.

As we were discussing the gate issue, I heard a large truck driving into the yard. It was Nick towing his equipment trailer. I went out to meet him while Pete hid in the barn.

I was greeted with a hearty, "Hello there, I got the gate earlier than I expected, so I'm going to install it, then top-dress the length of the drive. Is that okay with you? I'll need a couple of hours at least. I see you're busy, so if you need to go out give me a shout. I brought enough fencing so I can extend the fencing back into the tree line. With that done, folks can't walk or drive around the gate if it's closed. They could, but not without a lot of effort. I hope it meets with your approval."

"Thank you for thinking so far ahead, I do want it secure. I'll be installing an alarm in the gate area, so I'll know when someone comes into the driveway area. The wildlife will probably be the biggest offenders. I'll check on your progress later. For now, I don't need to leave the property."

Nick moved his equipment down to the drive area, and I returned to the task of trying to unload and organize my stuff, and figure out what to do with Pete and Luce. I still didn't know if the dog would tolerate Miss Joy or me. I needed to find out immediately.

When I stepped inside the barn, I saw Pete watching me from behind the truck parked there. I walked over to where he was standing and spoke quietly. "We have to find out if Luce is going to be friendly to me and my dog. It is imperative if we are to co-habit the property for the time being. Do you have a suggestion as to how we figure it out?"

Pete was pensive then shrugged his shoulders. "I can hear Nick's equipment running, and I know he works alone, so now may be a good time to introduce you to Luce. I think he'll be okay with you because he was watching you talk with me and hadn't moved. He saw your dog with you and didn't make a sound. Maybe he'll accept you as a pair. I honestly don't know. I wouldn't allow him to harm you or the dog. Do you trust me that far?"

I nodded my head, knowing the shotgun was still loaded and leaning against the wall behind me. I had an internal chuckle; I'd left Pete and a loaded gun here while I talked with Nick. He must be okay, or I would be having a problem now instead of meeting his dog. That was one hell of a way to establish trust in a new relationship. "Okay, let's see what he'll do. I hope he doesn't think I smell like a pig."

Pete laughed then moved his hand slightly, and the dog came out of the bushes standing at the entrance of the barn. He didn't seem apprehensive or curious. Pete urged him to come into the building.

He was a *massive* dog. The man at the lumberyard was correct in saying it was the ugliest looking dog he'd ever seen. He had a gray and white bristly coat. I was guessing he was a crossbreed of an Irish wolfhound and some mastiff. He looked like he weighed over one hundred fifty pounds, with the largest feet I'd ever seen on a dog, more like bear paws.

Luce walked up to Pete and sat at his feet. When sitting, the top of the dog's head was higher than Pete's waist. Pete placed his hand on Luce's head and spoke softly to him. "Luce, this is Nettie. She's our friend. I want you to be nice. Say hello and shake for her."

The dog stood and made eye contact with me. He had 'soft-eyes.' He walked forward, sat at my feet, facing me while extending his paw. I took his paw and patted his head. He seemed to be comfortable with me. I hoped he would accept Miss Joy in the same manner.

I had to be certain she would be safe with him, or we wouldn't be able to share the property. Miss Joy was getting older and I couldn't allow any abuse by an animal or a person.

I walked to the camper, picked her from the seat, and returned to the barn for a meet and greet with the giant beast. Miss Joy was nervous; I could feel her little heart beating a staccato in her chest. I held her in my arms and leaned over so Luce could smell her, and she could sniff him. I was surprised they appeared to be okay. Her heart slowed, and she relaxed in my arms. I carefully placed her on the floor by my feet. Luce moved his head forward and sniffed her again, then licked her ear. I hoped he was not just sampling her for a larger bite. Miss Joy looked up at the massive head and licked him on the end of his nose. I breathed a sigh of relief. Luce looked at me with a quizzical glance as if to say, "Did you think I was going to eat her?" I chuckled.

I glanced at Pete to see what his thoughts were on the meeting. He was grinning from ear to ear.

In the past, I had owned a big male Airedale who had a horrible odor to his skin and fur. Luce had no detectable odor other than fresh air and the clean river smell.

Nick finished the installation of the gate and the driveway work. He even left me a large gate lock. He insisted it couldn't be cut or broken even with bolt cutters. I paid him, and as he drove away with a big grin on his face, he said, "Welcome home. Call me if you need me."

I needed to get the security system installed at once. I'd never installed one. I would have to lay it out and do some reading of the directions.

Pete insisted he knew how to install it. I was worried about his being out near the road…what if someone driving by spotted him? I shouldn't have been concerned. While he was working, I couldn't see him, and I knew where he was. He had the cameras installed with the solar panels up and running in less than an hour. It would not be completely safe because someone could also arrive on the riverside of the property. It was a beginning.

Ten

When the installation was completed, Pete showed me where the pumping system was and how it worked. I was grateful he was there. I would have figured it out in time, but it was so easy with his assistance. He showed me how to run the generator, which would power the entire house, pump, and barn. He had built it into an embankment beside the barn, adding a small, insulated building so it ran quietly. The fuel for the generator was propane, thus explaining the large gas tank in the back yard.

On my next trip to a large city not too far away, I purchased field walkie-talkies. I got two with the battery packs. I made certain they were long range rated, even if used in heavy brush or timber. These became my source of communicating with Pete.

I was working out in the barn sorting my things while trying to decide what I would put into the cabin when the gate alarm sounded. I checked the screen we set up so we could view who entered the driveway, even though we kept the gate padlocked. It was a woman.

I called Pete on the walkie-talkie and alerted him. I needed to know if this was the *woman* in question.

While he hurried into the barn to check the screen, I busied myself putting my .38 revolver into the back of my jeans. My motto is stay safe, not sorry, or dead. So far, that had worked well for me.

Pete took one glance at the screen, paled, and then looked like he wanted to run anywhere but near here. "It's her, she came back. What are we going to do?"

I didn't know what he was going to do, but I certainly knew what I was going to do.

"Pete, quick, you need to take Luce and hide upstairs in the barn. I'll take care of this situation right now. Whatever you do, stay hidden until I return and call you."

I could see from the monitor she'd ducked under the gate and was walking up the driveway. She was a cheeky broad. I had carefully posted the property with signs stating 'No Trespassing and No Hunting.' This was trespassing at its best. She was most likely hunting as well. I would stop this in its tracks.

I put Miss Joy in the cabin and walked down the driveway to meet her. She spotted me. She stopped, and then continued to walk toward me. She was younger than I, although it was hard to gauge her age from that distance. We both kept walking, but I wanted to retain some distance between us until I knew the situation. "You can stop right where you are and state your business. You're trespassing on my property."

I gave her a ten for grit when she spoke, "I'm a Federal Agent, and I'm here on business. Who are you? What are you doing here?"

My response was simple. "I want to see identification, and I want to see it now."

"My business isn't with you. Who I am is none of your business. I don't need to show you anything. Now get out of my way."

Big mistake on her part; I do not bully easily or at all. Those days are long ago and far away. "If you don't produce some legal identification right now I *will* call the police and have you removed. Am I clear? I own this property and you have *NO* business here, or with me. Now either present what I have requested, or I'll take it from here, my way; choice is yours."

She stopped walking and seemed to consider her next move. She reached into her jacket pocket and produced what looked like a cardholder, opened it, and took out a business card. She was extending her arm to me when I stopped her with, "Either show me a legitimate badge or get out."

Her reaction was priceless. She stared at me as if I had two heads. "This is what I use… take it, or leave it."

I shook my head. "Time for you to get out of here and don't return."

She flung the card on the ground, spun around and, muttering over her shoulder something about a Federal warrant, she stormed off. I knew I hadn't seen the last of this broad. I looked at the card. I smiled…the card had her photo on it and a name, Mary Murphy, and stated she was an Agent of the FBI. No office or phone number listed. How dumb did she think people were?

I retrieved the card from the ground carefully, touching only the outside edges. I had her fingerprints. I would guard this for later use. I knew there would be a *later* with this bird.

I managed to get a make on the car registration. I would've bet it was a rental car. Nonetheless, I had the tag number. I also had the recording on the camera.

When I reached the barn, Pete looked like he was ready to give birth to a batch of live kittens. Luce was sitting at his feet looking mournful. He knew his master was upset.

"She's gone for the moment, but she'll return. We need to be vigilant until I get this straightened out."

After I said that, I wondered for the millionth time how I got myself into these messes and, furthermore, why it was up to me to fix them. I knew in the depths of my soul, Pete couldn't; he was too spooked. I, on the other hand, was just pissed.

We worked along for a couple of quiet days doing the repairs necessary to make the cabin comfortable. Pete was a great help with the repairs. There were no other callers to the property. I didn't relax my vigilance. Over the years, I'd encountered too many situations that went sour in an eye blink, and knew this would be the same.

I had enjoyed some kayaking in the early mornings and late afternoons. The river was wide in this area and with very little current. I managed to catch a few fish for my dinner. Miss Joy settled in comfortably. She loved to kayak, although she was not as keen when I fished. I didn't bring the fish into the kayak, but when they thrashed against the side of the boat, she looked worried.

I made a deal with Pete to pick up food and supplies for him when I shopped so he didn't have to venture up river unless he wanted to. He seemed content to putter about the property out of sight. *He was the invisible man.* I mowed, along with any grounds work requiring being in view of the road or the river. He worked in the barn and the back yard.

The day I knew would come *did*. Again, the gate alarm sounded, and the woman was back. I dubbed her a *slow learner* among other things. I alerted Pete, slipped the .38 into my waistband, and walked down the driveway. She seemed surprised I was still there. I, however, wasn't surprised she'd returned.

She was only about twenty feet in on the driveway when I met her. "I thought I made it crystal clear you were not to return to, or come onto, my property again."

She ignored my admonition, and snarled, "I have business here, Federal business. If you continue to interfere with my carrying out my duties, I'll have you arrested on a federal warrant. Now get out of my way."

I may be getting on in age, but I'm not a pushover. I stood my ground. "Get off my property or I'll call the law and have you arrested."

She sneered, "Law, there's no law here, and no cell phone coverage so *you*, smart ass, are screwed. Get out of my way." She tried to push me aside.

I've always been a strange person when it came to anyone invading my personal space. I don't ever allow anyone to touch me with violent intent. It triggers something in me that's almost primal.

When she touched me, I blocked her arm. She squared off like a boxer and was already swinging her fist toward my jaw when I kicked her so hard in the crotch I thought I'd broken my leg. She doubled over as I grabbed her hair and slammed her face into my knee just as I was bringing it up. She hadn't been a good-looking woman before, but now she was a mess. Blood was squirting from her nose. It was certainly broken in at least one place.

I was mad as hell and ready for her next move. She shook her head like a mad bull and charged at me; I stepped aside and tripped her. She sprawled in the dirt at my feet. I placed my foot on the back of her neck and stepped down.

At that moment, I would have cheerfully killed her. I knew my temper was out of control. I needed to get a grip or I would.

She was screaming like a wounded animal. I remained oblivious. She tried to roll over so she could grab my foot. I increased the pressure. Finally, she stopped. Her voice was low when she uttered, "I quit. Let me up before I bleed to death."

My retort wasn't helpful. "I've never heard of anybody who bled to death from a nose bleed.

"I told you twice to stay off my property, and you're too dumb to understand. I meant it. I'll take my foot off your neck long enough for you to crawl back down the drive. Then get the hell out of here and never return.

"If you make any move other than that, I *will* kill you. Do you understand? Don't come here again, ever. If you do, I'll make sure there's a warrant for your arrest for trespassing as well as bank fraud, a federal crime. Am I clear?"

When I mentioned the bank, I felt her stiffen as if I'd stuck her with a cattle prod. I finally got her attention… good bad or indifferent, I wasn't sure.

She muttered, "Okay, let me up."

"No, you don't listen very well, I said *crawl* down the driveway, and I meant it."

"Okay I'll crawl. Now let me go."

Without another word, she crawled on her hands and knees to her car. As she was getting into her car, she gave me the finger and shouted, "Next time you won't be so damn lucky."

What a dumb broad.

As I walked back toward the cabin, Pete stepped out of the tree line to meet me. He looked horrified. "How did you do that? I'm a man, and I couldn't have fought anyone like that."

"Pete, you've just never been pushed far enough. I'm going kayaking; be back soon."

I needed to unwind. It's never good for my state of health to get so much adrenalin flowing. I knew this, but I'd be damned if anyone was going to bully me. I'd rather die of a heart attack, or a stroke, than be a wuss.

When I returned from my paddle, I had managed to calm myself down to almost normal. I knew it wouldn't be my last encounter with her. My problem was if I called the police and told them what the situation was, they would do one of a couple of things… first think I was a nut-job or out Pete. I wasn't willing yet to risk either of those scenarios.

To make everything crazier, my sister e-mailed me begging me to come. She had a problem and needed my assistance.

I didn't think *crazy woman* would return for a couple of weeks at least. I thought if I hurried, I could make a flying trip to Virginia with the camper and be back in ten days. When I proposed this to Pete, he looked like the end of time was about to happen.

Pete shook his head. "I need to get away from here, and then she won't bother you anymore. You're going to get hurt trying to protect me. I can't allow anything like that to happen."

"Pete, I no longer think it's just about you; she's deranged and very dangerous. Now it has become personal between her and me. If I call the police, they'll think I'm crazy, and they might out you. I know there's a solution to this mess. I just need time to figure it out so neither of us loses. I'll work this problem out while I'm on the road. I'm going to get you a cell phone to have here so we can stay connected while I'm gone. We don't have good coverage out here, but it'll be better than no communication. If I got you a phone, would you use it?"

"Yes, although it's been a long time since I had one. What are you thinking about for a solution? When this first began, I tried calling the office that handled my case, and they plainly would not discuss it. It was as if I never existed. I couldn't even get to speak to the man I worked with throughout the whole problem. I became so frustrated I quit trying. This really isn't your problem. I should just move on."

Eleven

I made my arrangements, packed the camper, and headed out. Maybe a geographical change would help me figure a solution to the current situation. There had to be a way. Other than shoot the dumb broad and bury her on the back forty. I had to admit after our scrap in the driveway that looked like priority one to me. I was never a violent person and always looked for the best in folks and would help anyone in need. I realized the last few years had left their bumps and bruises.

I blamed my state of mind on a couple of failed marriages, business partners who would rather steal from you than work at a legitimate business venture, and then the state of the world in general. Perhaps a short junket would re-set my clock. I sure hoped it would. I didn't want to spend the rest of my life as a bitter, mean-spirited old woman.

Once on the road, as always, I felt free. My motor home was older with quite a bit of mileage but still willing to run. The trip down was without incident with the weather being pleasant.

My visit with my sister was fun and much too short. Although we corresponded on e-mail, we seldom spoke on the phone due to her hearing loss. To sit and chat had been a pleasure. It was always fun when I was there to take her out to eat. She reminded me of my mom. Before my mom died, I used to visit with her; she also loved to go out to eat.

We completed the tasks I came to do, said our goodbyes, and then I was back on the road headed for home.

I still hadn't figured out a solution to the problem with Pete and the crazy woman.

I hadn't had a call from Pete nor had I expected one unless there was a problem. No news was good news, or no cell reception.

I was making good time heading north while enjoying the country. I don't drive the 95 corridor because I want to avoid any of the large, congested cities. It is also cheaper for tolls and the scenery is pleasant.

I was in a hilly section of the highway late in the afternoon cruising along at a comfortable speed. Thankfully, there was no wind. Sometimes when driving the camper in the wind, it's more like sailing a large boat on a rough sea.

I had driven these rigs for most of my life, so I use the mirrors and stay cognizant of my surroundings. Things can change quickly at 70 miles an hour. I kept good tires on the rig and serviced it often just to avoid issues while on the road away from home.

Twelve

Miss Joy was taking a nap on her seat, all secure in her travel harness. I was enjoying the quiet time to watch the sun getting ready to set.

The one thing I really enjoyed about this camper was the large windows, and the light-colored interior. I also had the advantage of being able to see in my rearview mirror through the large windows in the kitchen area at the rear.

I had just thought these things when a movement in my rearview mirror caught my attention. I checked the side mirrors and could see the nose of a large red semi-truck cresting the hill behind me.

Something flickered into the rearview mirror. This time I took a longer glance. What caught my attention was sun glinting off his shiny trailer.

I checked the side mirrors again. I *knew* I had trouble. The tractor-trailer was barreling down the highway out of control with the trailer swaying from side to side using both lanes. Traffic had been light at this time of day… at that exact moment, we were the only two vehicles I saw on either side of the divided highway.

The road dropped off on both sides with no guardrails and we were going downhill into a sweeping turn.

He was closing the distance between us rapidly, but still out of control. I had to get out of the truck's way or he would ram us. I was as far over onto the shoulder as I could get without being off the road and down over the bank. I had managed to slow my speed considerably. I was praying as I had never prayed. I knew I couldn't panic, or we would die.

His trailer made a violent thrust and flung his tractor right at me. I knew we were going to collide. It was all in slow motion. He was going to drag me down over the steep bank in front of his rig. I made a quick decision for survival. I had to keep the camper from rolling, or getting run over. We would never survive. He hit my back bumper and swung me sideways. I was off the road onto the grassy slope headed down. I had a death grip on the wheel and I stood on the brake.

He didn't apply any brakes at all. His trailer was almost straight behind him at my last glance in the mirror. The impact was horrible. He caught the side of my camper with his bumper and front fender and ripped the side off the camper, taking my driver's door and front fender with him. I'd managed to stop my forward motion from the collision. When his rig sliced into the side of the camper, the couch directly behind me came partially free, pinning me in my seat against the steering wheel.

He plunged down over the bank landing in what appeared to be a swamp with the trailer against the tractor. I hoped because the ground was so wet it had slowed the trailer.

I took a deep breath. It hurt, and I couldn't move. I was wedged in with the seat against the steering wheel. I moved the shifter to park, shut the ignition off, but did not take my foot off the brake pedal. I took a quick inventory. I was alive. Miss Joy seemed scared but okay. The side he'd hit was not the side holding my propane tank. I found my cell phone in the console and tried to dial 911.

Finally, a voice was asking what my emergency was. I tried to stay calm and explain where we were and what happened. The dispatcher's reply was, "I need you to stay put, and help is on the way."

I giggled...stay put...I couldn't move. Had I forgotten to tell them I couldn't move if I wanted to? I *did* want to get free... I'm horribly claustrophobic, and I worried about fire even though I'd cut the ignition and set the emergency brake.

I heard sirens. People were arriving, more sirens.

A man was standing beside the camper talking to me. I couldn't figure out what he was saying. Why couldn't I hear or understand him? Was shock setting in? I needed to stay alert for Miss Joy who was whining, but I couldn't reach her.

The man tried again to talk to me. This time I could understand some of what he was saying. He was asking me if anyone else was in the camper with me. I tried to shake my head no. At least my head didn't fall off from the effort. That was a good omen.

Everyone, it seemed was invested in getting me out of the camper. I tried to explain to the man, he needed to turn off the valve on the propane tank located on the other side of the rig. Blessed be, he understood and ran around to do it.

He tried to move the steering wheel with the tilt adjustment. It wouldn't move. I was happy the air bag had not deployed. I'm short, and it would've broken my face. Odd the things you think about at a time like that. I wasn't in pain, or if I was, I didn't know it. I was having difficulty breathing and tried to regulate my breaths to keep them shallow. I was hopeful once they could get the seat pulled back and free me, I'd be okay.

My left arm had begun to hurt terribly. I didn't see any blood, yet. My seat was jammed against the wheel so it faced the passenger side of the rig, limiting my vision. Then my left leg and hip began to pound with pain. I prayed I hadn't broken my hip.

Several folks tried without success to move my seat back. The couch was wedged tight. They conversed, then took bars and tore the couch free from the outside of the camper and pried my seat back.

I was free from the steering wheel. I needed to get the seat belt off. It was strangling me because it was so tight. Someone cut it loose with a knife. I could draw a full breath. My chest hurt.

I was trying with all my might to determine my injuries. I hoped most of the pain was from the trauma of hitting the wheel. I wasn't sure how badly damaged my arm was. I guessed I'd broken it. I wasn't doing well on assessing the hip or leg either.

They were trying to get me out of the cab. I wanted to help. I wanted to stand. They didn't want any of my assistance. They laid me on a gurney in a prone position. My only thought was to get Miss Joy in my arms and be grateful I was wearing jeans.

The man who seemed to be in charge brought Miss Joy. She was shaking in terror. I held her close and tried to calm her. On his next trip, he had my cell phone and the fanny pack I used as a purse when traveling.

They were picking me up, getting ready to load me into an ambulance. I didn't want to go. I needed to keep my dog with me, and the camper was full of my stuff. They continued to ask me whom they should call. I told them nobody. I needed to get home fast.

I had one last glance of the truck and trailer down in the gulley. I wanted to know if the driver was alive. They wouldn't tell me. As they were trying to get my protesting self into the ambulance, I saw them carrying a person I took to be a man to the other waiting unit. The paramedics hadn't covered him with a sheet nor was he in a body bag. I took that as a positive sign.

The medic was trying to take my vital signs while Miss Joy was trying to stay as close to me as my skin. They were great with her, listening to her chest with the stethoscope.

I asked the medic what would happen to the camper. His answer was an attempt to be humorous; I wasn't ready for funny just yet. "They'll scoop it up and haul it all away. Don't worry; they will not cite you for littering."

I was beyond sad. How could this trip have ended so badly? I'd gone to do a favor, and ended up with this mess.

It seemed we hadn't traveled very far when we arrived at a low building. I knew nothing about the area so I had no idea of population or towns. I felt it was very rural, but that could have been a misconception because I was on a major interstate highway, which by-passed small towns.

It was getting dark, or I thought it was. I had no sense of time.

They backed into a bay, opened the rear doors, and unloaded me into what appeared to be an emergency room. There were several staff members there. They wanted to take Miss Joy. I wouldn't let go of her. She was cowering in fright with all the noise, smells, and strangers. They were insisting I let go, and I was getting louder by the second in my refusal.

A man in a long white coat stepped forward and spoke only one word, "Stop." It was obvious he was in charge. He was a tall man of about my age with thinning hair. He wore wire-rimmed glasses

They stopped. The man walked to my side. "I'm so sorry for the commotion. I'm Doctor Roberts, and this is my clinic. Your dog can stay with you. There'll be no further discussion about it." With a glance around the assembled staff, he'd dismissed the issue.

"Come in and let me see what damage has been done. Can you hear me all right, and how is your vision? I noticed your glasses are bent; I'll adjust them in a moment." As he was speaking to me, he had been directing the staff into which exam room he wanted me placed.

He put me into a small cubicle where they slid me from the gurney.

The doctor's voice was calming and resonant while he spoke slowly and precisely. I felt myself relaxing as he was making a visual inspection of my arm, head, hip, and leg. He carefully touched my ribs where I had been pinned against the steering wheel.

His questions were thorough but easily understood. I could feel the cold seeping over me. This was never good for me. I tend to go into shock quickly, and the deep and penetrating cold was always the first sign.

I managed to utter, "Doctor, I need to be covered up with blankets. I have a problem with going into shock."

I'd never seen medical personnel move so fast. They wrapped me in warmed blankets with a heating pad so quickly I was amazed. Miss Joy snuggled in.

The doctor asked more health-related questions, and then told me he needed to have x-rays of my arm and hip. He would go with me, and if I would allow him to, he would hold my dog.

After the examination of the films, he determined I had broken my upper arm but had not damaged my shoulder…he would cast the arm. My hip seemed only to be badly contused. There wasn't any fracture in the leg or foot.

I could say when he applied the cast to the arm he was the gentlest person, medically, I'd ever encountered. I was so thankful he was not rough or loud. I think if he were, it would have finished me off.

I was beginning to feel the rigors of the accident. I was alone and frightened. I was also in a strange place. I had no idea what town or city this was.

Thirteen

I heard the doctor speaking with a gentleman outside of the cubicle. I heard him ask if he could speak with me, so I assumed he was from the police department.

Dr. Roberts escorted the man into the space, but didn't leave. "Nettie, this is Dom Giovanni. It was one of his trucks involved in the accident. If you can, he would like to speak with you for a moment. It's your choice."

The man was tall, trim in a muscular way, with black hair graying at the sides and a black mustache. His eyes were as black as coal. Although his appearance was formable, he didn't disturb me or set off any internal warnings. He waited for me to open the conversation.

I wanted to be careful in what I said. I took a moment to collect my thoughts. "I hope your driver is okay. I think he was ill while he was driving because the rig was going from lane to lane when he topped the hill. It appeared he didn't have any control, nor was he braking at all. Perhaps the rig lost the ability to brake. I couldn't avoid him."

A strange look came over his face, and a tear ran down his cheek. I was afraid he was going to tell me the driver died. My heart sank, even though it hadn't been my fault. I didn't cause the wreck, but I still felt horrible.

He sensed my angst. He reached out his hand and touched my uninjured shoulder. When he finally spoke, his voice was commanding but quiet. "I'm so sorry you're injured, and so grateful you didn't die. I have no idea how you kept your rig upright and got it stopped. Another five feet and you would've plunged straight down into the gulley. If you'd turned the wheels on impact, he would have rolled you over and down the slope.

"I had to come and make certain for myself what your injuries are. I've spoken to John about what you'll require for aftercare. He can release you to a nursing facility."

I began to sputter. "I need to go home. I am not leaving my dog anywhere. I need a short time to figure out how I'll transport the dog and myself along with my stuff, what's left of it, to Maine. I'm never going to a nursing facility for anybody. Is that clear?"

He smiled. Now I was provoked. Who did he think he was? I wasn't impressed. It was obvious he was used to getting his own damn way, not with me, not now or ever. Before I could speak, he raised his hands as if in defeat.

"I wasn't planning on shipping you to a *nursing facility*. I don't think you want to be here in the clinic either. I was going to have you transported to a very nice motel close by where I have a very dear friend who will care for you as if you were his mother. He has medical training with years of experience. I spoke with him a short time ago.

"He would welcome you. The dog is icing on the cake. It's going to take you several days to be ambulatory with all the bruising and battering you've endured. Will you please avail yourself of these services?

"John is a phone call away and will check you frequently. He and Wade have worked together for years, and they are very trustworthy. What do you say?"

Well, don't I look like an idiot, "I need to stay somewhere for the night. Tomorrow I'll see about renting a car to get home. It is imperative I return at once. I have been away for over a week."

Dom spoke and seemed quizzical. "I understood you were single and alone. Do you have animals at home needing care? Is there someone we should notify about the accident?"

"No, your assumption was correct that I'm single, and there aren't any animals needing care. I have a very bad situation at home I was trying to rectify. I can't tell you anything else about it. It involves another person's welfare.

"I would appreciate a ride to the motel for the night's stay, if you could arrange it for me.

"Dr. Roberts, I need to give you my Medicare and insurance cards to copy for the treatment here at your clinic."

Dom's response was instant and almost curt. "I've taken care of the clinic. I'll see you tomorrow in the morning."

Dr. Roberts had us delivered to the motel in question by ambulance and remained in attendance. When we arrived, they brought me into a lovely room. It was a combination of bedroom and living room with a fireplace blazing away. He introduced me to the kindest looking man in his late fifties or early sixties. I liked him at once. His personality and mannerisms were comforting.

"Nettie, this is Wade Sommers; he'll take care of your needs. I must warn you, he loves dogs. He'll spoil her as if she were a child."

The room was homey with a large adjustable bed placed close to the picture windows that overlooked a manicured lawn with flower gardens and a pool.

Wade explained this was his mother's suite until her recent death. He'd returned home to run their business, but primarily to care for her. He was a registered nurse and physical therapist specializing in elder care.

His love for his deceased mother was apparent when he spoke of her enjoying being home for her end of life experience.

I was beginning to shake with the early onset of shock from the trauma. I knew from past accidents I needed to get warm and try to relax, or I would be in big trouble. I was also beginning to experience massive pain, mostly in my hip and leg.

They carefully placed me on the bed while Wade set about covering me with soft, warm blankets. I was still fully clothed, but I would worry about them later after I got warm.

Wade and Dr. Roberts conferred, then the doctor left, promising to return to check on me in a short while. I was beginning to relax when I remembered I was still clutching Miss Joy to my chest. She seemed to be enjoying the warmth and comfort of the covers, so I let her stay.

We must have dozed off because I awoke suddenly to realize I didn't know where I was, or what had happened. Most of all I hurt all over. The room was warm, and softly illuminated with lamps; I thought it must be nighttime. I had no idea of what time it was, or where I was. My panic level escalated. I tried to get off the bed. Bad move on my part. I really hurt and to make things worse, I couldn't move.

My only thought was I needed to get home quickly to make sure Pete was not in danger.

I tried again to move, but to no avail. Now, Miss Joy sensed I was upset. She whined and tried to lick my cheek to comfort me.

I heard a man's voice saying, "You're all right, remember me, Wade, I'm here to help you. You had an accident, and they brought you here to the motel so I could care for you rather than leave you at the clinic. Let me see what I can do to make you more comfortable." He changed the position of the bed, easing some of the pressure on my back and hip, and fluffed the pillows. The slight change in position helped. I began to remember the wreck, the clinic, and Dr. Roberts. With clarity, I began to calm myself so my mind would function better.

Wade inquired, "How do you feel?"

Easy answer, "Like I was hit by a truck." I'd offered a feeble attempt at a grin after my small bit of sarcasm; it prompted a return smile from him.

"Are you hungry or thirsty? Should I take Miss Joy out for a stroll? I have some dog food, should I feed her? What's your pleasure, I'm here to take care of both of you." He delivered this dialog with a slight bow and a sweeping gesture of his hand.

I was certain she would be hungry and in need of a potty break; that should be task one. I needed a bathroom break also, but I wasn't sure I could walk however far it was to the facilities. I hadn't thought about food because pain seemed to be the most pressing thing at that moment. I finally managed to convey these thoughts to Wade: "Dog first… she needs potty, food, and water. She didn't seem to be hurt. Thank God for her travel harness. Then I need to use the bathroom. I'm not sure I could walk there, but I need to clean up and use the facilities."

I was grateful he was willing to attend to Miss Joy; I knew I couldn't walk her. He seemed to be kind, and she wasn't frightened of him. Neither, for that matter, was I.

With the dog's agenda taken care of, he turned his attention to me. My attempt at sitting up failed. I tried to roll on my side to try again still no success. I *had* to get off the bed and try to stand, or I was in big trouble.

Wade left the room for a moment to return with what looked like a mesh covered patio chair with wheels on the back legs. He positioned the chair next to the bed, then raised the bottom to form a chaise lounge while tipping the chair back lower. With a practiced movement, he slid the partial sheet I'd been lying on, along with me, onto the chair.

He wasn't a large man, but he was stronger than I would have expected. He carefully wheeled me into a spacious bathroom. It was handicapped accessible. He was so matter of fact, I wasn't embarrassed with his assistance in the least. He moved me to the vanity area, then left the room to return with a pair of fleece pjs in a hot pink color and foot warming socks of the same fabric and color. In a matter of a few moments, he had me sponge-bathed, toileted, and dressed for bed.

"I need you to eat something so you can take the pain meds. What sounds good to you? I can get you anything you want."

I wasn't hungry in the least but the pain was washing over me in waves, so I knew I needed something in my stomach. "Toast or anything easy will do, thank you."

Wade went out through a door I hadn't noticed before and returned in a matter of minutes with a tray containing toast, scrambled eggs, and a pot of herbal tea.

He raised the head of the bed slightly and placed the tray on my lap. From the bedside table, he selected a pill bottle. He placed it in my hand, so I could read the label. It was a narcotic. I didn't want anything that would impair my thinking so I shook my head *no*. He replaced the bottle, and passed me Advil. Those I would take. Wade placed three on the tray. I managed to eat some of the food and swallow the pills.

I was so worried about Pete's safety I couldn't relax, even though I knew I had to. Wade was quiet in his approach, so when he asked me what the problem was I tried to give him a short explanation of my concern, and the anxiety it was causing me. He listened intently, then surprised me with his answer. "I know who can help you with this situation. It's Dom; you have hit the jackpot, lady. I'll give him a call."

I must have looked at him as if he were an idiot. He chuckled and put his hand up as if in surrender. Then, he explained. "Dom is like my father. If it hadn't been for him, I would have been doing hard time in some penitentiary making little ones out of big ones".

His reference to old prison slang was humorous.

"After my dad died, I was a lost cause, and I gave my mom a run for her money. I got into all kinds of trouble, and she was at her wit's end with trying to run the business and keep me out of jail.

"One day, she expressed her concerns to Dom, who'd been a long-time friend of the family. He came to visit me in jail. He told me what he was going to do, and what I was going to do. He was clear and concise what the ramifications to me would be if I didn't comply.

"That conversation changed my life, and I've never looked back. He sent me to a private school to finish out my high school, then to culinary school and last, but not least, to nursing school.

"While I was away growing up and getting an education, he made certain my mom was okay. When I came home after her health failed, I ran the business and cared for her. She passed recently… it's why this room is set up the way it is. I miss her terribly.

"Over the years, I watched Dom do some incredible things for people. He's a good man with a great sense of justice in his heart. He isn't a pushover, and when people tried to take advantage of him, or others he cared about, it was never good. He has the capacity to be as bad as he can be good and kind. He hates injustice of any kind. He knows a lot of people in the right places to make things happen. I'll call him right now."

"Wade, it's the middle of the night. You can't wake him just because I'm upset. He'll be angry with both of us."

Wade laughed out loud as if I had told him a great joke. "Trust me on this one; he will be here in fifteen minutes or less, and he would be madder than hell if I hadn't called him."

Dom arrived shortly, dressed in an impeccable white shirt, dark suit with a subtle striped tie. He was clean-shaven with the exception of his jet-black mustache. He looked as though he had just stepped off the pages of a man's fashion magazine.

When he entered the room, it was as if he sucked the oxygen out of the air. "Wade, what's the problem? Why didn't you call me earlier? Nettie, how can I assist you?"

Wade remained calm. "I just learned of Nettie's issue and knew you could resolve the problem. Nettie will explain it to you while I fix us all some breakfast, with the usual for you Dom, and coffee for you, Nettie. I'm off to the kitchen. If you need me just sound the buzzer."

I wasn't sure how to approach the subject with Dom; I didn't know him at all. I thought about it for a few minutes, figured what the heck, I'd always been forthright and honest, so I gave it a shot. I explained the situation to him as I had with Wade. As I finished, I realized his expression hadn't altered one iota, nor had he asked any questions. The only change I could detect was in his eyes. I knew he was listening to my commentary, and he understood what I said. When I explained my run-in with the crazy woman, I saw a crinkle at the edge of his eyes. I explained the fact I was frightened for Pete's life, his eyes hardened to a point where they resembled chunks of coal.

Wade entered the room with a food trolley, which he set up with ease. His service was as fine as any up-scale hotel I had ever been to. We ate our breakfast while Dom and Wade exchanged polite conversation. I picked at the food and sipped my coffee. I marveled at the fact that, despite all the information I had just dispensed, there was no mention of the situation.

Wade cleared the dishes and re-filled our coffee cups while Dom explained, "I never discuss serious matters when I'm eating. Food should be enjoyed along with the company you're sharing it with."

My pain was subsiding some with the help of the pills. As so often happens, when I share my concerns with someone else, it eases my mind. As part of my narrative, I included the fact I was certain the woman had blackmailed others in the program. I expressed to Dom that I felt she was crazy enough to do real harm to other mild-mannered folks the same as she'd threatened to do with Pete and his family.

Dom nodded to me, excused himself, and walked out onto the patio through the sliders. He had his cell phone in his hand as he closed the doors. He appeared to be in earnest conversation with hand gestures and head nodding. I wondered whom he was talking to at this hour of the early morning. He returned to the room with the cell still in his hand. The phone buzzed, and he answered it while never taking his eyes off me.

I couldn't read the man at all; good thing we were not playing high-stakes poker, I would lose big time. He spoke softly, so I could barely make out any of his words, then he offered the phone to me. I had no idea whom he had been speaking with, perhaps the local insane asylum. Oh, what the hell, I took the phone.

"This is Agent Carter, Adam Carter at the FBI. I just had a conversation with Dom, and he instructed me to speak directly with you. I'll tell you I have verified you are Nettie Small, and the current recorded owner of the property in question. Can you give me more information regarding the man referred to as Pete? Where did he work, what was his position, what his name was prior to the change of identity, and which office he worked with during his case? Do you need some time to gather this information?"

"I can only give you partial answers as I know them. However, I also need to have information verifying who you are and what your role is before I converse further with you. I understand you're a friend and an acquaintance of Dom's. I have only recently met him through a situation involving an accident. I must tell you up front, I *am not* a very trusting person."

The reply was instant and delivered with a hearty laugh. "My badge number is eight nine dash six three three. You can call or go on line to get my professional profile. They recently promoted me to this division and, if this problem exists, I am happy to be aware of it. Please verify my information, then call me back directly. I'll wait for your call."

I glanced at Dom and noticed his expression had remained unchanged. Wade looked horrified I had questioned Carter's credentials. I didn't care. I wasn't looking to be blindsided by another scam.

Wade provided a laptop and assisted me in gathering the information necessary to verify who, what, and where Carter was.

I then contacted Agent Carter and gave him the information I knew. I told him Pete had worked for the firm of Dunn and Bradley in

Hartford, Connecticut. He was their lead CPA and had worked there for his entire career. When the owner died suddenly, his son took over the practice, although he was not a CPA. That was when the problems began. I would have to speak with Pete to gather the other information and names he was requesting. I explained Pete did have a cell I had left with him; however, the reception in the area was sketchy at best. If he wished to speak with Dom, I would try to get Pete on my cell. I passed the phone to Dom and took my cell from Wade.

I prayed Pete would answer. He answered on the second ring. His first question was, "Are you doing okay, and when will you be heading home?"

I ignored both questions, feeling the information I needed was more important to the crisis than chatter. I also didn't know when I would be able to start home, but didn't want to tell him so. "Pete, I need some information from you quickly, regarding the FBI. Can you remember your social security numbers, both the old one and the new one?" It was at that moment I realized I couldn't hold the phone and write with one arm. Wade noticed my plight and held the phone and the pad for me. Thankfully, I am right handed.

"I need to know the office of the FBI your case was handled in, and the name of the agent you worked with, if you can recall it. I also need your real name and the approximate date it all took place. If you can remember the name of the crazy woman, it would be helpful. I think I may be on the trail to resolving our issue, and I'll keep you posted." I was writing as fast as I could, trying to get it all on paper, not trusting my memory. "Has anybody been around the property? I may need to call you back with more instructions or for more information, so please stay where you are because the reception seems good. Talk to you soon, bye."

Dom returned his phone to me, and I relayed all the information I'd obtained. The agent seemed satisfied then took my cell number and told me he would be back to me directly. I finished the call with the thought in mind it would be an 'if and when' call if I spoke with him again. I'm not an optimistic person.

Dom made no move to leave the room or return to his home or office. It was clear he had unfinished business with either Wade, me, or both. He pulled his chair closer to the side of the bed and sat.

When Wade began to move the trolley toward the door back from where it had come, he put up a hand in a halt gesture. "Wade, I want you to be part of this conversation I'm about to have with Nettie.

"Pull up a chair; you can take notes for her. First Nettie, I want to thank you for your patience about the accident. I also want to thank you for saving my son. The driver of the truck who hit you was my youngest son. I'll be honest, he was high on drugs, and he'd passed out at the wheel. He got injured, but he'll recover. For now, he is in a rehab facility.

"Now I want to tell you what I'm willing to do to make this right with you. You have every right to sue my ass off if you want to, or we can work this out together without others involved in it.

"First I'm going to deposit the amount of one hundred thousand dollars directly into your bank account. I'll replace your motor home, and also provide for the entire medical and rehab care you need. I'm going to pay off the mortgage on your home, and I'll deposit the amount of four thousand dollars a month into your account for living expenses for the remainder of your life. I need you to tell me what else you feel you need from me to make you whole."

Before I could even grasp any of what he just said, or draw a breath, Dom's cell phone buzzed. "Dom here, what did you find? As bad as that? You don't say. It looks like we opened up a real can of dead worms. What do you want to do now?"

Dom nodded and passed me his phone. "This is Carter… you uncovered a doozie here, kiddo. You need to contact Pete at once and tell him there will be two agents down by the gate posing as a survey team. They should arrive there within the hour. They'll identify themselves by calling out numbers. This is important so make sure he understands. They will call out *'three-six-nine-eighty-eight and one quarter.'* He is to answer, *'one twenty and a half'*. These two agents will stay with him twenty-four-seven, and he is to stay with them.

"You were correct, he wasn't the only victim. We have three we cannot account for. Let's make sure he won't become the fourth.

"What I understood from Dom is that you are also in danger. Can you get this message to Pete at once? They'll not enter the property until they make the appropriate contact with him. In the future, I'll contact you, if necessary, on your cell phone directly. Get well and be vigilant, so you remain healthy. Thank you for your assistance in this matter."

I passed Dom back his phone and took mine to call Pete with the instructions. I prayed he would follow them.

I was exhausted as I fell back onto the pillows. I knew I had done everything I could. It was someone else's problem from now on. I wouldn't stress anymore about the outcome. For once, I felt happy not to be in charge. I looked at Dom knowing he would understand about having to wait for an answer regarding any settlement with me and just faded out, not waking until late afternoon.

Fourteen

When I opened my eyes, the pain was back worse than before. I did know where I was, and why I was there. That was an improvement. I needed to address the discomfort.

Miss Joy had curled up on the pillow beside my head watching me. Wade sat in the recliner reading. With the opening of my eye, it seemed the whole room began to function as if I'd pushed the 'on' button.

Wade came to the bedside and inquired about how much pain I was experiencing; Joy licked my cheek for reassurance. My brain was telling me I needed to get out of bed, but my body was in full rebellion.

"Would you like something to eat or drink? Do you need a transport to the bathroom first?" Those had all been logical questions, but I seemed to be having an issue setting the priorities. I just nodded my head. Damn, the pain from that move stopped any further thoughts from forming for an instant. I recognized it as whiplash. Not my first bout with it; I would need to be easier with my movements.

I was finally able to ask about Miss Joy's needs. Wade assured she had eaten and been out to play with her Frisbee. How, I wondered had she gotten her toy?

Wade must have read the question on my face, so he explained, "The guys from Sandy's RV where they took your camper brought a few of your personal things over. She helped herself to the toy, so I knew it must have been important to her."

With Wade's care and assistance, I began to heal. He was a great physical therapist. He coaxed me into sitting, standing, and attempting to walk on my own with a cane.

During that time, I considered the offer Dom had made for a settlement. I knew if I sued him using a lawyer, it would take months, and the results wouldn't be any better at my age than Dom's offer. He had been more than generous. I wanted the replacement of the camper, my medical bills paid, and something set aside for any later complications I might encounter from the injuries. I felt he had covered all of those issues and more. I had to admit, after his immediate response to Pete's problem, I trusted him more than I would have in a fight with an insurance company using a lawyer.

My problem was the injuries were all on the left side so I couldn't hold the cane for support with that side. With Wade's assistance, I could manage to walk out to the patio, and rest on the padded chaise lounge in the sun.

Dom arrived each day to check my progress, and Dr. Roberts came twice a day for a wellness visit. I knew they were keeping in touch with Wade by phone.

One morning, Wade inquired if I could tolerate a short ride in a car. I explained to him that if he could help me get back out, I thought I could.

Later, Dom arrived with a large sedan, and Wade loaded both Miss Joy and me into the car. We drove into Sandy's RV sales lot not far from the motel. Dom drove to a building at the rear of the lot. True to his word, Wade helped me out of the auto then, with Miss Joy under one of his arms and me on the other, we made our way into the structure.

There, sitting in the middle of the floor, were the remains of my camper. It was a wreck, torn to shreds. I hadn't seen it other than a glance when they loaded me into the ambulance. I felt my knees beginning to buckle. Wade had a firm grip on my arm, or I think I would've fallen onto the cement floor. I knew I had taken a substantial hit from the truck and that, at the least, campers were not sturdy. This was worse than I envisioned. I really didn't want to see the inside.

A man arrived with a large golf cart and began chatting with Dom. They introduced me; his name was Sandy, the owner of the business.

He was a man in his late sixties with a big smiling face, and when he offered his hand for a handshake, I just continued to hold onto Wade for fear of falling.

He shook his head. "Sorry, not my smartest move today. I'm pleased to see you could come. I selected three campers at Dom's request to show you to replace this one. We removed everything from the camper and, other than the things they brought to you at the motel, they are stored in our secure storage area. Because we perform a lot of repair work, I have a locked storage building on site. Will you be comfortable riding in the cart?"

I hoped I could navigate getting into it, so I just nodded my head. Wade all but lifted me onto the seat, and they all piled in. Miss Joy was sitting on Wade's lap as if we did this every day.

Sandy drove us down to the office building where there were three campers parked with their slides extended. He stopped in front of the first one in the line and was busy explaining all the features. I was not paying attention. The unit was brand new, top of the line, and incredibly expensive. There wasn't any point in even looking at it. I would never pay that price for a camper. Mine had been an older used one when I bought it, and I'd driven it many miles since my purchase. I couldn't even guess at what the cost to register or insure this one would be.

Sandy looked perplexed at my lack of interest in the rig. I needed to clear the misconception around replacing my old camper. "The unit is lovely, and I'm certain the interior is great. However, I only need a small used unit to replace mine. Do you have one on the lot?"

I thought Dom was going to swallow his tongue. His face darkened and his eyes hardened. It took him a few seconds to gather himself before he spoke. "Nettie, you will *not* be paying for this equipment, nor do you need to be concerned about the cost to register or insure it. *I* am replacing your camper, not you. Do you understand what I am telling you?"

Wade leaned over and spoke very softly, but urgently, into my ear, "For God's sakes, say 'yes'."

I complied with Wade's request, and then we walked up to the steps leading into the camper. They were all waiting for me to go first. This was a challenge. I hadn't tried any steps and wasn't sure if my left leg and hip could or would support me to climb up into the rig. I knew I needed to try, but I was very embarrassed to be feeling this unstable. There were three steps. I placed my right foot on the first one while leaning on Wade and managed to step up. We repeated the procedure for the other two. I needed to sit down quickly because I was shaking and sweating with the required effort. I was also worried about how I would get back out again.

I sat in a large white leather chair closest to the door and tried to collect myself. I didn't want to seem ungrateful to Dom. He had told me he would replace my camper, and I anticipated he meant with a like unit. This camper was beyond elegant. It had two slides, one on each side making for a very spacious living area. I could see the driver and passenger seats were of the same white leather. I looked into the kitchen portion, which was well appointed. I didn't know how to tell them it was too nice as well as way too expensive.

Sandy spoke up when he realized how difficult it had been for me to enter the unit. "Nettie, please sit and rest for a moment, and I'll be right back with a better solution for the stairs." He left with his golf cart.

Dom stood in front of me looking sad. "I'm so sorry I didn't realize the effort it required to get into one of these. I've never even looked at any of the travel units available. I'm sure Sandy has a plan or we can do this another time when you're feeling better."

"Dom, thank you for your concern, I'll be okay in a minute. I do want you to know I appreciate what you are trying to do for me, but it's not necessary to be this elaborate. I just need something similar in size to mine. This unit is diesel and mine had a Ford V-10 Triton motor that produced all the power ever needed to push it over the road with ease."

I didn't expect Dom's response. He threw back his head and laughed. "You are the first woman I have ever discussed engines with in my life. I love it. Have you ever used a diesel engine?"

I explained indeed I had, when I hauled a 5th wheel with my Ford diesel and had loved the equipment.

Don continued to chat with me about how many campers I had owned and where I traveled with them.

Sandy returned with a lift. He folded the electric steps away and brought the lift even with the camper floor so I could walk out onto the lift on Wade's arm. He lowered us to the ground; this worked much better.

Sandy took us to the next unit he had displayed. As with the first, it was too elegant, and expensive. I looked and listened but made no comment. We repeated the effort with the next unit in line. He was waiting for me to make a selection. I wasn't ready to do anything with any of them. He gave me, or I should say Dom, brochures for me to read before making a selection.

Thankfully, we drove back to the automobile, and I returned to the safety of the motel for a chance to rest. The trip had rattled my old bones into a spasm of continuous pain. I needed to have some Advil and lie down.

Wade understood how much pain I had. He went to get something for me to eat, so I could take the pills. He was the kindest person I'd ever met. When he returned with a tray of sandwiches and drinks, he quickly added the Advil to the tray. I said the blessing, and we ate in silence. I knew it would take some time for the meds to work. If I could relax, they would work quicker.

When we finished our lunch, I asked Wade to go and take care of business. I didn't want to hurt his feelings, but I really wanted to be alone. I was distressed. Seeing the wrecked camper, not being able to get into the ones Sandy wanted me to see, and the degree of pain the exertion had given me were such shocks. I just wanted to go home. I didn't know how I was going to be able to get there. I knew I couldn't drive even a rental car right now. I didn't like feeling vulnerable. I hate wimpy people, and now I was one.

After Wade left to return the tray and check with his office, I tried to get out of the recliner on my own. I struggled through several attempts before I was finally able to stand. I had the cane, which seemed to be of no use to me, but I hung onto it hoping I could navigate some alone. I managed to get to the bathroom and had to sit on the hamper to catch my breath. I was so close to crying, I was ashamed of myself. I shook my head with a resolve to make it work somehow and attempted to stand again. It was easier because the hamper was taller than the recliner had been. I finished my bathroom break by washing my face in cold water, hoping it would revive me for the journey back to the bed.

I was almost to the bed when I decided to see if I could make it onto the screened patio and use the chaise lounge. In my mind that was progress; at least I would not be in bed.

I awoke with Miss Joy snuggled up next to me. At some point, Wade had put a light blanket over us. I didn't know he had been there.

Wade was sitting in the recliner reading reports when I woke again. He came out onto the patio and inquired if I would like a drink and to change positions.

I was blunt but not harsh in my answer. "I want to go home. I want you to have your life back, and I want to be me again."

Wade smiled his benevolent smile. "You've made remarkable progress. I see you made the journey to the bathroom and out here on your own. It is going to take a while for the muscles to recover from the bruising, and the arm and shoulder to heal. I do have my life back. Thanks to your arrival, I have finally been able to grieve my mom's passing. I didn't think I would ever get over losing her."

Fifteen

I had to laugh at Wade because he knew I was frustrated about things I couldn't change, so he went into the room and returned with a small bottle of diet Coke; my favorite. I smiled my thanks when he unscrewed the cap and passed it to me.

He took Miss Joy out to the grassy area and played Frisbee with her. He was a very considerate and caring man. They had just returned from play, and she was looking for her treat when his buzzer beeped. He excused himself and left abruptly for the front area of the motel.

When he returned, he was talking on his cell phone. It was obvious he was upset. I had no idea who he was speaking to or about what. He pulled the other patio chair closer to where I was sitting. Something was wrong. *Oh, Lord I prayed, please don't let anything have happened to Pete or Luce.*

"Wade, what's wrong? Are you going to share the information with me?"

He continued to look troubled, and then appeared to make a decision. "Nettie, someone just came to the front desk to inquire if the woman who was involved in the accident was still staying here or if she had left. My front desk clerk buzzed me; that was why I left. My clerk informed the person we don't give any information about our guests to anyone. The woman left the office. Could you speak with my clerk? I want to know who it was, and why she came here."

I was shocked. "Of course, I'll speak with her! I need to know who she was, and why she was here, too."

Wade phoned the clerk and asked her to come to the room. She arrived in a matter of minutes. She explained a woman had come to the desk in the motel lobby and made the inquiry. She assured me she had not given her any indication I was in the motel.

I asked her to describe the person for me. When she was done, I knew it was the 'crazy woman.' How had she known about the accident or where I was? I also knew I was a sitting duck here. There was no way I could defend myself. This realization shook me to the core of my soul.

Wade thanked the clerk, and she returned to her station. He was concerned; it showed in his wrinkled brow, along with the fact he kept running his hand through his hair. Miss Joy sensed there was something wrong, so she hopped up onto his lap.

Dom arrived just after the clerk left the room. He was not alone. He had a young muscular man with him who looked like a thug in nice clothing. "Nettie, this is Bruce. He'll be here for the time being until I get this sorted out."

When Dom's cell phone rang, he answered it quickly. He spoke with the person in a clipped manner, then closed his phone. He addressed all of us. "Mystery solved as to how she found you here; she went to Sandy's and spoke with the man who works for him in the back repair shop. She told him she was an insurance adjuster so she needed to inspect the damage. She asked him if the driver was in the hospital, and he had no reason not to tell her, so he sent her here. Is this the nut job the Feds are looking for?"

Now, I was even more concerned. I knew I was in mortal danger. She could finish me off with a slingshot, and I wouldn't be able to do anything about it. Bruce was looking better to me now.

Dom sensed my angst. He made an awkward attempt to pat me on my good shoulder to reassure me it would be all right. I didn't believe him, and he knew it.

"Dom, I wonder how she got the information as to where I was. I didn't tell anyone other than Pete I was going to Virginia, and even he didn't know what town in the state. I wonder if she has an accomplice in the Bureau."

Dom took his phone out and relayed this information to his contact at the Bureau. When he finished with the phone call, he informed us he would be getting information as soon as this person found it. I didn't anticipate anything would be forthcoming soon.

With Wade's assistance, I reentered the room. I was content to rest on the bed with Joy by my side. I needed to talk with Wade privately. My opportunity came when Dom left and instructed Bruce to guard the door in the hall.

"Wade, when they brought my things from the camper, do you recall if they found my revolver? I would like to have it handy if doing so won't distress you too much."

Wade's grin said it all. "Hell no, it won't bother me. It'll make me happy to have you guard me, although it will ruin my reputation as a badass. Let me see if it's in your bag. There was quite an assortment… a Bible, and a gun. You're my kind of woman."

Wade searched and found my .38 Colt Detective Special in its carrying case. It was still loaded with the five bullets I carried in the cylinder. I always left the sixth cylinder empty with the hammer resting there for safety.

That evening Wade thought a change of venue would perk up my sagging spirits so he wanted me to go to the dining room for dinner. We would leave Joy in the room. With Bruce monitoring the hall, we felt she would be fine.

We were sitting in the booth enjoying our appetizer and chatting when a movement caused me to look over Wade's shoulder. It was *the woman*; she was walking slowly out of the dining room toward the outside patio area of the restaurant. I grabbed Wade's hand so hard he flinched. "She's here and is walking out through the door over there. Get Bruce quick!"

Wade sprinted through the door leading to the corridor. I got out of my seat with difficulty and walked as fast as I could to the door through which she exited. She was walking toward the parking area with something stuffed in the front of her jacket. I heard the yelp of pain just as I pushed open the door, and realized she had Miss Joy bundled in her coat. I called as loudly as I could, "Miss Joy, COME QUICK!" I saw her twist her little body as the woman squeezed her hard enough to make her cry out in pain again. Miss Joy bit her on her cheek. The shock of the bite made her lessen her grip on the dog, and Joy bolted out of her grasp, running toward me as fast as she could. She dashed through the open door and sat on my foot looking up at me. I wanted to scoop her up into my arms while trying to hold my balance. The waiter came to my rescue and lifted her up into my good arm. I stood there leaning against the back of an empty booth and just sobbed. She was shaking like a leaf, and so was I.

Wade flew into the dining room with Bruce on his heels, but they were too late to get a plate number from the car.

Wade helped me back to our booth and tucked Miss Joy into the corner beside me. He was as white as a sheet. His hands were shaking. I reached over and patted his hand. "It'll be okay, please, don't worry." From the look on his face, I thought he was going to cry. I patted his hand and gave it a gentle squeeze. None of this was his fault. Somehow, I'd brought the mess with me.

I knew I'd never let Joy out of my sight again until I knew the bitch was dead. How dare she touch my dog? I was wild with anger. If she messed with me that was one thing, but to touch a harmless animal was another.

Dom entered the dining room like a thundercloud. His face resembled a bust chiseled out of granite… his eyes were jet-black, cold, hard, and the set of his shoulders scared me. There wasn't any semblance of Mr. Nice-Guy. Wade had warned me once, Dom wasn't a man to trifle with. He looked at Bruce and nodded to the exit door. He hadn't spoken a word to anyone. I felt sorry for Bruce as he followed Dom across the parking lot.

"Wade, do you think we should remove this distraction from your dining area? I'm so sorry to have created a problem for you. Can we return to the room?"

With Wade's assistance and Miss Joy in his arms, we made our way to the peace and quiet of the suite.

When we entered the room, we found a stranger there. It was obvious Wade didn't know who he was as he stopped abruptly, stepping in front of me. The man put his hand up in a halt signal while he moved his suit coat aside so we could see he was wearing a badge on his belt. "I'm Agent Samson, FBI; I've been assigned to shadow Nettie."

He sure didn't look like any Sampson I'd ever imagined. He was small in stature, looking more like a bookie than a protector should. All I could think of was Don Adams when he played an agent named Maxwell Smart. I noticed when he moved his jacket to show us his badge he was carrying an automatic pistol in a shoulder holster. Even wearing a badge didn't help my attitude toward him. I instantly did not like him. He looked shifty and so far, nothing he had done had adjusted my thinking.

Wade slowly let his breath out with an audible sigh. I think all of the excitement had been too much for this mild-mannered man. I needed to get away from here and out of his life.

Dom walked in without even knocking, sized up the situation, and nodded his approval. He addressed Sampson directly. "Can you explain to me in ten words, or less, how the hell this could happen? Your agency can't catch this damn woman, and yet she has been here two times with enough information to hunt Nettie down. How did she get into this suite and take the dog? If you are going to stand there and offer me some insipid excuse, spare me. Save your breath and my time."

Sampson's reply surprised me; he wasn't the least bit intimidated by Dom. "Sir, I can tell you how she got in here. That was simple; she picked the lock on the patio door. How she developed her information, we don't know. We are investigating inside sources. If I gather new information, I'll keep you posted as per my instructions."

I spoke directly to Dom. "I need to get out of here before someone who has no skin in the game gets hurt. I need to go home at once. She'll follow me because she wants revenge, which will remove her from your area, and let things become peaceful again."

Dom looked at Wade and softly spoke to him. "You need to put Nettie into a chair or the bed before she collapses. I think the same may be true for Miss Joy. If you hold her any tighter she'll stop breathing." Then Dom smiled, softening his expression.

Wade chuckled and put Miss Joy on the bed where she promptly made a little nest with the pillow and laid down. Wade offered me his arm and seated me in the recliner. I was relieved to sit.

I realized the whole dog-and-pony-show had probably taken only three minutes, but I was exhausted. I was so tired I couldn't even feel if I had any pain; it was a first in my life.

Sampson excused himself to step outside on the patio to take a call on his cell phone.

Dom put a hand on Wade's shoulder in a fatherly fashion, while he explained everything would be okay. "Now, Wade, how about you break out a glass of wine for us, and then we'll talk?"

I could see Wade's expression soften as his shoulders relaxed and a grin spread across his face. The old Wade had returned. He left and returned with a tray containing a bottle and three glasses. He opened the bottle and poured us all a glass while Dom pulled a chair closer to the recliner. Wade slid his hassock beside my chair so he could sit closer and be inside the group. We toasted each other and sipped while Miss Joy napped. Life seemed good for the moment. I knew it wouldn't, and couldn't, last. This was just a lull in the mayhem.

Sampson returned to the room to inform us they hadn't found the car or the woman. He'd alerted the state police and all local law enforcement. There were also two other agents on the premises, and all three would remain for the duration of my stay.

I asked Sampson about any progress in checking on the relatives of Pete and other people she had victimized. He told me he didn't have any information, but would check with his supervisor and get back to me.

Dom waited until Sampson left the room then inquired. "Nettie, why is she so hell bent on getting you? She could have just walked away with the money she defrauded the bank out of and no one would have been the wiser. I don't get her vendetta with you."

I smirked. "I beat the crap out of her physically when she returned to the property for the second time. I think *that* made it personal. She doesn't like me. The woman is totally deranged. When you look at her when she's angry, she even presents as insane. She was nearly unstoppable. I was serious when I said I needed to leave before she harms any of you folks. I would appreciate any assistance you can give me to make it happen."

There was a soft knock on the door. Wade opened the door and admitted the caller. Dr. Roberts entered with a warm greeting. The good doctor took in our social circle along with the wine bottle. "I don't recall prescribing that medication for you, Nettie. Where's my glass? I'm not sure I'm fully protected from whatever is going around here, so I need some of the antidote."

Wade returned with another glass, and an additional bottle of wine, and pulled a chair for Dr. Roberts into the circle. We sipped and brought Dr. Roberts up to date on our antics. His only comment was, "I thought I said bed rest and quiet. What happened to the doctor's orders?" The entire comment was delivered with a hearty laugh.

Dom looked directly at Dr. Roberts and said, "I forbade Nettie to leave here until she is healthy and you release her. What is your opinion on the matter? I think she would be safer here with us, three FBI agents, and four of my men around the clock."

Dr. Roberts nodded. "I agree with you, Dom. I wouldn't want her to bungle the healing on her arm to say nothing of her other injuries. If she were going to do hand-to-hand combat, perhaps we should buy her a Kevlar vest and an Uzi."

I needed to have some answers, so I asked. "I understand this seemed funny, but I must tell you, from years of experience, I'm really concerned about the folks in the 'change of identity' program they can't find. What happened to their relatives? This woman has a lot of moxie to just show up and demand money for not harming their families. She had, and I firmly believe still has, access to files on whom, what and where. Nobody dared to blow the whistle on her for fear of what she would do. She had free rein. Most of the people who entered the program thought, wrongly, the government would keep them safe. They were just work-a-day people reporting a wrong because they were nice honest folks. They probably never even had a check bounce. How could they deal with the likes of her? If they stood up to her, I believe she would have no problem killing them.

"After our dust-up, she promised to return and kill me. Perhaps her quest will be satisfied. Presently, I'm a little defenseless, if you hadn't noticed. Doctor, perhaps you could install a shiv in a hard cast, so I could at the very least beat her on the head with it."

You could have heard a pin drop in the room. I could see from their expressions they never thought about how serious and far-flung the situation was.

After a few moments and some brief chatter, Dr. Roberts excused himself and left. Dom said his goodbyes with cautions to be careful and stay safe, and then departed.

Sixteen

When Wade and I were alone, I questioned him about whether he had a car. His response was humorous, "Do you want to run away with me?" We both enjoyed a good laugh.

"Tomorrow, will you take me to Sandy's? I want to look at something he has for an RV." We made our plans, and then Wade took Miss Joy for her evening stroll accompanied by one of Dom's men while I prepared for bed. It had been a long day. I was ready to rest.

Wade arrived with a breakfast cart and a devilish sparkle in his eye. I think he was ready to have a small adventure. We ate our breakfast and read the morning paper. I had a plan. I was ready and rested enough to get it done. While Wade returned the food-cart, I dressed for the day. Nothing fit well anymore; it all seemed too large. Having my arm in the sling made it more difficult to maneuver getting dressed.

Wade took Miss Joy and led us to a small silver truck parked out back. We drove to Sandy's lot. I directed him to a second row of RV units. When we stopped in front of the camper I wanted to see, we heard Sandy arriving on his golf cart. We hadn't called ahead because I needed time to scrutinize the rig without any fanfare.

Sandy greeted us, but seemed a little surprised at our being there. I explained I wanted to see the interior of the unit. Sandy explained the history. Although the rig was new, it was a two-year old model. I already knew the information because I had looked it up on his website. He unlocked the door, and while Wade held Miss Joy, I made my way up the steps into the camper.

I liked it. The unit was nicely appointed and typical of that manufacturer, having the full kitchen I wanted and a similar floor plan to my old camper. The exception was having two slides, where mine had none. There were chairs and a table, instead of booth seating. I walked to the rear to check out the bathroom. *Wow*, was my only thought. It was larger than mine had been and was much nicer. I liked all the large windows with the day/night blinds. It was tastefully decorated, and very upscale, different from anything I'd seen.

Sandy and I discussed the running gear and history of the unit. He had ordered the unit when they were having a promotion for smaller, more upscale models. It was a beautiful camper, but everyone wanted larger units at the time, so it languished on his lot.

"I would like you to start it, and I want to take it for a road test if you could arrange it now." Wade's expression was one of pure horror. I was certain from his expression, he thought I was going to ask him to drive.

Sandy assured me he could jump the battery, move it ahead out of the line, and we could check the slides. I would see how spacious it really was. In a matter of minutes, we were sitting in the middle of the lot with the slides extended and the motor purring away. I liked the camper. I had to determine if I could drive it with only one arm.

Sandy closed the slides and offered to go with us to drive. Sitting in the driver's seat, I declined his offer while I made the necessary adjustments to the electric seat. The adjustment was difficult because it was on my left side. I managed the task, and smiled at Wade who sat tentatively in the passenger seat holding Miss Joy as if she would protect him from danger.

"Okay there, Mr. Wade, buckle up and get your prayer beads out. We are leaving the lot." I knew we were being followed by at least one man… who he belonged to I didn't care. I was taking my life back. I needed to know how capable I still was, even while I healed from the accident. God was not done with me, so I was required to step up to the plate, and play my part as well as I could.

I eased the rig into gear and started out of the lot. I'd downloaded the area map, so I knew if I turned right, I would be on a secondary road with little or no traffic. I would also have ample places to turn the rig around without too much effort. I stopped at the end of the lot to adjust the electric mirrors, then drove out onto the road.

After about a mile, I noticed Wade begin to relax and loosen his grip on the dog. I smiled. I knew I would be okay to drive this camper. I wasn't sure how far or for how long, but this was a start. That was all I needed to put my plan into place. I pulled into a small business with a nice circular drive and turned back toward the lot. I was happy it had been a successful trial run.

When I drove back onto the lot, Sandy was waiting. He looked relieved and had a huge smile plastered across his face. I parked, wanting to see if I could exit the cab and get onto the ground with only one arm and a bad left leg. I did; although it wasn't the most graceful exit I have ever accomplished. Nonetheless, I succeeded without any assistance.

I told Sandy I would take the camper. Because the unit had been on his lot for a couple of years, I wanted him to install new tires and do an overly careful servicing of the unit.

His reply struck me funny. "I called Dom and told him you were here and had selected a camper for a road test. When he asked me who was driving; I explained you were. He chuckled and mentioned that you were 'one damned independent woman.' I told him the rig was a holdover from two years ago, and he wanted me to get the same thing, but newer. After some wrangling, he told me to give you whatever you wanted. I'll change the tires, service, clean and load your things into the unit. I could have it ready tomorrow if the timing works for you."

"Sandy, what do you know about the campground out on the lake near here? I found only limited information when I researched it on the web."

He smiled, "My uncle owns it. The park is very nice, well run, and quiet. Do you want me to give him a call?"

"I may after I check it out. Thanks. If you get this ready, I'll let you know where and when I want it delivered. I appreciate your assistance. I don't need to tell you I don't want anyone else to know what I have selected or the timeline of it being ready to leave."

We got into Wade's truck to leave. I realized he hadn't said anything at all while we did the test drive or talked with Sandy. "Wade, what's wrong? Did you not approve of my selection? I've never known you to be so silent."

He looked sad. "You're planning on leaving soon, aren't you? I worry you'll get hurt by the crazy woman or be too exhausted to drive and have another accident. I know you want to go home, but I think it is far too soon, considering the state of your health."

Wade was a sweet and caring man with a good heart. He would have no basis upon which to understand the turmoil going on in my mind. I'd lived my entire life, with God's help, taking care of others and myself. Seldom, during all my years, had I ever been so incapacitated. I was unable to protect anyone including myself. I needed to end this cat-and-mouse game with the idiot woman so I could get on with what was left of my life.

I found it extremely annoying that the Bureau and local law could not catch one person. I needed to be free of her threats in order to move on. I knew she was predatory in her thinking. I also knew she would keep trying to get me as long as I appeared to be a victim. *She was in for a surprise.*

I asked him if he would take me to the RV Park Sandy told us about. The request caused him more distress. "You can't be thinking of staying out there. Who would protect you?"

Easy answer. "Me…it isn't the first time in my life someone has hunted me with ill intent. It'll be all right. I want the danger away from you and the motel staff. You have been so kind and caring, it would break my heart if you were injured or something happened to your business."

We rode on in silence. I knew he was troubled. I intended to change the state of his thinking.

As we approached the park, there was a paved road passing through a thick stand of mixed trees shielding it from the main road. We passed through a large, mowed meadow, giving a neat appearance to the entrance. The road curved and meandered around the small pond allowing campsites to be on both sides, then a row of lakefront lots. All of the lots appeared to be large enough to accommodate substantial rigs. Some were obviously seasonal or yearly lots with campers installed on them.

As we drove slowly through, I spotted a corner lot suitable for my purpose. I made note of the lot number, and the fact there wasn't a unit placed there. We finished our tour and returned to the motel in time for lunch.

I phoned Sandy and asked him to speak with his uncle to see if the lot I'd selected was available. If it was, could he please plan on delivering the unit to the lot and set it up for me?

Dom arrived shortly after I placed the call to Sandy. I wasn't surprised. He wanted to talk with me about my plans. He, of course, knew we had been out to the park because I was certain Wade had enlisted his assistance to convince me I was nuts.

"I'm delighted you found the camper you liked. I have taken care of it with Sandy. However, I don't want you to go out to the park and stay. What in hell are you thinking?" I could see he was getting a little upset, but I was still going to implement my plan.

"Dom, I was never a person who ran scared. I'm not stupid or careless. I won't allow the crazy bitch to control my life. I know I've said this before, but I think if they ever investigated all the files she'd been involved with or still is, the circumstances would be dire. I don't have much faith they'll even try. The fallout would give the agency a black eye. I need to end this for me, right now!"

He shook his head and looked to Wade for support. "I'll give you as much backup as I can, but I'm worried it won't be adequate. This is like shadow dancing with a spook."

My answer floored him. "She's hiding in plain sight, which is why no one can find her. I need to draw her to me, on my terms. That will level the playing field."

I could see the dawn of awareness spread over Dom's face. He reached for his cell phone, excused himself, and left without a good bye. It was evident he was on a mission.

I busied myself packing my personal belongings getting ready for my move to the camper the next day.

Later in the afternoon, Wade joined me on the screened patio. He arrived with a tray of munchies, a bottle of wine, and two glasses. I smiled at him and expressed how much I was going to miss these services. He grinned as if he knew something I didn't. I allowed him the pleasure of his secret.

In the evening, we ate in the dining room. We were in a private room. The room was quiet with a large table set for several people, decked out with fresh flowers everywhere. When we arrived with Miss Joy on her leash, I was happy we would perhaps not disrupt the other diners tonight as we had on our last trip to the dining room.

The door opened, and Dom arrived with a lady on his arm. She was as striking as he was handsome. She had startling green eyes and beautiful long black hair with just a little white showing at her temples. The lady was tall and slender with an athletic figure. Dom introduced her as Cher, his wife. She had a good grip in her handshake. I would've bet she played a mean game of tennis.

Dr. Roberts arrive a few moments later with a woman I assumed was his wife. Then two younger men with ladies on their arms came. It had turned into a gathering. The two new men were almost carbon copies of Dom, so I surmised they were Dom and Cher's sons with their wives. Everyone was making an effort to introduce him or herself, so I would know who everyone was.

The waiter wheeled a cart into the room and began dispensing wine and drinks for everyone. Wade secured a glass of wine for me. Another cart arrived with every imaginable canapé and cheese selection. This was quite a party. If I had known they would celebrate this way, I would have left earlier. However, by waiting until now, I could at least stand and walk with my cane.

There was a knock on the door, and Dom went to admit whoever was there. A young man was there with another older man. Dom hugged the young man and shook hands with his escort. Cher moved to Dom's side and embraced the young man.

Dom escorted the new arrival to me. He introduced him as Anthony, but told me to call him Tony. The young man had been the driver of the truck in the accident. I was pleased to see he was well. It was obvious Tony wanted to talk to me, so we stepped away from the crowd to a quiet corner of the room.

When he spoke, his voice was strong but gentle. "I needed to personally tell you how sorry I am that I hurt and scared you. I also want to thank you for saving my life. When I saw you on the gurney after the wreck, holding your dog, for the first time in my life, I saw the true face of God. Please don't think I'm blowing smoke at you. I want you to know I was born and raised into a very strict, loving family; well educated, church going and all the right things. I blew off my responsibilities and skated through life, thinking I was entitled to everything. I got into drugs big time at college and never stopped. I had connections, along with the funds, so I did as I pleased. I stayed just straight enough to fly under the radar; it worked well enough to get me by. When I saw you lying there, I wasn't certain if you would live or not. It sobered me completely. I realized I could have rammed your camper down the embankment with the tractor, and smashed you, and it, to hell and beyond. I can tell you this with no fear of ever having to apologize again to anyone; I will never drink or do drugs again. I wanted you to know this from my lips, not someone else's. I know my dad took care of your expenses. I'm grateful we could. I'll always owe you my life. If you ever need anything, please call me. I don't care how big or small, I will take care of you. I have to return to the center now; I'm out on a pass. I need to finish this re-hab, then get back to work. Please take care of yourself and stay safe." He gave me a big hug with a kiss on my cheek, said his good-byes to his family, and was gone.

I needed some space to process everything I'd been told. I was flattered he'd made the effort to come and speak with me. I prayed he could get his life back on track and keep it there. Drugs were killing off our young folks at an alarming rate.

Seventeen

Early the next morning, Sandy called to inform me the camper was already at the lake and installed on the lot. He had left the keys with his uncle.

I coerced Wade into taking me shopping at the local supermarket for provisions, then we went out to the park to see if everything was in order. Sandy's installation of the unit was perfect. I could see the lake and still have privacy. I also noticed there were several new campers that had not been there on my previous visit.

I blessed Wade for carrying the provisions into the camper for me. Sandy had placed all my belongings from the wreck in the cupboards and closets. It would take me a while to sort through and see what had not survived the accident.

I thanked Wade and told him he needed to return to his work and his life. He didn't want to leave me there alone. Finally, he voiced his concern. "I don't like you being here without me and some coverage from the agents. What will you do if she shows up here and catches you without backup?"

"Wade, I know she'll show up out here. It's just a matter of time. I'll be fine, and I won't be worried about harming you or your business. I have my cell phone, and I checked the coverage when we were here the other day. If something happens, you will be the first to know. You need to go to work and enjoy some time without having to babysit." I gave him a warm hug and sent him on his way.

While it was still daylight, I wanted to explore my surroundings and learn the lay of the land. I took Miss Joy for a pleasant stroll around the park. I noticed the three campers next to mine were from Sandy's lot. When I walked behind them toward the meadow, I made note that none of them was registered. Had Sandy supplied housing for either Dom's men or the FBI agents who had been at the motel?

When I returned to the camper, I put out the mat along with the folding chairs and tables so we could sit out under the awning and watch the sunset across the lake. It was a pretty setting, and I intended to enjoy what I could of my freedom. I had to admit I should have asked Wade to put the rug and the furniture out for me. With only one useable arm, it had been somewhat of a struggle to get it done. Hindsight is always 20/20.

As darkness began to fall, I busied myself with fixing dinner. It was a treat to cook again. Although the food at the motel was great, I had missed some simple things. I didn't indulge in my usual glass of wine with dinner. I needed to be alert and on guard. I knew in my bones, tonight I would have a visitor.

I fixed a place in the sling on my arm where I could carry my revolver. I was as ready as I was going to be, considering the circumstances.

I waited until it was dark with the only illumination being the park lights, before I took Miss Joy for her evening walk. If anybody were watching, that person would only see someone casually strolling along the park road walking his or her pet. I walked the whole loop being pleasantly surprised at the lack of bugs. I always like to be grateful for the small things in life.

I returned to the camper carefully checking the surrounding area. Interestingly there had been no activity in the camper next to mine, and there were no lights showing. I brought the dog in and settled in the chair to see if I could access the internet with my laptop.

Although it had sustained damage in the accident, I was certain it would still work.

I had been playing with the computer for a few minutes when Miss Joy began acting anxious. She wasn't whining, but something was troubling her. She was getting more agitated by the second. I quieted her, then told her to stay. I couldn't hear anything out of the ordinary, but I knew something was not right.

I'd taken precautions before settling in for the evening by placing tape over the button for the cab lights on the driver's door. I also checked if the door would open without any noise from the hinges. I sat in the driver's seat, carefully opened the door, and slid out to the ground. I stood still as a statue and listened.

My heart was beating so hard, I was sure they could hear it in the office. I made an effort to calm my breathing, then crouched by the front wheel. As my eyes adjusted to the darkness and my night vision improved, I began to hear a rustle in the grass coming from the meadow. I'd hunted since I was a young child, so I was keenly aware of night noises and movements.

My patience paid off in dividends as I watched a figure emerge from the edge of the meadow onto the grassy surface of the lot. I recognized the gait of the woman. I held my breath and waited to see where she was heading.

Soon it would be *show time*.

I silently prayed Miss Joy would not become more alarmed or begin barking and scare her off. As I looked under the camper, I could see her legs, silhouetted by the park lights, walking along the side of my unit. She was getting down on her knees for some reason. I watched for a moment then realized she was opening the compartment housing my propane tank. It was time to stop the foolishness before she had time to do something dangerous.

I stepped carefully around the front of the rig with my .38 in my hand, cocked and ready. She was so invested in what she was trying to do she didn't sense my presence until I pressed the revolver to the back of her neck with a warning. "Don't even breathe. It's loaded and cocked. Put your hands on your head, and stay right where you are." She stiffened when I touched the gun to her neck then slowly raised her hands and placed them on her head. She had not uttered a sound. I knew I was handicapped in the fact I only had one hand. If she moved, I would have no problem shooting her, somewhere.

At that moment, a male voice said, "What in hell is going on here? Nettie what are you doing? Let her get up. I'll handle this matter from here. I need you to stand down now." I recognized the voice as Sampson, the Agent. He did not appear to have a weapon drawn, which I found odd, considering he was there and had obviously been watching what happened.

The woman stood up, turned, faced Sampson, and then spit in his face. He was so shocked he stepped back a step, nearly knocking me down. In that instant, she was gone. He ran toward where he thought she'd gone, but found nothing. She was like chasing a wisp of smoke in a gale. I was beyond furious. I'd had her. It would have been over. The dumb ass had helped her get away, yet again.

Before Sampson returned empty-handed, as I knew he would, I had Dom on the phone with a request to have his friend, the person in charge of this idiot, call me directly. The whole mess smelled to me and not in a pleasant manner. I promised Dom I would update him as soon as I finished speaking to Agent Carter.

My cell rang and Carter was on the line asking what the problem was. I gave him a quick synopsis of the last few minutes and the fact his man, Sampson, had again assisted and allowed the crazy woman to escape. I told him my honest feeling there were most likely more sticky fingers in the pie than anyone realized. I wanted Sampson removed, and out of my way, or he was going to get me killed while he was *playing* protector.

Agent Carter remained silent for several seconds when I finished my rant. When he spoke again, he was calm and very firm saying he was leaving and would be there before daylight. He inquired if I thought she would return during the remainder of the night. I assured him if she did, I would be ready and waiting. I was done with intimidation from her, his men, or anyone else. I was clearly finished with this whole situation.

I got a chuckle for a response and a, "See you in the morning. I like my coffee fresh, black, and strong."

Sampson returned just as I rang off from the call to Adam. He wanted me to think he had run for some distance chasing her. I knew better because I heard a car start and drive away out by the front road. The second clue was that the grass in the meadow was taller than the lawns on the lots. The meadow was heavy with early evening dew and very wet. Sampson's shoes were damp just above the soles. *Sorry, I just look dumb.* He gasped out, "I couldn't catch her."

I ground my teeth, but said calmly, "Get the hell away from me before you get me killed. Don't come near this unit or me again. Do you understand me?"

He looked like I'd taken a swipe at him. He kind of puffed himself up for bravado, then spat out, "I was told to guard you. I was doing my job. What in hell did you think you were going to do…a one-armed cripple of an old woman against her? I should think you would be happy I scared her away and saved your sorry ass."

Now I was *pissed*. "Look, you stupid son of a bitch, if I needed protection I wouldn't call on some sorry-ass pretender. You stay away from me, or I will personally shoot you with no remorse. Now get out of here and stay away."

He was mad as hell; too damn bad for him. I took out my phone and took a photo of the cutters she had dropped on the ground under the edge of the unit by the propane tank. I made certain there was enough of the camper in the shot so if the cutters were moved or removed, I would know.

As if by cue, I heard a car coming into the drive of the park and headed to my lot.

Dom and Wade arrived with another man I'd never seen. I knew Adam had called either one or the other of them. I was certain it wasn't Sampson. When they pulled into the parking space, it seems they all exited the vehicle at once. When they reached where I was standing, Dom was the first to speak. "I told you this wasn't a good idea. What happened? Why are you standing out here?"

"I was waiting for you folks to arrive. Did Adam call you? Then you know what happened here. I was just taking a photo with my phone of the cutters she left behind because I was certain they'd disappear before daylight. You can see them for yourselves. I don't know if she was planning on cutting brake lines or the propane tank lines. Either way I stopped her before she got the task completed. Come on in and sit for a moment. Let's see how long it will take for the cutters to move."

Dom asked, "Where is Sampson? He was supposed to be guarding you and the area."

"I assume he is sulking somewhere because I chewed his ass about his behavior or lack thereof. He botched getting her. Then he lied to me about chasing her across the meadow. I told him to get away from me before he got me killed."

We entered through the coach door. I reached in and closed the driver's door I'd left ajar when I exited to catch her. I snapped the electric door lock to secure both doors.

Dom introduced me to the new man, Fred. He was middle aged, rugged, of medium height, trimmed beard and a cropped haircut. He had a keen eye; one of those people you knew was quick to assess his surroundings. He looked capable of handling himself in almost any situation.

Wade hadn't uttered a word. He was just standing there as if he'd lost his best friend. Miss Joy came and sat by his foot. He scooped her into his arms and began to pat her. From his expression, I thought he was trying to soothe himself more than the dog.

Dom asked Fred to check out the perimeter, stay out of sight, and to keep an eye on the pair of dropped cutters. Fred exited the camper and walked away as if he were going to the area where the public bathrooms were. I watched him disappear into the shadows created by the lack of illumination from the streetlight in that area by the road. I knew he would double back to my lot under the cover of darkness. I liked his style.

I made a pot of coffee, and we sat and chatted about nothing too important until we heard a scuffle at the side of the camper. I didn't get up, but Dom was out through the door like a lightning bolt. Wade decided he would stay with me. He spoke softly, "Sampson is either an idiot or had a death wish to cross Dom… *that's never healthy.* I'm certain if Adam Carter sent him, he also told him not to mess with Dom.

"Fred is a good guy. You can trust him with anything. I have a feeling whoever he just tangled with is not feeling too well, at the moment. I wish you would return to the motel. I don't think there is any way you can be safe here alone."

Just as Wade finished speaking, Dom came back into the camper. He sat in the chair he had vacated and reached for his coffee cup as if he'd just stepped out for a cigar or something. He made no mention of where Fred was or what happened. I didn't ask because some things are better unsaid.

Dom checked his watch and said, "Nettie, I think you better make another pot of coffee. Adam will be here shortly, and he really does like it fresh, hot, and black. I expect he'll be arriving in about five minutes."

I smiled and made a new pot of coffee.

Eighteen

Adam arrived in six minutes, according to the clock on the microwave. I was pleasantly surprised. The man stood about six feet six inches, with a muscular build. He was a large, handsome black man with an even larger smile. His face was clean-shaven with his hair close cut. The only thing about him that wasn't a surprise was his voice. He looked nothing at all, as I'd imagined him. He seemed to fill the space in the camper with energy that flowed from his body.

Adam helped himself to a mug of coffee, then sat in the passenger seat rotated toward the living area. "Okay, let's get this dealt with; bring Sampson here. I want to talk with him face to face.

"Nettie, I'm sorry this happened. I'm learning more and more about several things in my department I was totally unaware of, including this case. I took the position about a year ago, so I missed the history of these cases. I've done due diligence after I spoke with Dom and you.

"A clerk I trusted and brought with me when I transferred performed most of my research. As far as I know, that person and I are the only ones who know what we have uncovered. I need to warn you some, or most, of it was not good."

Dom left the camper, returning with Fred who had Sampson in tow. Sampson was sputtering insults to Fred about what he was going to do to him for roughing up a federal employee. Fred all but hoisted him into the camper. When Sampson spotted Adam, all the bluster left like a deflated balloon.

When Sampson finally pulled himself together, he spoke directly to Adam. "Sir, I'm glad you're here and can get this straightened out directly. This group of people has treated me abysmally. I saved her from danger, then she insulted me and told me to get lost. I was making a check of the unit and this goon tackled me, and the other one egged him on."

Adam looked at Sampson as if he were a cockroach. "Shut up, Sampson. You're a disgrace to the agency. You are also dismissed. There'll be a car here shortly to take you to lockdown where you will remain indefinitely, until I'm finished with the investigation. Pass over your service pistol, identification and any other weapons you're carrying along with your cell phone and any electronics."

Sampson began to argue with him. "You can't do this. Who do you think you are? I'm entitled to an attorney along with a fair hearing. I know my rights."

Adam stood, dwarfing the smaller man, "Either hand them over, or I'll personally search you, and it won't be to your liking. Do it now." He took a step toward Sampson, who would have stepped back except Fred was blocking him.

He tried to make a break for the door beside Fred who quickly clamped him around his middle, pinning his arms to his side. His feet were not touching the floor. I dare say I didn't know how he could breathe with so much pressure around his middle. Strangely, I didn't care. Fred removed him to the waiting car and continued his surveillance of the camper.

Adam turned his attention to me. "Nettie, I *have* done some checking into this matter. First, let me express to you how sorry I am you became the brunt of the problem. The woman you thought was Mary Murphy doesn't exist. She worked for the department after leaving the army on a medical discharge. She was in basic training when an accident occurred. They gave her an honorable discharge due to medical circumstances. She applied for a clerical position with the Bureau. She worked her way up through the ranks quickly, until she reached the whistleblower's section. Her real name is Janet Mason. There were no adverse personnel records until after she'd been in the division for about eighteen months.

"Problems first surfaced because of Janet's spending habits, which was a dead give-a-way when her lifestyle became extravagant. They made an inquiry; she abruptly left the job without notice and disappeared. We hadn't any reason to pursue her until I got the call from Dom.

"When I got his call regarding Sampson, I ran his recent profile and bingo! He was a close friend to Janet when she worked in the office. He had continued a relationship with her; however, I'm unsure as to what it was, or is. We need to get you to a safer place until we catch her, or she'll harm you. I truthfully believe she is deranged."

He hadn't asked for my opinion, but I offered it anyhow. "I'm not hiding out for the rest of my life in order to avoid her. That's not my style. I want to go home and see if I can piece my life back together. I must admit I find it ridiculous nobody can find this woman, yet she can find me. She'll come back for another go at me, I'm certain of that fact. She may wait a day or two, but she'll come, and I'll be here."

Dom and Adam shook their heads like two bobble dolls. Dom spoke first, "Nettie, I'm sorry but I can't allow *that* to happen."

I laughed. "Dom, I'm an adult and, even with all your generosity, I can't allow you to run my life. I appreciate your concern. I need to get this finished now. The longer it goes on, the more time she has to dream up a higher level of mayhem. Shit is shit, no matter how you present it. The stench always remains. I will stay here until I finish with her, or she wins."

Adam was the next to add his two cents. "Nettie I'm ready and willing to give you coverage. I need her found more than you do. When I began checking the records of folks admitted to the program,

I had an issue finding several of them. This information cannot leave here, is that clear? I also don't know if there are others involved in this shakedown scheme.

"Dom, how many units did you have placed in this park? Where are they located? How are they linked?

"Nettie, I want you to wear a device so we can talk and track you at all times. If you're out walking the dog and see anything out of order, even if it's all right, I want it reported so we can check it out. Do you understand?"

I appreciated the fact that Adam had been thorough in his thought process in the attempt to cover me and to catch her.

Nineteen

We sat and discussed a plan of attack with the goal of catching Janet. Giving her a name didn't change my mental choice of calling her *crazy woman*. It had worked for me, so I was going to stick with it.

When dawn finally brightened the sky, they all thought it would be safe for me with only Fred and another man on duty. We didn't think she would show up during daylight. I had the link where I could contact Fred in an instant without using a phone. The small microphone was wireless and transmitted from a small unit in my jeans pocket.

After everyone left, I took Miss Joy for her morning walk and returned for a short nap. It had been a long night for both of us.

In the afternoon, we sat under the awning while I worked on the new computer Dom had left me. The accident had damaged my old one beyond my ability to repair it. I called Pete to see if he was doing okay. I didn't share with him the crazy stuff going on with my life.

Joy and I had an early dinner then went for our stroll by the lake. I was noticing the fact most of the campers were empty. Most likely, the owners came on the weekends to enjoy the lake. I prayed it wouldn't complicate our catching Janet. We returned to the unit where I closed the blinds as if getting ready to retire for the night. I didn't intend to sleep during any hour of darkness until they found her, but the first night passed without incident.

Miss Joy and I kept to our usual routine with walks and reading under the awning in the afternoon.

On the second night, I felt a real sense of uneasiness that wouldn't leave me. Later in the evening, I wondered if I loosened the binder on my arm, it might make me more comfortable. I wasn't going to be lying down so I could keep it stable with just the sling. I removed the binder and it seemed to be more comfortable while I was sitting in the recliner. I left the .38 colt tucked into the fold of the sling just in case.

I loved the fact my passenger seat became part of my living space when it was swiveled around and put on the recliner setting.

I had turned off all the lights with the exception of a small night light I burned each night in the kitchen area. It would appear we had retired for the night.

It was so quiet in the park you could hear the crickets singing and an occasional owl would hoot. I loved being out in nature, especially at dark. You heard sounds that never happened in the daylight.

The thought of listening to my dad teach me those things when I was a kid brought a smile to my lips, and a warm feeling to my core. How fortunate I was to have had him in my life if only for thirteen years. His wisdom had served me well throughout my life.

I was thinking those thoughts when I realized the cricket song had stopped. It meant something was moving close to the camper because I could hear the song from the meadow.

I carefully slid out of the seat and into the driver's side so I could open the door that still had the tape on the light button. I eased myself to the ground with my still weakened left foot and then managed to shift my weight to my right foot, stepping to the edge of the extended slider.

I either heard or sensed a movement. My reflexes kicked into high gear as I threw up my left arm to protect the side of my head when the blow came. The ensuing blow was so forcefully delivered it shook my whole body, causing me to lose my balance. An array of lights burst in my head. I heard her grunt a guttural sound like a mad animal, and her stench filled my nostrils. I could feel her lifting whatever she was using for a club again. I couldn't get away from her, and I hadn't enough breath to scream. I tried in my semi-conscious state to roll under the camper. My arm hurt like hell where she'd hit it and blood was streaming down my face where she had struck my scalp.

I had to get under the rig or I would die right here. Everything hurt; I had to move. On my last attempt to slide under my hand touched my revolver, which had fallen out of the sling onto the ground when I fell. I grasped it with all my might. I could barely see the outline of her leg, but I aimed and fired. She screamed.

I prayed Fred would come to help me. I felt so helpless at that moment. I wasn't even sure if I had enough strength to cock the revolver for another shot. I was getting woozy. I realized it was not a good time for me to check out.

I heard running, and Fred's voice calling my name. I couldn't answer him. I had to let him know where I was so he could help me. I knew he was trying to enter the camper door, which I had locked. He ran around to the driver's door and when he opened it, I croaked, "Fred, I'm under the camper." Darkness came.

I don't know how long it took Fred to find me. My next memory was waking up in the emergency room of the clinic and hearing Dr. Roberts talking to me.

"Nettie, speak to me. I need you to wake up. Nettie, can you hear me?"

I managed to open one eye out of courtesy, but was unable to speak. My mind wanted to talk; I just couldn't get my mouth to work. I tried harder to concentrate on talking and finally managed to say, "Hi."

Dr. Roberts must have been holding his breath because I heard him exhale, loudly. Why, I wondered had he been holding his breath? I wanted to go back to the darkness and not wonder about anything.

The sudden burst of pain in my arm brought me back into the emergency room. I could hear someone moaning; it sounded like me. I sounded pathetic. That would never do. I hated *pathetic*. I opened my eye again. It seemed only one eye was working… not good. I tried to move my arm to check why my other eye wasn't opening. Another burst of pain! Damn! I tried using my right arm. I could move it but before I could raise it to my head, Dr. Roberts touched it, stopping my reach.

"Nettie, I have a bandage on your head covering your eye. You've taken a substantial beating. Your left arm is broken again, and you have a large gash on your skull. I need to get x-rays in order to determine how bad these injuries are. Do you understand what I'm telling you?"

I wanted to nod my head. Not a clever idea, I just looked up at his kind face and tried to smile.

He and his staff wheeled me off to another room where he completed the x-rays. He informed me he would need to give me some medicine to relax me while he repaired the arm. He quickly assured me the old fracture suffered in the accident was still intact. However, the new incident had broken both bones in the forearm.

He was appalled because the blow was so violent that while the arm had been in a semi-hard cast, it still crushed the cast and shattered the bones.

The good doctor told me I didn't have a skull fracture, although he couldn't figure out why not. He was certain I would have a concussion, at the least, and a long scar to contend with.

I was tired, almost too tired to care anymore when the thought of Miss Joy popped into my nearly vacant brain.

I panicked. Dr. Roberts must have seen the change on my face. "Nettie what's wrong?"

"Miss Joy where is she? I left her in the camper when I went outside. She'll be frightened. I need to go get her."

A soft smile stole across the good man's face. "She's with Wade, being spoiled. I should have told you before. You are going to need to be here in the clinic at least twenty-four hours after the surgery on your arm and to watch for concussion."

I relaxed. I knew both the dog and I were in good hands for the time being. I remembered drifting off to sleep peacefully.

When Dr. Roberts roused me from my sleep, we were in a hospital room; I was lying on the bed. He was speaking quietly to me. "Nettie, can you hear me? I have placed you in a private room with my best nurse, Nancy. She'll stay here in the room with you at all times, and Fred is in the hall, so you are safe and can rest. I will be staying in the clinic for the remainder of the night in case they need me. You go to sleep. I'll see you in the morning when you can give me hell about my barbering job on your hair."

The nurse stepped closer to the bed and said, "If you need anything, either speak or push the button I've taped to your right hand. Do you hear me? I will be sitting close to your bed in my chair."

"I hear you. You smell nice, like clean linen hung outside to dry."

That was the last thing I remembered until something in my brain kicked into action. I could smell a putrid stench. I *knew* that smell. I had smelled it before, but now it was so intense it was making me gag. I came fully awake…the crazy woman was here…in the room. I got my good eye open just as she was reaching out her hand with something in it toward my arm. I had to do something to save myself. I'd swung my right arm across my body while pushing the button taped to my hand. She stepped back beside the bed and I kicked her with all my might with my left leg, sending her crashing into the bed tray at the foot of the bed. She regained her footing and lunged again. This time I knew it was do or die, so I aimed my kick at her midsection. She fell back, knocking over the chair by the bed. All hell broke loose in the room. The overhead light came on, and Fred was there. I could hear feet running as Nancy flew into the room. Somehow, in the melee, the nut case was gone again.

I could hear Nancy asking what had happened while Fred was almost yelling into his phone to lock down the hospital. I was trying to get myself back onto the mattress so I wouldn't slip off onto the floor. Nancy was getting me repositioned when Dr. Roberts came into the room. He looked so upset I felt sorry for him. I couldn't resist a tease. "I told you to send me home. I'm more trouble than I'm worth, and this time you have to take Medicare payments as this was entirely my fault."

It seemed a male nurse had approached Fred and told him he was there to give Nancy her break. Fred didn't think anything odd about it, but Nancy had mentioned to him she was under the impression from the doctor she would be the only one tending me during the shift. When Fred saw the light over my door blinking red and heard the ruckus, he stormed into the room. His focus was solely on me, allowing an instant for the intruder to get away.

They locked down the clinic and searched every square inch of space but, as always, she was gone like the ghoul she was. Someone had to find her soon or she was going to succeed in killing me. I was rapidly running out of reserves.

Wade visited me in the morning with Miss Joy, lifting my spirits. Dom arrived while Wade was still there, and he had Adam with him. Neither of them looked like they'd slept a wink in days. I wondered if they'd been sitting up all night rekindling their friendship. It was odd to see Dom when he wasn't immaculately dressed, shaved, and on top of his game.

They pulled up chairs and sat facing me. It seemed they had gone to Adam's office to use computers to check records and gather some data that neither thought made much sense. I didn't know Dom's connection to Adam and didn't ask.

They found Janet Mason was a foster child who had lived with Sampson's mother when she was a young teen. The two had formed a close friendship lasting into adulthood. Sampson had encouraged Janet to apply to the agency for the clerk's position. He had personally recommended her, without telling anyone about his or her previous connection.

All went well for a time, until Janet discovered most of the folks she was processing for the witness protection program were ordinary working people who were terrified. They were worried about having their new lives disrupted or harmed, by the people they had blown the whistle on, and turned over to the law. Evidently, she fed on their fears, realizing they would be easy prey for her to shake down for money.

At the onset, Sampson didn't know anything about what she was planning or doing. He knew she was taking time off from work for various reasons, but he never questioned why.

When she overstepped her boundaries by copying files she shouldn't have access to, her supervisor reported her. They began to look into her personal habits and realized she was living way above what she could afford on her salary. They questioned her about the spending, and she left abruptly without giving any notice.

After she was out of the office, she maintained the relationship with Sampson to gain access to new folks coming into the program. He didn't question her interest in these people until she paid off a large loan for him. He'd been late on several payments to an aggressive loan shark. It seemed he liked to gamble. Sampson was worried about the agency discovering his vice and losing his job.

Janet began using him to *help* her persuade victims to pay up or have their covers blown to the wrong people. On one of those ventures, Janet had gone too far and the victim died, making Sampson an active participant to the crime. He assisted her in the cover-up, then couldn't walk away. He became her minion.

When they visited him in custody with their information, he told them he would cooperate for a lighter sentence.

Twenty

It pleased me to know they were at least working on some of the cases. Although, I had to admit selflessly, I was more concerned about my own safety.

They informed me there would be even more protection from Adam. I quickly pointed out that so far it hadn't worked very well. They agreed with me that the most likely way to capture her was by using me for bait. She was totally fixated on killing me.

I wanted to get out of the clinic and be in my own space with Miss Joy. I was smart enough to realize I couldn't protect myself physically now. I was also not in any shape to drive the motor home. I felt very vulnerable. Thankfully, it was a feeling I seldom needed to face.

When Dr. Roberts came to check on me, he found a sad and discouraged patient. I persisted on wanting to leave and even though he was adamant about the extent of my injuries, he told me he couldn't keep me against my will. He called Wade and informed him I could leave, but was not to be alone.

Poor Wade arrived to take me back to the camper. He was distraught because he couldn't persuade me to go back to his motel and stay. I couldn't risk putting him or other guests at the motel in danger. This woman was crazy, and I had no idea of the lengths she would take to rid herself of me.

Wade's report to me was there were agents hidden all over the RV Park. There were reportedly several canines as well. We could only wait to see if she made a move.

The first evening Wade stayed with me until it was almost eleven o'clock. I was exhausted, so I had to trust someone was guarding my camper, and I went to sleep on the couch with Miss Joy curled up by my side. We slept until daylight was streaking the sky.

I made coffee, fed the dog, and then took her for a short walk and returned directly to the camper. I enjoyed my coffee with some breakfast Wade left me. I showered as best I could and dressed in sweats and running shoes. I noticed there were several people walking their dogs around the lake area. I felt it would be a good time to take Miss Joy out for a slightly longer outing. I assumed some people were part of Adam's group.

I was careful to lock the camper before we started on our walk. Without being obvious, I was paying strict attention to the units as we walked along. One of the units I recognized was a Cardinal fifth wheel. It had been there either when I first arrived in the park or was placed there shortly afterwards. I knew the unit because I owned one exactly like it a couple of years before.

We enjoyed the long walk, returning to the camper relaxed and ready to settle down to read a new book I bought. I placed a snack with a diet Coke on the table beside the recliner, and settled back with Miss Joy beside me for a good read.

My cell phone rang, pulling me away from the story. When I answered, all I heard was heavy breathing on the other end. I knew who it was. I was infuriated instantly so my retort was most likely not well thought out. "Is that all you've got, stupid?" The line went dead. Good. I was sick to death of this idiot. I thought, *the death part may be sooner and truer than I knew.*

The rest of the day was peaceful and quiet. I opened the windows for fresh air earlier in the day, and I managed to nap in the middle of the afternoon. By early evening, prior to dark, I felt ready to take the dog for another good walk. I knew the walking was fun for her, and would help rebuild my stamina.

We set off for our stroll, foolishly without checking to see if the other dogs were out walking. I was about half way around the walking path when the thought crossed my mind.

I didn't change my pace or direction, even as I was acutely aware I was not carrying my .38. *How could I be so stupid to overlook these things,* I wondered as I plodded along. I knew it would still be daylight when I returned to the camper. I wasn't as alarmed as I would have been later in the evening. My senses were all on screech mode.

When I reached the camper, I was watching Miss Joy for any reactions while I scanned the unit prior to unlocking the door and entering. I felt better as soon as I was inside and had tucked the gun into my sling.

I prepared dinner while I watched the news on television. I missed seeing my Maine news and wondered what was going on with Pete. I would call him later.

There had been no sign of the men Adam had assured me were here, so I guessed that was a good sign. When the evening air temperature began to cool, I started closing the windows. That was when I smelled her; the same acrid odor I'd smelled in the room at the clinic. I panicked.

How could I reach the men who were supposed to be on guard? I fumbled out my cell phone and called the number Adam programmed into it. No answer; it didn't even go to voice mail. Now I was scared. I shut Miss Joy in the bathroom to keep her safe. I didn't want her harmed if there was a showdown here. I called Wade. Thankfully, he answered on the first ring. Before he even got a chance to speak, I told him the problem. He told me he would call Dom, and he was on his way.

I had not turned on any of the lights in the camper, and I wouldn't. There wasn't any point in giving her a better target if she wanted to shoot me. I was certain she had something more devious in mind than just shooting a hole in my sorry hide.

I heard soft footsteps on the gravel base by the camper. It would be too early for Wade to be here, and I would have heard his truck. The back of my neck started to prickle as my hair began to stand on end. Not a good sign; it meant danger had arrived.

Someone was by the front of the camper but with the window covering over the windshield I couldn't see out. Then I heard someone moving under the camper. I freaked out. Even with my revolver, I was no match for a scrap with anyone. I knew I couldn't even best a stray cat. *What an insipid thought to filter through my mind.*

I had to get a grip and do something, even if it was wrong!

I heard a scuffle at the side of the camper; no voices, just grunts, and then I heard a man's voice say, "Shit." I still had no idea who was there or what had transpired. Then there were sounds of running, and a dog panting as if pulling hard on their leash. I heard conversation noises, but not loud enough for me to understand.

There was a soft knock on the camper door. Fred's voice spoke, "Nettie, open the door… its Fred."

When I unlocked and opened the door, he stood there holding in his hand what appeared to be a woman's shoe. He entered the camper looking sheepish; an odd sight on a man of his size and tough demeanor. "I was lying under the camper waiting for her to make another move when seemingly from out of nowhere I saw these two legs at the front of a vehicle moving toward the driver's door. I hitched myself over to that direction. I knew I wouldn't have time to slide out from under the camper and grab her, so I alerted the others on our team with the silent beeper. I don't know how, but I think she knew I'd spotted her. She was stepping back with one foot when I grabbed her other one. She was gone, and all I got was her shoe. We sent the dog off on her track but it got into something in the grass that caused him to go into a spasm of sneezing. By the time we got another dog over to the area, it was too late."

When I looked at the shoe he was holding in his hand, it was identical to the ones she'd worn the first day we met in my driveway at the cabin. This seemed odd to me… women don't usually wear the same style and color of shoes all the time.

Wade arrived and was relieved to see the troops were with me and I was okay. We talked while the men continued to search on foot and with the dogs.

The rest of the night passed without further incident.

The next morning, I followed my usual routine of taking Miss Joy for a walk around the park and the lake. When I passed the Cardinal fifth wheel, something in my brain clicked, stirring a memory. It was so quick and so elusive I couldn't grasp any meaning from the fleeting thought. I dismissed it and continued with my walk. I felt comforted because I was able to spot where the men had been stationed, providing me with more security while walking.

I returned to the camper, fixed coffee and, because it was pleasantly warm outside, I decided to sit under the awning and enjoy at least a few minutes of the day.

Miss Joy wandered to the front of the camper and was busy looking at something in the tall grass growing on the edge of the lot. I could hear her growling. I needed to check. She was staring at a small cylinder in the weeds with a short hose connected to it. I had no idea what it was so I beeped Fred. He arrived at once; perhaps he had been hiding under the camper. I called Joy to come, and sent Fred to investigate whatever it was. He informed me it looked like something an exterminator would use. He didn't have any idea what was in it, or how anyone would intend to use it. We knew from the location where someone discarded it into the grassy area, it hadn't been there very long. He suspected crazy woman had thrown it there last night. He would send it to the lab for analysis, and then keep me posted with the results.

I enjoyed my coffee, and watched the lake for a time and reflected on my situation. The whole problem was, seemingly the crazy woman materialized from nowhere and returned to the same place, without anybody seeing her. The only concrete thing we had was her shoe. Ghosts do not leave shoes behind. She was definitely not Cinderella. I reflected back to the night I shot her in the leg. No one found any blood at the scene, yet I knew I injured her. I could still remember her scream.

My mind was too involved in these thoughts to try to read.

For every problem, there's a reasonable solution; I needed to figure this out and quickly. With this thought running through my mind on a short-loop tape that just kept replaying, I decided I needed to walk. I found most of my answers to problems when I either walked or drove.

I was half way around the park road when I knew part of the answer. I returned to the camper and beeped Fred. He was there in an instant.

"Fred, I know where she's hiding. It's right under our noses. I need you to gather some information for me as quickly as possible. It is imperative we know when and why they discharged her from the service for an injury, and what her disability was. Can you do it from here?"

He looked stunned, nodded his head, and pulled out his phone. He talked for a few moments, then said he'd wait for a return call. "It may take a few minutes or more to get the record pulled and read, and then they'll call me. What's going on in that mind of yours, if you don't mind my asking? By the way, the problem with the dogs last night was the grass was loaded with about a pound or more of pepper."

"I don't mind sharing with you what I know. I could be all wet, but I don't think so. Can you or one of the men go to the office and inquire who owns the Cardinal unit on the second lot from this one? They need to find out if it is a rental unit and, if so, when they rented it, and for what length of time. This is important."

Fred called one of the men, sending him off on the fact-finding mission. He looked dubious, but I think he thought he would humor me, anyway.

His phone rang and when he answered, although his face registered surprise, other than to say 'hello' he hadn't spoken a word and was just listening. Finally, he spoke, "Tell me the dates again, the extent of the injuries, and the resulting surgeries. Yes, it does make sense to me, but I wouldn't have suspected it on my own. Nettie brought this to my attention. I'm waiting on more information on another aspect of this. Nettie thinks she knows where our errant spook is hiding. Yes, I'll keep you posted."

Fred's phone rang again. "Really; why didn't we know this information before? I need you to round up the others and stand-by out of sight until I get a plan in place. We all need to be wearing our Kevlar vests; this could go very wrong, very fast. I'll call you with the plan when I'm ready."

Fred looked at me and shook his head. "I think you may have cracked this thing wide open. She was in a Jeep accident on the basic training course. They were learning to drive during maneuvers while under fire. She miscalculated when she spun the vehicle and rolled hers over, injuring her right leg severely. They did surgery trying to repair the break but in the end, they amputated her leg just below the knee. She has worn the prosthesis since then.

"The information on the Cardinal unit was what you suspected. The folks who own it come for only a couple of months in the summer. They let the office rent it for the rest of the season. The office rented the unit to a couple, with the term beginning the same day your camper arrived in the park. The park owner said he hadn't seen any activity around the unit that wouldn't be too unusual with a rental. Most people used them a few days at a time. They rented the unit for two months and paid in full on the internet. Now, what are your thoughts?"

"I know that model of camper because I owned one just like it for a short period of time. When I went by there this morning on my walk, I paid attention to the storage areas. Because they had it backed onto the lot and parked, even with the slides out I was able to check the closures on those doors. This configuration is a 'basement' model. The design is for use when the weather is colder. The ductwork for the furnace runs under the floors, keeping the storage areas from freezing. It has heated fresh and gray water tanks. The point I want to make is, there was a laundry chute with a net bag in a space below the floor. You could access it through a trapdoor in the floor as you went up into the gooseneck where the bathroom and bedroom area are. I didn't know it was there until the salesman pointed it out to me. It also gives you access to the entire storage area under the gooseneck. You could access the area from the front of the unit through the larger storage door or on either side through the smaller doors. Most generally, those doors would be latched shut and locked so there wouldn't be a draft, varmints, or bugs to get into the underside of the living space. I noticed on the big front door the latches were in the correct position, to keep it closed tight; however, on both the side doors even though the latches look closed, both of those doors were ajar.

"When I was not wearing a cast, or recovering from a wreck, I could easily pop into the side doors and fit up through the trap door into the bedroom area. Once inside the camper, there are several places where someone could hide. Under the bed is a large storage area; under the seats in the dinette would be another. I don't think she leaves the unit at all unless she's stalking me.

"Have you found her car? I doubt she stored it in the park. My guess is it may be in the woods either out front, or at a business nearby, like a garage. She would need it close enough so she could access it to leave the area without anyone seeing her. I may be all wrong, but I don't think so."

Fred just sat and shook his head. "Logically, it makes sense, and yet, it seems like a bad story book tale. I'm going to see if we can find the automobile first. If we get close to her, I don't want her to escape again. Her wearing the prosthesis makes the fact there wasn't any blood when you shot her fit. The shock of the shot to the limb would have created a great deal of pain, resulting in the scream you heard."

"Fred, for your information, there would be lights in the basement area of the unit. I think if I Google the model on the computer, we can get a diagram of how it's laid out, if it would be of assistance."

I opened my laptop to begin the research and produce the necessary prints of the Cardinal; then I had another thought, which had not occurred to me. *Perhaps she used the Cardinal for just a pass-through to another unit.* "Fred, we need to know if they rented any other units in the park either at the same time or shortly after I came. She may be using the fifth wheel as a temporary hiding spot then moving on to another unit when the chase dies down. It's worth investigating, don't you think?"

Fred called his man to check more thoroughly with the park owner. *I'll bet the poor park owner is sick and tired of me along with the group of men who invaded his space.* I was sorry for the problems this mess was causing to innocent folks, but we couldn't stop looking for her. She was dangerous, not only to me but, to anyone else she thought was an obstruction to her final plans.

Fred's phone buzzed, and when he answered, his face told the story. "They rented three units for a family reunion, according to the reservation. They paid with a pre-paid credit card and instructed the owner to leave the keys in the locks so they could access them when they arrived. He did as instructed, and had not seen anyone associated with the rental group, but the keys have been removed from the locks."

"Is there any way you can put listening monitors on those units? If we search any one of the campers and she isn't there, it would alert her to the fact we're looking for her. She could just disappear again; we would have to wait for her to reappear."

"We need to wait until dark to attempt to bug them. In the meantime, I have assigned a man to each unit. One of them is right next to the camper we've been using. I may deploy a couple of the guys to camp out in the woods so she thinks we left the area."

Fred's phone buzzed again. "Fred here; what have you got? Okay, where is it? How long has it been parked there and why?" He listened intently, nodded his head, and finished the call.

"We found the car. You were right; she parked it with a bunch of cars at a garage out on the main road. It's been there for several days. The owner of the garage said a person called to arrange to park there because they would be camping with a large group here in the park. They told him they would have too many cars in the party, so they needed to leave it outside of the park. He said he thought it was strange because when there are large parties the park owner puts the overflow of autos in the field out front. He said he had mentioned this to the caller, but they insisted on having it available in case they wanted to leave without disturbing anyone."

Fred shook his head. "I never in all my years worked so hard to capture one person. We need to get her this time, so planning is crucial to success. I'm going to have a meeting with the guys and see if I need to bring in anyone else to make it happen. Will you be all right while I'm gone? She isn't apt to make a daytime appearance, and I'm just a short distance away."

"I'll be fine. Take your time and let's get this over with so I can go home and live in peace and quiet." I wanted to be home so badly I could almost taste it. I wanted to kayak on the river, sit on the porch and listen to the night sounds, sip a glass of wine and enjoy some peace. It seemed like it had been years since I had done those very things. I sighed, my frustration evident at something so simple, yet seemingly, so hard to accomplish.

Fred returned after his meeting with the men. They worked out a plan for early this evening to bug the units and deploy men to the woods and field area in case she decided to leave.

"Fred, you missed an important piece of the puzzle… did you forget about the lake? There are kayaks all along the beach area with paddles in them for guests to use. At night, it would be easy to slip away in a boat without a sound."

Fred's answer said it all. "Shit, we didn't cover the water side because we were so focused on the car and the highway. I'll take care of the oversight right now."

I noticed the kayaks because I love to row with Miss Joy. At one point during a walk, I wondered if I could perhaps use one with just one arm. I discounted the idea as foolhardy. At least I hadn't lost all my common sense during this fiasco. With that thought in mind, I collected my drink and book to sit in the afternoon sun and relax for a spell.

I was enjoying my read in the warm autumn sun when I got a whiff of the stench. My neck hair bristled, and the hair on my forearm prickled. Miss Joy had been asleep on my lap and was startled awake. She began to growl. I reached into my sling and cupped the butt of the .38. The breeze had been blowing softly from behind me, but I couldn't see over the chair back. I was not in a good position. I pressed the silent beeper to alert Fred. I hadn't attempted to get out of the chair. I would be surprised if she decided to make a daylight assault on me. The stench lessened. She either moved away from me or was out of the path of the breeze. I hadn't relaxed.

When Fred arrived, he looked perplexed. "Did you beep me?"

I nodded yes, and spoke quietly, "She was here, behind me. I could smell her and no, I am not nuts, I have a nose like a bloodhound, and she reeks. She smells like a decaying animal or one with distemper."

Fred walked behind me to the front of the camper. He returned quickly. He was truly agitated. He was holding a piece of paper in his hand. He was so angry his hand shook. He passed me the paper. It read, 'YOU CAN RUN AND HIDE BUT I AM GOING TO KILL YOU', printed in bold childlike print. He'd found the paper taped to the hood of my camper.

Twenty-one

She was getting bolder. Would we get her before she got to me? I wondered if perhaps I'd truly met my match. I shook my head to clear away the negative thoughts. I knew I needed to stay sharp in order to survive. I firmed up my resolve, rose from the chair, and entered the camper.

"Fred, it's time for me to be gone. I need to get out of the way, so you and your guys can work. I'm going to call Sandy at the RV lot and have him send his work truck for supposed repairs to the camper. Once he arrives, I want him to pull alongside so I can take Miss Joy and get into his truck without anyone seeing me. I could stay with Wade for a couple of days if necessary.

"I think you'll only have one shot at getting her and if you blow it, she'll go underground. She is way too dangerous to leave free.

"I'm going to ask Sandy to bring another man with him. When they arrive, if you're here along with the two others, I think I can get off the step and into his truck without anyone noticing my legs and feet during the step needed to enter his truck. It will be a chance I have to take in order to get out without detection. I want to do this in the daylight, giving us the best chance of seeing her. Although, as you can plainly see, she came in full daylight to the front of my rig not five feet from me, yet nobody noticed her. How do you think it was possible?"

Fred looked defeated. "I don't know how it happened. I do know for a fact it did. Did you hear any sounds when she was there?"

"Nothing, the smell tipped me off." I understood why he felt defeated… we were not on top of this game. We were just pawns in a game we knew nothing about. It was too important to me; I had to win this one.

Sandy arrived with his truck and the helper. He pulled alongside my camper as I requested. They stood talking for a moment, then walked around the entire rig while gesturing with their arms and seemingly surveyed several areas on the camper. Fred stood just outside the entrance to my rig, and off the step, while he watched Sandy and his man.

Sandy said something to his man who nodded. He then spoke with Fred for a brief minute while he opened his truck's side service door. He reached inside for a tool he handed to his worker.

Fred spoke quietly through the screen door to me. "Grab the dog, and when I say 'ready', get into the service truck as fast as you can."

I picked up Miss Joy under my arm, but found my balance was not good with my other arm in the sling. I jostled her into a better grasp, and prayed I could do this without falling down or dropping her.

Sandy's man slid under the camper while Sandy squatted down as if to assist him, and Fred said, "Now."

I got the screen door open and stepped carefully down the steps. I was not steady on my feet, but I clung to Miss Joy as if her life depended on it. The service door on the truck was higher than I anticipated but, thankfully, Sandy had left a toolbox there to use as a step. There was nothing to grab onto to help me get up into the truck. It took every bit of energy I could muster to make the step up and literally fall into the vehicle onto the floor. Miss Joy moved inside without a sound, and I crawled in far enough so nobody could see me from outside. Certainly, it was not one of my finest moments.

I could hear Fred checking in with his crew while Sandy, and his man talked about the maintenance they were doing.

I hunkered just inside the door on a cushion placed there. I leaned against the truck wall and tried to catch my breath. Miss Joy came and sat on my lap. I was so out of shape physically, I was alarmed for my own and her safety. I had to face the truth sitting there in the back of a service truck… I was almost out of luck and options.

My age, the accident, and the resulting injuries from the assault had taken a bigger toll than I'd realized. It was a difficult truth to face. I'd always prided myself on being able to take care of anything. Now I couldn't even take care of myself. I was more discouraged than I ever remembered. I was truly stunned about this self-revelation. I shook my head trying to clear away the negative thoughts. It hadn't worked, and I didn't have time for a pity-party. I had to face the truth, and make a plan. One I could execute if I were going to get out of this mess alive. I snickered to myself. As beaten up as I was, the only next logical step *was* to stay alive; somehow. At least I hadn't lost the ability to laugh at myself.

Sandy came to the doorway and replaced his toolbox. His man stood beside him and handed him the tarp they'd used under the camper. Sandy closed the door. I could hear him saying, "I think we have the leak fixed, Nettie. If you experience any more problems with it, give me a call. I may need to order a new part. Talk with you soon."

Sandy got onto the driver's seat and his man got into the passenger seat. We drove out of the park and waited until he was out on the highway before he called back to see if I wanted to change seats with his man. I assured him I was fine where I was, and thanked him for the cushion.

When we arrived at the shop, Sandy drove into the large building where Wade was waiting. He looked worse than I felt. It didn't make me happy to see how stressed he was. I was delighted to see him.

I thanked Sandy and accepted a hand down out of the truck.

When I sat in Wade's pickup, it was more comfortable. I was exhausted. I couldn't remember when I had a good night of rest, or even a long nap, when I hadn't kept one eye open and both ears trained for the next sound. It seemed even my nose was tired of sniffing the air for bad smells. My whole body was shutting down. Perhaps I'd waited too long to leave the chaos behind. It was my last remembered thought.

When I awoke, I had no idea of where I was or even who I was, for a moment. It appeared to be early morning, or maybe it was twilight. I couldn't tell. I tried to focus, but couldn't. I drifted away. My next awareness was the smell of coffee and cigar. My mind snapped to attention: *cigar*. I never allowed smoking in my home. What happened? I tried to lift my head. It was too heavy. I got my eyes open. All I could see was the ceiling. Where was I? What was wrong? A small black and white furry face came into my line of sight. I smiled as Miss Joy gave me a kiss on the cheek.

Wade stood beside the bed with an anxious look on his pleasant face. "Welcome back, sleepy head. I thought you would never return. Are you ready for a cup of coffee? I'll crank the bed up. We have company."

I wasn't sure I wanted to return, although the coffee tempted me.

I took the cup Wade offered, finding it was too heavy to hold even though it was only half-full. Wade assisted me in getting a few sips. It tasted so good. He offered another half cup, and then even though there was company in the room, I needed a bathroom break. Wade cleared the room and helped me into the familiar bathroom. I told him I could manage on my own from there, so he waited outside.

I glanced in the mirror while washing my hands. I was grateful I was leaning against the vanity when I looked or I would've fallen to the floor. In the mirror was a person I couldn't relate to or recognize. I knew I should know who she was, but I just couldn't put the pieces together in my mind. Perhaps later I would figure it out.

As I touched the door handle, Wade opened it and skillfully sat me in the wheelchair he had waiting. How could he have known what I would feel when I glanced at myself in the mirror, I wondered.

He wheeled me into the large room, placing me next to the butler's cart of skillfully prepared breakfast foods. "You need to eat something. I don't know when you last ate, but you've been here for almost twenty hours. You are as thin as a rail. That's part of the reason you're having a difficult time getting your thoughts together. I want you to drink this first… it's a protein shake. I loaded it with everything you need. I made it in case you couldn't or wouldn't eat.

I snickered. "When would I ever not eat anything you prepared? I may be a little out of it, but I'm not stupid."

Wade laughed. Such a nice sound; I needed that.

He was correct in his thinking; the nourishment helped. I sipped the shake carefully trying to remember to swallow and not choke. I finished most of the shake feeling my body as it responded to the refueling.

"Wade, I smelled a cigar when I was waking up. Were you smoking?"

I got my reward immediately, with the biggest belly laugh I had ever heard from him along with an instant reply. "Not me sweet lady, I couldn't even stand a puff, or I'd keel over in a heap. That smell you can blame on Dom. He only smokes when he is worried or happy… perhaps he's both. My mother, God rest her soul, would have thrown him out the door if he lit up when she was here. I sent him and Adam off to the dining room so you could get settled before you talked with them."

I appreciated Wade more and more. He was so considerate and understood my need to gather myself before going forward. I was ready to find out the outcome from the trailer park. I had to plug back in and know what I would be facing.

Dom and Adam returned to the room with Fred. From the look on their faces, I guessed the raid was a success. I needed to hear it from their lips, saying I was safe from the crazy woman along with the rest of society.

Fred was the first to speak. "Hi there, good to see you're still interested in my career path. For a while, I thought I needed to take up goat herding or something.

"You were right about how she used the trailers to move and hide. When darkness fell, she thought you were still in the unit and snuck over through the field with a homemade napalm cocktail. I hadn't a clue how she would have known how to concoct such a thing.

"We had her covered six ways to Sunday because we didn't know what she had, or what she intended to do. We were aware whatever it was, it wouldn't be good. She slid under the back of the unit while trying to light the wick she'd fashioned out of paper toweling. I reached down under and grabbed her by the foot. I was ready to give a heave to pull her out from under the camper. When I grasped her foot, I remembered she had an artificial foot or leg, so I grabbed both feet and yanked as hard as I could.

"Thankfully, she dropped the lighter in the scuffle. She hung onto the bottle, though. I figured it was just gasoline. If I had known what was in the bottle I would have been more careful. Once I had her out on the ground, she flung the bottle at me, covering me with the fluid. She kept fumbling for something in her pocket.

"She flipped over and made a dash for it. She was in remarkable physical shape. She dashed past one of the men and fairly dove into the side compartment on the fifth wheel. If you hadn't alerted us to the strategy, we would have lost her. When she popped out on the other side of the unit, I had a man standing there just in case it happened. He tackled her.

"We restrained her in a straitjacket in order to transport her. Because she was so erratic, they transported her to the hospital to have her evaluated. She is truly crazy, along with some medical issues. I understand now what you were saying about the stench."

I was appalled. "You mean she is at the clinic here?"

Fred was perplexed at my question. It showed clearly in his expression. "We had no choice except to incarcerate her in a medical facility. She is clearly out of her mind as well as needing medical attention. Why would that be so upsetting to you? We have a guard there 24/7."

"I understand she needs help; however, this is her avenue for escape. She's familiar with medical facilities, and will be out of there within a matter of minutes or hours. She's a master of escape, character changes including gender changes. Mark my words; she'll walk right past your guard. He won't even be aware of who or what she was. We witnessed this when she attacked me in the clinic with the guard sitting in the hall. They never found her then. How long has she been there? Have you actually checked to see if she is in fact still there?"

Fred looked hurt; Adam looked concerned, and Dom probably thought I'd lost what was left of my mind. Nevertheless, Fred stepped out onto the patio with his phone in his hand. We watched through the closed glass as he placed the call. He face went from being passive to astonishment then horror in a matter of seconds. I knew the answer before he opened the door…*she was gone again.*

Twenty-two

I watched as the faces of Dom and Adam quickly reflected the fact we were doomed to finding her again. I was the only bait available to bring her out of hiding. I shuddered. I'd become so emotionally and physically drained; I couldn't go another round with the crazy woman. I also knew, with dread in my soul, I didn't have any choice. I couldn't allow this woman loose on society if I could play a part in capturing her again.

Wade patted my shoulder; I was unsure if he was seeking to reassure himself or me. I was certain we all needed some assistance in the courage department.

I knew I needed to contact Pete, and let him know she was on the loose again. All he had been aware of was she'd stayed in our area, and the men Adam sent for Pete's protection had been recalled and assigned to other duties. I checked in with him every few days to be certain everything was okay. Although I doubted she would go there, with me remaining in this area, I felt he needed to be aware of the danger.

I wondered if I was well enough to drive the camper back to Maine. I didn't necessarily need to go to the house to stay. Perhaps I could move around enough to avoid her until she got tired of the game, or she dropped dead from gangrene. With the last thought still floating through my tired mind, I knew I was blowing smoke at myself. *Shame on me, I abhorred stupid behavior.*

"Well guys, where are we going from here? We have no idea of where she is, or where she will go. I bet, depending on how long ago she left the clinic, she is close to here. My next bet is the RV Park. Is her car still parked out at the garage by the park?"

My flurry of questions started a free-for-all of looks, phone calls, orders, and people moving. Scary what a few words from a silly old lady can do to a bunch of men.

Dom spoke first. "Nettie, please don't worry; you're safe here. Wade can take good care of you and Miss Joy. See if you can get some rest. I'll return in a short while."

I wondered about Sampson, where he was, and if she would contact him. "Adam, do you know if she has contacted Sampson?"

Adam looked slightly confused. "Why would you ask a question like that? Sampson is in a Federal prison serving his time. If it makes you more comfortable, I'll call right now and check."

He took his phone from the case and made the call. To watch his face, even though I couldn't hear his conversation, was a contrast in emotions. When he finished the call, he looked from me to Dom with utter disbelief on his face. When he addressed us, I understood why. "Not only had she contacted him, she visited him in person, posing as an agent. They transferred him to solitary confinement immediately after the visit. I'll have someone there shortly to find out what in hell is going on. They are transmitting the tapes and film as we speak."

How this group could be so out-smarted by one crazy woman was beyond me. I was certain of one thing: none of these snafus would ever be public knowledge.

I couldn't waste any more of my strength and mental ability to worry about her. I needed to take care of me, then get Miss Joy and me home safely.

As much as I wanted to return and retrieve my things from the camper, I knew it would be unwise to consider the thought. I would have to create a new and better escape plan.

At that moment, my plan was simple: I needed to get well again before I stepped back into the fray. I was too exhausted; I couldn't even devise a plan, let along carry one out.

I allowed myself the luxury of just taking care of me for the next couple of days. Wade was delighted at the fact he had someone to take care of.

Adam and Dom arrived late one afternoon looking defeated and sorrowful. There had been no trace of the crazy woman. I knew they had left nothing off the table in order to trace her. It's hard to trap a vapor.

We were batting ideas back and forth when I suddenly knew what we were missing. I spoke directly to Adam. "Can you get me the records from the hospital along with whatever interviews you did there? I may have an inkling of where she is. I would also like to see the conversation with Sampson at the prison. I know all this is classified, but I *am* the victim here."

Adam made a series of calls, then the screen on his computer came to life. He moved the computer across the coffee table so I could read the information with him.

When she was examined at the hospital, it was determined the stump of the amputation was beyond septic, bordering on gangrene. She had treated it with what limited knowledge she possessed to keep it somewhat under control. While she had been on the run, her care had been sketchy and the infection had gotten serious. They explained to her that in order to save her life, they would amputate above her knee, and fit her with a newer and better limb. She freaked out. When they explained she had no choice since she was a prisoner, and it was their duty to preserve her life, she begged them to leave her old prosthesis in her room until they took her to surgery. Because it seemed a moot point, the staff allowed her to keep it with her. Because of her mental state, they had her on strong doses of drugs, which seemed to keep her calmer. When the night nurse came in to give her the pre-op meds and explain the procedure for the next morning, she attacked and nearly killed the nurse by bludgeoning her with the artificial leg. She then attached her leg, stole the nurse's clothing, walked by the guard, and was gone again. The guard had no knowledge of what happened until sometime later when he heard moaning from the room, and asked another nurse to check and see what was wrong with the patient.

She had a good head start by then. They had not a clue where she would be going or how she could get there. They put out an all-points bulletin with no results. They couldn't even describe her, what she was wearing… nothing...and they got nothing in return.

"Don't you folks find it odd she always seems to have funds available to her? She doesn't carry a computer with her, a purse, or any identification, yet she travels easily to wherever she wants to go. She's able to rent campers, buys gas, stores her auto, etc. Have you searched for bank accounts for her or even Sampson? He has to know where she gets money. She rented the campers with a payment on the computer. Have you checked that out? Does anyone have any idea how her car is registered, who's on the title, her address, anything that's relevant? Is it still at the garage, or did you impound it? Were the campers searched for anything personal?"

Adam snapped his head up, grabbed his phone, and for the next twenty minutes he gave orders. It must have worked because soon his computer screen lit up with the beginnings of information.

Someone in the office had traced the rental payment to an active account. Not surprisingly, it was a joint account for Janette and Cal Sampson. They also discovered her disability check from the service was direct deposited to this account. There were other withdrawals from a debit card. One was today at a car rental agency outside of the city where the hospital was. When the agent questioned the person who rented the car, they remembered the transaction well. It had been the first rental of the day, and the person needed the car delivered. The address given was not to a home address, but to a large garage on the outskirts of town. The person paid for the car with a debit card over the phone and gave the driver's license information as well. They sent the car out for delivery with the usual young man and an extra car and driver to bring him back. When we asked, they said it didn't seem to be unusual, because that garage used them frequently for rentals. They gave the agent the make, model and plate number of the rental.

When they checked the garage where she'd parked her own car, it was gone. They didn't find the rental car there either. She was gone again!

They checked the campers and found no one had been there. Other than some old trash, there was nothing to indicate anyone had ever been there.

We were, once again, at square one, with the exception of the bank account. If any activity happened, Adam would know while it was going on.

We contacted the hospital again for a guesstimate on how long she could survive without medical attention. Soon either blood poisoning or gangrene would stop her. They told us when they checked the med closet on the floor, they found a large cache of antibiotics, and syringes were missing, along with some opiates. The locked cabinets in the med room posed no problem to her. The nurse who was tending her had provided not only a uniform but the keys. She could hold out for a time, but only until the drugs were gone, or she acquired more somehow. They had no positive idea of how long she could go.

Adam got a positive hit on the bank later in the day, for a large withdrawal, in a town near the prison where Sampson was incarcerated. He contacted the authorities there and informed them if anyone came to see Sampson, for any reason, it was imperative he be notified at once. He stressed the fact it didn't matter whom or what the reason was, he needed to know of any change from his solitary confinement, even if the contact came from inside the prison. There would be no exception to this.

When Adam's phone sounded, he stepped out of the room to take the call. He was still talking when he quickly re-entered with a look of disbelief shrouding his face. "HOW COULD THAT HAVE HAPPENED?" he yelled into the phone. "I left specific orders no one was to see, speak, touch, or anything else to this prisoner!" He appeared to be listening carefully to the explanation offered before he just signed off without a word. A look of total disgust wreathed his face. He shook his head as if to clear away the confusion in his mind before he spoke. "Sampson is dead. They found him lying on the floor of his cell. They told me the only person to be near him was a guard. When they went to speak with his guard, they found him in a storage closet passed out and stripped of his uniform. How can this be happening? We know who did this; but how? I don't think we'll ever know the truth."

We were back to zero again. It became a waiting game. What would she do next, and to whom?

I looked at the faces of the folks around me... all I saw was shock and dismay. I was certain I wore the same expression. There seemed to be no end in sight.

"Adam, what time did Sampson die? Was it before or after the withdrawal at the bank? Do they know what he died from, and if death was instantaneous? This is important. Did he leave any clues to what happened? Did they look or just move the body out of the cell?"

He whipped his phone from his pocket and began an intense conversation with whomever he had contacted. He posed his questions and waited while they replied, then ended the call. He turned his attention back to us as he passed a hand over his face. "When they discovered he was down on the floor of his cell, they tried to revive him without any success. It had just happened. The only video they have is the guard entering his cell and exiting after only a few seconds. They didn't process the cell as a crime scene because of the circumstances. They're going to check it now. They'll do an autopsy to determine the cause of death. There were no visible wounds to the body.

"What do you suppose she did to him, and how did she get in and out of there so fast?" he asked no one in particular.

"My guess, for what it is worth, is she drugged him or shot him up with a dry syringe to give him an embolism, then left at the change of shift. She's a master at comings and goings. Now it's a waiting game to see where she strikes again. Let's pray we live through the next round."

Twenty-Three

Nearly a week passed with no sightings of the spook. It hadn't lessened our angst to any degree. It seemed strange for her to be silent for so long when she obviously felt getting rid of me was priority one, even while her health was failing.

Fred stopped by to give me his usual daily update late one morning. He seemed more like a defeated hunter than a man on top of his game. I sensed it when he spoke. The total lack of contact or clues had him completely stymied. "I have nowhere to go with this, Nettie, and I must admit I'm out of ideas completely. Do you have any suggestions of something I may have overlooked?"

"Fred, did you ever return to Sampson's home after he was arrested? She was living somewhere and, as tight-knit as they were, she most likely had access to his space. I would venture it would be worthwhile to take a look."

Fred's face instantly took on a look of new determination. With a smile and a wave, he left. He was a man with a mission. I wondered quietly to myself why they hadn't thought to check it out before. What did I know? They were the professionals.

Later the same day, I had the answers to many of my questions when Fred and Adam paid me a visit.

They had checked Samson's home, and found Janet there. She'd been dead for several days. Her problems with her leg were too severe to overcome with just her doctoring.

She left a long rambling letter addressed to me. I assumed it was for me. She'd addressed it to the *Bitch.* It had been written over a period of days as was witnessed by the deterioration of her writing and mental state. In the letter, she blamed me for ruining her 'business,' stealing her love, Sampson, and in general making her life hell. Her only regret was that I was still alive, and she couldn't physically kill me. However, she hoped I would die a long and painful death, alone, as she had.

I was truly sad when I heard about her death. She had been so sick mentally and physically, but could have survived with medical and mental health care, if she'd asked for help.

The good side of the investigation to Sampson's house was the fact she had retained a filing system and computers there. The agents were able to recover information necessary to check on most of the others involved in her extortion scheme.

With the mystery finally solved of how she traveled from place to place, with seemingly no funds or paperwork. She had made a compartment in her artificial leg where she kept her debit card, driver's license, and a variety of identification cards.

I was now free to go home! I wasted no time in getting Sandy to deliver my camper. I appreciated all of Wade's care, but I was anxious to leave for Maine. We all enjoyed a delicious dinner prepared by Wade with Dom, his family, Dr. Roberts, his wife, Fred and Adam. It had been a nice way to say goodbye to many folks who had been great friends and diligent supporters of my care and cause.

The trip home was long because of my needing to stop and rest more often than usual, but thankfully, uneventful and enjoyable for both Miss Joy and me. It was wonderful to be home and feel safe in my own space again. I recovered well, and was soon feeling more like my previous self.

Twenty-four

Pete and I regained the rhythm of our lives with me living in the cottage while he remained in his tree house. We were free to work together on the grounds without hiding. Freedom never seemed so good to either of us.

We still hadn't figured out what to do about the property. He wouldn't accept any money because he insisted I owned it. He told me he liked being a squatter with no taxes to pay. I, however, had a plan in mind to make us joint owners. I would go to the city and take care of it legally. I needed to get my computer looked at so I planned my trip around the appointment.

Crazy woman was dead. I hadn't heard from Dom for a while. He'd not deposited the monthly amount we agreed to into my account for a couple of months. I didn't care. He had been more than generous with me, so I wrote it off completely. There was no reason for Adam or the others to stay in touch with me. Life was once again good in my part of the world. Or, so I thought…

I told Pete I was going to Bangor for the computer repair, inviting him to come if he wanted. He declined. Later, I would be grateful he had.

Miss Joy and I started our trip in my beloved older Ford Sport Trac with the radio playing, and just enjoying the day. It was so good to be me again. When I left my drive, I stopped to close the gate out of habit when I noticed an older gray sedan parked on the side of the road.

I wasn't a nosey person by nature, but I always try to be aware of anything out of the ordinary. When I passed the car, I noticed it was a Buick, and it had out of state plates. Not anything too odd about that, we get lots of tourist in the area. I noticed there was an older man behind the wheel. He was wearing a cap and had his face turned away from me, most likely checking his map.

The age of GPS was a joke in parts of our state; it would send you down a snowmobile trail or an old logging road. A good map was mandatory in this area.

I drove along, enjoying the scenery and thinking ahead to my visit with the attorney regarding the deed change. I glanced at the rearview mirror and noticed the gray Buick was behind me. He must be going to Bangor as well. When we came to a straight section of the road, he passed me. I drove up the ramp onto the interstate and again noticed the same car, or so I thought, behind me; about two cars back. It seemed odd, but not troubling.

After the mess with the crazy woman, I must admit I was, or perhaps could be, a tad paranoid. I stayed alert.

I was early with plenty of time to spare, so I decided to visit the computer store first. The store had an odd drive and parking lot that required patrons to come up an incline and around to the front of the store. It was actually the top floor of a building which housed several other businesses in the lower level serviced by a parking area on the other side at ground level. I parked, entered the store, explained what I wanted to have done to my equipment, and agreed on a time to return to pick it up later.

As I exited the store, I saw the Buick parked at an odd angle in the driveway. I saw a man who looked like he was tying his shoe or picking something up off the ground just behind my vehicle. He straightened walked to the Buick, and drove off down the ramp.

Miss Joy was letting me know she needed a pee break. I started the truck, pulled down the ramp and parked on the edge of the tarmac. I attached her leash and out of habit grabbed my purse. We walked off to the grassy area to find a spot for her business.

I was maybe a hundred feet from the truck when it exploded, shattering the windows in the building behind me. The blast knocked me off my feet. I was stunned. I could hear sirens heading our way. *I was also damned mad.* I pulled out my cell and punched Dom's number. He answered with a hearty, "How great to hear from you. Is everything okay?"

I was not as hearty. If he wanted to ignore his commitment for the monthly amount, then he could have just not paid it. I would have been fine either way. He didn't have to destroy my truck. When I relayed this load of unpleasantness to him, all I got was a dead silence. I thought he had disconnected. I was ready to do the same when he shouted, "What in hell are you telling me? I personally set up the payment system and it was automatic. What are you saying? Somebody trashed your truck, how? Are you telling me someone bombed it or the motor quit? Nettie, talk to me. Are you hurt? Is Miss Joy all right?"

I took a deep breath, then explained carefully, with great attention to detail, what had transpired with the truck and my reasoning that perhaps he had something to gain with my death. *I will never make that assumption ever again if I live to be one hundred.*

Wade had been correct when he said I never wanted to see or hear Dom mad.

"Nettie, where are you in Bangor? Do you know where the man driving the car is now? As soon as you finish with the police, have them take you to the Bangor airport. Check into the hotel there, and stay there without letting anyone know where you are until I get there. I'm heading for my plane right now. Do you understand what I am saying?"

I assured him I did, and then returned my attention to the officer who was trying to figure out what had happened.

The officer seemed impatient with me because I was talking on the phone. Too damned bad, he could wait for a minute. I offered him my full attention. "I'm sorry I wasted your time; however, the call was important. How may I assist you?"

Officer Friendly was not amused. "What happened here?"

"I honestly don't know. When I came out of the computer store, I noticed a man by the back of my truck stooped over, and it looked as if he was tying his shoe. He stood, walked over, got into the car parked across the drive behind me, and drove off. I got into my vehicle and came down the incline to where I could let my dog walk for a minute. I was perhaps fifty to a hundred feet away from the truck when it exploded, knocking me to the ground. Other than those facts, I guess I can't be very helpful."

"Did you know the man in the car?"

"No. Earlier in the day when I was leaving my home, I saw the same car on my road. It's a very rural area, so I took notice of the fact it had out-of-state plates. Lots of folks get lost out there. The GPS signaling is very sketchy, so I thought he was checking his map. He passed me again when I was on the interstate just outside of Bangor. I was surprised to see the car when I came out of the store. I really didn't think much more about it until the truck exploded."

"Did you get hurt when you fell? Is your dog okay?"

"I'm fine other than finding it hard to hear at the moment, and she seems alright. Thank you for asking. What'll happen to my vehicle, and what should I do?"

"I understand the department has called the state police, and they'll make the call as to where it will go, and what they'll do with it. Can I offer you transportation to somewhere? The other officers will want to talk with you, so stay close by."

"Thank you. I can call a cab. You have my cell number and home address. I'll be staying in town until I figure out what to do with the transportation problem. Can I leave now?"

"Sure. I'll call you if I need any additional information."

The cab dropped me off at the airport hotel where I got a room. *Here I go again,* was my thought. Had I made a fatal error calling Dom? I didn't know. Had I opened a can of whoop-ass for myself? My guess was I would soon find out.

While I waited for Dom's arrival, I received a call from the state police inspector who informed me they were impounding the truck, and would be in touch. He left me his name and badge number. He told me he was checking the surveillance cameras in the area of the computer store and the lower level businesses.

Dom arrived with Fred. I was surprised to see Fred. Dom entered the room with his usual gusto, proclaiming he couldn't believe I would distrust him, and felt he would ever harm me. I admitted to feeling sheepish, but who else, I asked, would want me off their list of liabilities? I was practical, if nothing else.

I again retold the facts. When I mentioned the older man in the gray Buick, Dom was paying particular attention. I didn't know why.

Dom directed his first questions to the settlement. "When was the last payment you received for the monthly allowance I set up?"

"It has been a few months. I believe the first one not deposited to the account was during the time I was at the RV Park. I really hadn't checked the account until the first month I returned home. Thanks to you, I didn't need any additional funds so I ignored it. I was grateful for all the assistance you'd already provided. I thought that would be the end of it."

Dom looked like a thundercloud. I noticed Fred blanched and took a step back. *What had I done?*

It was several minutes before Dom calmed himself down and spoke. I could tell he was having a difficult time with his control factor. "When I tell someone what I'm going to do; *I do it.* There was never any doubt what I meant, or what I would do. I set the fund up for your lifetime, not for a short term."

He pulled the cell phone from his pocket, punched a button, spoke to someone, and then requested some information by return call ASAP.

Dom looked at Fred and spoke softly. "Marty is not in the office. They said he's been gone for a few days. I want you to call his home and find out where he is, and why he isn't at work." Fred left the room just as Dom's phone rang.

The conversation was brief; however, I got the impression he received the information he wanted. When the call ended, he came and sat in the chair facing me. "I would never leave you without support after all you've been through. You saved my son's life. I owe you more than you'll ever know. Then you had the mess with crazy woman, even though it was not of my creation, I admired your tenacity and daring-do. You're my hero. I'll get this straightened out directly.

Fred returned to the room to brief Dom on his findings. Marty's wife didn't know where he was. Her husband told her he would be away on business for Dom. He also told her he would be back when he damn well got there. She was worried because, although Marty had been sober for a few years while working for Dom, recently he began to drink heavily again. In the process, he had become abusive, something he never was before. She shared with Fred she was packing and getting ready to leave before he returned. Marty had been ranting and raving about some dumb old broad being financially supported by Dom while he worked his ass off and could barely pay his own bills.

At this inopportune moment, the police detective arrived at the door. I introduced Dom and Fred as friends of mine. Detective Jones was a tall man about Dom's age with thinning sandy colored hair and a firm handshake. He had a military bearing to his stance, but when he spoke, you knew he was a native of the state. He quickly relayed the facts from the security camera at the computer store. It showed a man as he opened my gas cap cover then closed it again before getting into his car, the older gray Buick I had described, and then drove off. The reason he stopped behind my truck was he'd dropped something in his haste and stopped to retrieve it. The initial result of the tests on the remains of my truck, was that a form of Centrex with a pencil timer had blown it up. I was lucky to be alive. I was out of the truck maybe three or four minutes before the explosion. He wanted to know who and where this person was.

Dom spoke to Jones directly. "I believe I know who this was. I don't know where he is presently. He has been an employee of mine for the last few years. With the information I've just received regarding this situation, I'm exploring if perhaps he's been embezzling funds from my company. We have contacted his wife; she doesn't know where he is, either. He can't be far away, and his car should be easy to spot."

Jones shook his head. "We found his car at the next shopping plaza. We have a stakeout on it, but I think he left the area or changed transportation. Do you think once he knows you are still alive he'll look for another chance to kill you?"

The question startled me. "I don't know. If I'm not dead, I think he would know I might call Dom, and his game would be over."

I needed to alert Pete. If this character showed up at the cottage with some cock-and-bull story, Pete would be in danger. I called his phone with my fingers crossed he would answer.

I got lucky...not only did he answer he was in an area where he had reception. "Pete, a man may show up at the property looking for me. He's older with gray hair and glasses and very dangerous. If he comes to the gate, don't open it. Do not engage with him in any way. Call the police; they're looking for him."

As I was speaking with Pete, the detective handed me a card gesturing he wanted to speak with Pete directly.

"Pete, Detective Jones wants to speak with you." I passed the phone over to him.

"This is Detective Jones of the Maine State Police. We have a serious situation going on here. If this dude shows up or you spot him, call this number pronto. It's my phone, and I'll answer. Under no circumstance do you talk to or try to apprehend him. I repeat; he *is* dangerous. Are you ready to take this number? I would suggest you program it into your phone on speed dial." He gave Pete the number, and then passed the phone back to me.

"Nettie, how do I know you and Miss Joy are all right? Has there been another incident? Do you need me to come get you?"

"I'm fine. I'll fill you in when I arrive home. I may not be there tonight. I'll let you know later. Don't worry; just stay hidden and safe."

Pete's reply was classic for him. He was a man of few words, "Shit, not again?"

"Not to worry; it'll be okay. I'll call you later."

Jones told us he had to leave, but would stay in touch by phone. He inquired if I would stay at the hotel or attempt to return home, and did I need someone to stand guard until they found the *person of interest*? I assured him I would be returning home as soon as I acquired transportation.

Dom spoke up, "I'll make sure she has someone with her 24/7 until we resolve this matter."

Twenty-five

When I finally arrived at home with Dom and Fred as escorts, Pete was so glad to see me he gave me a big welcoming hug. I'm not sure who was more surprised at the gesture. I introduced Dom and Fred to Pete.

Although Dom knew all of the circumstances around Pete hiding out here in Maine, he was still curious. In typical Dom fashion, he was busy questioning him about his past work experiences and skills. Pete was comfortable and at ease with the conversation. I took Fred on a tour of the property so he would have information related to his surveillance, if necessary.

Fred was impressed with the buildings and the skill displayed in the construction. I didn't take him for a tour of Pete's tree house. Although I knew about where it was located, I'd never been there. I felt it was Pete's private space.

As we were leaving the barn, I heard a rustle in the bushes just as Fred reached for his weapon. I grabbed his arm and said, "No. Stop! It's okay!" Just then, Luce, Pete's dog, stepped out of the edge of the woods. I heard the quick intake of Fred's breath when he saw the large animal. He still had his hand on his weapon.

"Relax Fred; he's just a big teddy bear as long as you don't pose any threat to me or Pete." I reached over and gave Luce his favorite treat, an ear scratch. He sniffed Fred, looked at me, and sat. I knew I would have to introduce him to Dom. I smiled to myself... *that might be humorous.*

I, however, missed out on the task because Pete and Dom came out on the porch just then. The look on Dom's face said it all. I couldn't decide if it was horror or mirth at the sight of the giant animal.

Pete took Fred on a tour of his tree house while Dom and I chatted. Dom said he knew so much about the property and Pete, he felt like he'd always known him. He then asked me if I thought Pete ever missed doing the type of work he had done so well for many years.

I gave Dom an honest answer to the best of my knowledge. "I think he did miss it for a long time because it was *who* he was, but with all the crazy stuff going on, he may have reluctantly closed the door on that chapter of his life. I'm certain he missed his family, even though they wanted nothing to do with him during the court cases or afterward when they knew he was right. I don't think he even knows where they are, or if they're still alive. Now, with Janet's death, I think he can safely find that information if he wants to. Why do you ask? I know you well enough to know if you are asking questions, you're planning something."

Dom smiled, then asked. "Do you think Pete would like to work for my company? Would you be upset if he moved from here? You could move also if it was important to the both of you."

I began to laugh in response to Dom's statement. I couldn't help it. "Let me clarify something for you... Pete and I are friends, nothing else. I think you would have the most honest, sober individual you would ever find in Pete. I don't know much about the size and scope of your company, but Pete is well qualified for the job. Perhaps you can reinstall the 'trust factor' for him. It was taken away when he did the right thing and lost everything."

Dom nodded smiling as if to a private thought of his own.

Pete and Fred returned, talking as if they had known each other for a lifetime. I had never seen Pete interact with anyone except me, so I had no idea of how social he was or could be. I was certain he must have missed male company in the years he was hiding or on the run. It was great to see him with a smile on his face.

Fred was the first to speak. "Dom, you have got to see this tree house; it is a work of art. You could stand directly under it and never know it was there. The inside is cozy, roomy, and so well designed I want it."

The alarm on the gate sounded. We all froze. Pete checked the monitor. No one was there. That meant either somebody was trying to get around the gate or side fencing, or backed away out of camera range. Whatever, it needed to be investigated and quickly. Fred and Pete headed through the side woods toward the driveway. Pete left Luce behind to stay with Dom and me. I put Miss Joy in the house to rest.

The men were gone for a long period before they returned. They hadn't found anyone, but did see footprints on the gravel drive where somebody walked up to the gate then retreated. Fred had called Detective Jones to report the incident. He was sending men to patrol the area in unmarked cars and on foot.

Dom's phone sounded its odd ring. He answered, requested a piece of paper, and began taking rapid notes. I left him to continue his conversation along with giving instructions to whomever was on the phone. I went to join Pete and Fred out by the barn.

When Dom joined us, I could see he had an agenda. He was a man who was never without a purpose. I think it's what made him appear so dynamic all the time.

He came directly to the point. "Fred we've got problems. I just spoke with Ethan. He's a great worker and skillful, although he has never needed to check many of the things I instructed him to do as the clerk to the comptroller. He was concerned because some things have become 'password protected' and he can't access them. Ethan has no idea why those accounts would be blocked, or have unavailable or secret passwords. He did find ones he could access... they had unauthorized activity regarding funds. He told me he was frightened when Marty found out he'd accessed them, that he would be angry and harm him. He explained Marty had been acting strangely the last few weeks, telling him to stay out of his office and mind his own work, or he would have him fired.

"Ethan also told me when he pried open one of Marty's desk drawers, with my permission and a witness, he found a few bags of what he thinks could be heroin, and perhaps it explained why he was so edgy lately.

"I've called security, denied Marty access to any of our sites, and gave instructions they should detain him with no questions asked."

I could plainly see Dom was troubled. I understood his frustration when he continued. "When Marty first came to me about a job, and he was still in the re-hab program trying to put his life back together, I knew he, and his family, were struggling, so I gave him a clerking position. He worked hard, did a good job, so I expanded his work responsibilities. He seemed to be performing even better than I had expected. I helped them out by paying off their mortgage on the house and giving him a company car to drive. Marty seemed to be grateful and continued to work well. When our office manager retired, we decided he would fill the position and grow with our company. I've paid him a good salary with benefits, along with a good bonus each year. I don't understand why he would suddenly begin doing this."

Pete joined the conversation with a sad shake of his head. "This didn't *just* happen. It never does. It's been going on for some time. I think when you trace it back; the timeline will shock you. They tend to take a little, then a little more, until it becomes too big to hide. At some point, they know it's just a matter of time until the hammer falls. Panic ensues, and then it begins to get ugly. I know this from years and years of chasing these things. I'm sorry for you because it's always hard to re-create the trust-factor again. Sometimes it never happens with anyone you hire."

I was surprised Pete had spoken up. Usually, he was a man of very few words, and those, carefully processed prior to uttering them. Although we'd spent considerable time working together on the property, Pete never discussed his previous employment skills, other than the first day when I caught him in the barn.

Dom seemed to process Pete's words carefully, and nodded his head as if agreeing with a conclusion of his own. He looked Pete square in the face, then made his request. "Pete, I would like to hire you to replace Marty. I've heard great things about you from Nettie. I want you to know that Adam, a very close friend of mine, who works for the FBI, ran information on you when Janet was terrorizing Nettie. You had a sterling reputation in your field and, without the competent work you prepared for the cases, they would never have been prosecuted."

Pete looked stunned. He was standing there in his usual work clothes consisting of camo pants, plaid shirt, and wearing heavy work boots. He hadn't had a professional haircut since I met him, and was sporting a full beard. I chuckled as he glanced down at his attire running a hand over his face and hair. I thought, *he's taking a personal inventory.*

When he finally spoke, I knew I was correct in my assumption. "I no longer hold my CPA Ticket; I stopped using anything traceable, including my driver's license. I would also point out to you that I don't look like much of a professional man any longer."

Dom and Fred threw back their heads and roared with laughter. When they could gather their wits about them, Dom explained. It seemed when he met Fred, many years ago there were similar overtones.

Fred was an ex-Marine and a brawling longshoreman who thought every day was a total waste unless you had at least two good knock-down-drag-out fights. He loved to drink and fight with no sense of direction beyond that. A much younger Dom had arrived to pick up a load with one of his trucks when a riot broke out. The gang of rival men from another pier was badly beating Fred. Dom assessed the situation, realized they were going to kill Fred, and stepped into the fray.

Dom later admitted he hadn't enjoyed a 'damn good scrap' in years. His father, who owned the trucking company, told him if he didn't stop brawling, and grow up; he would never amount to anything. His dad threatened at one time to make him a janitor in the warehouse until he could mature.

Long story short, Dom grabbed Fred, chucked him into his truck, and took him home with him. They became good friends, growing into good men together. Dom's dad highly approved of the men they had become.

Pete spoke softly. "Sir, I appreciate your offer, but first of all, I can't leave Nettie here alone with what's going on. I have Luce to consider while I'm also wondering if I still possess my original skill set. I'm certain you'll find a competent person for your company. Thank you, but no. I haven't even been out in society for years because of hiding."

It was time for me to get involved. I saw a golden opportunity for Pete to re-discover himself, and I wanted him to take it. I trusted Dom to take good care of him and gently thrust him back into the real world. He was a young man, compared to me, with many productive years remaining. Perhaps he would find a lady to rebuild his personal life.

"Pete, you can't hide behind me on this one. You know I'm perfectly capable of caring for myself, and this homestead. Luce can stay with me until you decide what or where you want to be. It's time for you to step back into the real world. I can tell you truthfully, if you want to re-enter the work force, Dom is the person who can make it happen. I've offered my two cents, for what it's worth; I'll keep my mouth shut, go kayaking, and let you folks figure it out. Good luck all of you."

As if on cue, when I began walking to the shore, Luce and Miss Joy went with me. I guess it was a clear message that Luce would like to stay here.

When I returned from my paddle, Luce was still sitting on the shoreline waiting for me. I truly enjoyed the big furry mutt. He was as attentive and kind as any dog I'd ever owned. I had already made up my mind if Pete didn't stay here, I would get another large dog to be with me.

The men had moved the conversation onto the screened porch where Dom could smoke his cigar. The smell of his smoke evoked memories. I often smelled the same scent when trouble was brewing, or when it was over, and Dom began to relax. At that moment, there was no indication of which it would be.

Dom had convinced Pete to come for a short time to assist in and straighten out the finances within his company. Luce would stay here with us. Dom was going to leave Fred behind until we found Marty and he was in custody. Pete and Dom would leave tomorrow.

Dom charged Fred with the task of helping me replace my truck. I explained to him that I was more than capable to purchase my own vehicle. This was reminiscent of buying the motor home with Dom insisting I buy way more than I wanted. I had prevailed then, and I would now. A sinister smile must have shown on my face because Dom shot Fred a warning look.

The men left the next morning for Pete's new adventure. I hugged him goodbye and offered a short prayer he would be okay out in the big, bad world. It would be so unfamiliar to him after all these years. Dom gave me a big hug and a kiss on the cheek with a whispered, "Don't worry about Pete. I'll keep him safe."

Once they were in the plane, Fred and I looked at each other and grinned. "I wonder if there is still any oxygen left in the air for us to breathe."

Fred's response was a hearty laugh. I think he felt the same way I did. Then he had a reflective smile on his face as he said, "I wonder if he'll teach Pete how to fly the plane on this first trip. He taught me to fly on my first flight with him. He told me I needed to know in case he died while on the flight. It scared the living hell out of me. I learned to fly, and we both have our private pilot's license. Pete will get one also, just wait, you'll see. This will be good for both of them."

Twenty-six

His first question was funny. "Okay, kiddo, where will we spend Dom's money on a new car for you?"

"No, we're not spending *his* money. I'll pick out and pay for my own vehicle; that is the end of the conversation. It's going to be hard to replace my Sport Trac as they stopped making them. I want a similar vehicle, one to fill all my wants and needs."

We made several stops at car dealers without much success. I was looking for used, while Fred was looking at new and pricey. I hate to shop, so I called a truce, and we went to lunch.

Fred stepped outside of the restaurant to take a phone call. When he returned he was smirking...sorry but that was what he was doing. I could guess who had placed the call. I'd seen this group in action before. He grabbed the tab, and we headed for the door with his smirk still firmly in place.

"I want you to do me a favor. Will you please try?"

"Depends on what you want me to do, or to whom, and at what personal cost to me." I felt the statement covered all my bases pretty well.

"You want a used unit with the same configuration and comforts of your old one, right? I saw something you should look at, humor me, and at least take it for a ride?"

My energy level was waning, even with lunch onboard, so I nodded my agreement.

We returned to one of the lots we visited early in the day. Fred went inside returning with the salesman with a dealer plate in his hand and keys. I must admit, I was curious. When we were there earlier, I looked at a full-sized crew-cab, truck but it didn't have things I wanted, so I'd written it off. Perhaps Fred was as tired of shopping as I was. Perhaps, he thought I should at least drive it. He and the salesman talked for a moment, and then the salesman strode off, returning with a handsome Lincoln truck with a beautiful, deep red, custom metallic paint color. An old friend of mine owned one of those years ago, so I was familiar with the price point. I told him I'd drive it, and I would, but that would be the end of it.

I climbed in, adjusted the seat, checked out the dash, and running gear. This would be the shortest demo drive in the history of this lot. I planned to take it out one exit and drive it back into the entrance on the other end.

Fred spoke, "Can you please take me to the computer shop where they blew your truck up? I need to check something out. It'll only take us a minute. It's important, or I wouldn't ask."

What could I do? It was a reasonable request. I just drove on to the computer store. I needed to pick up my laptop anyhow.

I was exhausted and totally invested in the completion of the errand, for both of us. I couldn't even think of how comfortably the truck handled and rode.

Fred went into the shop with me and was busy talking to the owner while I paid for my equipment. When we left, it seemed like second nature to get into the truck, back away and drive down the ramp. I had to admit I liked the truck, but knew I wouldn't like the price.

We returned to the dealership where Fred talked to the salesman for a few minutes. Meanwhile, I strolled through the lot looking to see if I could spot something to satisfy me. I found nothing new since our earlier foray. If push came to shove, I could always buy a clunker from Nick, the man who fixed the road and installed the gate. He always had a couple of old trucks there for sale. I even considered asking Pete if I could buy his old truck rather than have it just sit in the barn gathering dust.

When Fred returned, he announced we would need to take the rental he was driving back to the airport. He explained he had rented it for a short stay and needed to redo the paperwork for a long-term rental.

It sounded reasonable to me, then I wanted to go home; I was getting tired. My stamina wasn't at its best. I knew Fred would understand. I also didn't like being away from the property for too long when I didn't know where Marty was. I had left Miss Joy in the house, and told Luce to guard. I would bet she was on my bed sound asleep, and he was on the porch in the sun stretched out sound asleep. At least, that was my hope.

We finished Fred's business with the rental agency, and he drove us back to the dealership. I smelled a rat. "Fred why are we here?"

"Simple, you forgot something in the truck. Don't you want your computer?"

I was so embarrassed for being careless and forgetful, I just hung my head in silence. I really was too exhausted, or something.

Fred returned without the computer, and my heart sunk. Had they lost it this quickly? All my stuff was on the laptop. Fred opened my door and walked me over to the truck we had demoed and passed me the keys. "I'll follow you home. Drive carefully; I'll be right behind you."

He opened the door and, for a second, I thought he was going to pick me up and sit me onto the seat. I was speechless. Now what had he done? He closed the door, smiled, and got into his car. I noticed a post-it stuck to the dash. It said, "If you hate it, you have 7 days to return it without charge." Oh, what the hell! I knew this was an argument I wouldn't win, so I started the truck and followed him to the exit. Once out on the highway, I took the lead and headed for home. I did like the luxury of the custom leather heated seats, and the stereo was killer.

Twenty-seven

When I pulled up to the gate at the end of my drive, I could see something was amiss. I jumped out to unlock and open the gate while examining something on the top metal pole of the device. It looked like dried blood to me.

I walked quickly back to Fred's car, "Do you have your gun with you?"

A look of alarm spread over his face as he opened his door. "What's wrong?"

I pointed to the smear of blood on the gate. "There was some sort of scuffle here on the inside. It looks like whoever was here came over the gate and met Luce. I've never known the dog to be aggressive. I've got to find him. I hope and pray no one hurt him. It would kill Pete if something happened to his dog."

I left Fred to close and relock the gate and drove rapidly to the house. As soon as I came to a halt, I began calling for Luce. He didn't come. My heart was beating almost to the point of stopping as I continued calling. He'd always come when I called him. I could hear Miss Joy in the house barking. I let her out, hoping it would encourage Luce to come, if he could.

Fred arrived to park beside me. He could see my dismay at not having found Luce. "Do you think he would be over at the tree-house? Do you want me to head over there to search for him?"

I was so distressed at that moment, I wasn't sure of what I should do. Miss Joy had run out to the woods, and I assumed she was going to pee, but she didn't come back to me. I was going to find her when I heard her whining on the edge of the tree line. I ran as fast as I could, telling her I was coming. I found her sitting beside Luce and licking his big face. He had blood on his snout and the front of his neck going down to his chest. I nearly fainted at the site of him covered in blood. I would need to take him to a vet. First, I needed to determine where, and how badly, he was hurt.

I spoke softly to him, and I knew he could hear me because his ear perked up. I tried to coax him to stand on his feet so I could get a better look at his injuries. I prayed someone hadn't shot him. The blood on his face looked more recent than the smears on his chest.

"Come boy, stand up so I can see how badly you're hurt. It's okay… you did the right thing. You're not in trouble; come here." With great effort, he stood and walked slowly toward me with his head down as if I would scold him. I'd never seen him like this.

When I got him to an area, where I could feel and check his body for wounds, I was astonished he didn't appear to have any, other than the one on his nose and his mouth. He seemed to be able to walk and move without pain. I began to draw a breath of relief.

Fred was inspecting the bushes where Luce had been lying when I heard his chuckle.

"What have you found?"

Fred held up what looked like the remains of a man's flannel shirtsleeve. All evidence indicated someone's arm was still in it when torn off, because it was soaked with a substantial amount of fresh blood. "All we have to do is find the rest of the shirt and a person with a very sore arm. We'll then know who our visitor was."

Luce stood looking at the shirtsleeve, then to me as if he were uncertain about whether it was his trophy, or he was in deep trouble. I gave him a reassuring pat along with an ear scratch.

I didn't know if Luce would let me clean his battle scars or not, but I was going to try.

Fred returned to the gate area to look for footprints and, perhaps, a blood trail. Whoever received such a severe bite would require a doctor's care. I didn't know if Pete had given Luce his shots for rabies.

When Fred returned, he briefed me with his findings. Someone indeed had climbed over the top of the gate. They were perhaps three feet in on the driveway when Luce nailed them. Fred was certain it was a man because of the shoe size. He theorized once Luce locked onto the arm he wasn't going to let go. He had dragged the person about ten feet from the gate before they hit him with something. They hit him hard enough so the dog either sat or fell back onto his butt. Then, as Fred said, the chase was on. He could see where Luce had dug into the driveway with his claws for traction.

I was so grateful Luce hadn't jumped the fence in hot pursuit. I knew he could clear the height of the gate easily if he wanted to.

Fred lost no time calling the state police contact to inform them of the situation. They assured us they would check medical facilities and drug stores. They were also sending a person in an unmarked car for posting where they could watch the driveway.

Fred seemed relieved. I was not. After my recent trauma with Janet, I wasn't going to trust anyone to keep the dogs and me safe. I went into the house and put on my shoulder holster. Carrying my .38 made me feel more in control and safer. I was certain our caller was Marty. Similar to Janet, Marty saw me as a person who had ruined his life. He was most likely as unhinged as she had been. Although it was hard for me to imagine I could encounter two people who were so mentally disturbed in such a short time span. He wasn't as clever, and he was using drugs, which would further impair his judgment. We also didn't understand his motive for wanting to eliminate me.

I received a call later in the evening from Dom inquiring how my day had been. I laughed, "You know perfectly well how my day went.

You've talked with Fred. I can tell you, I'm not keeping the truck I drove home. It was a thrill to drive and ride in, but too rich for my blood. It would be the same as living in a tent and parking a Mercedes beside it; too rich for my tastes. I'm also sure he told you we had a visitor. Have you told Pete about Luce? I don't want to upset him. It's the first time he ventured out into the real world, and I don't want to give him any excuse to return prematurely. How is he doing?"

Dom laughed, "Ask him yourself, but first open your computer so we can Skype."

I did as Dom requested. When we finally got connected, Fred stood looking over my shoulder. He was holding one of his hands behind his back. I wasn't paying any attention because here on my screen in living color was someone I would never have recognized. Pete was sitting in front of a giant desk piled high with files grinning like a kid in a candy store. He was clean-shaven, with a super new haircut, wearing a light-colored shirt and a tie. With his sleeves rolled up ready for business.

My heart sang. I wanted him to find a life besides hiding out and running. He had done the correct and ethical thing when he blew the whistle on the businesses. He had experienced nothing but grief and frustration for his efforts, until now. All I could say was, "Wow, you clean up some good, as we say in Maine. Are you happy? Things are good here, and Luce is a treasure. I am beyond happy to have him with us."

Fred leaned into the range of vision showing Pete the newly acquired sleeve and grinning. "I bet you had no idea what kind of a watch dog you had, Buddy. Now, even I'm scared, although probably not as scared as the person who lost this."

Pete looked shocked. That information wasn't what I wanted him to hear, but it was too late. "Don't be concerned. Luce is fine, with the exception of a bump on his nose and a slight cut on his lip. Has he had his shots? Should I take him to the vet for them?"

Pete threw his head back and howled with laughter. It took him a minute to regain control, then he wiped away a tear running down his cheek, gasping for breath. "The only time I ever took Luce to a vet he was about half the size he is now. Even with a muzzle on him, the vet couldn't get near. The vet told me a dog with that much stamina and energy was damn well healthy, and he gave me a lifetime supply of meds for him, and the needles to administer them. I have given him his shots and wormed him ever since. He'll let me give him the shots without any argument. He has another two years to go with his rabies, so he'll be fine until I return."

We all said goodbye and signed off. It had been a good and positive ending to a long and stressful day.

I asked Fred what he would like for dinner and if he would like a beer or a glass of wine. I received a classic Fred answer. "You cook, I'll pour, and then we eat."

Twenty-eight

Even though it was early fall, it was still not cold, just cool, so after dinner we sat on the screened porch and watched the last of the sunset, and the beginnings of twilight.

"Does Luce ever bark?" Fred inquired as the evening darkened.

"I've never heard him bark as long as I've been here. Why do you ask?"

"How would I know if anyone was lurking about?"

"I guess when he returns with another shirt sleeve, or we hear a cry of pain, and perhaps a plea for help. I don't know what to tell you. To be honest, Pete taught him to be quiet because, when Janet was stalking him, she couldn't find him in the woods. Pete told me once she was looking for him in the woods, and he climbed a tree and just sat there. She walked within a foot of Luce and never saw him. I think if anyone ever touched Pete, the dog would do a number on them, without any thought of harm to himself. He loves Pete. They've been together for a lot of years.

"I'm going to bed and sleep with my .38 close at hand. Unlike Luce, Miss Joy would wake the dead if anyone comes. What are you going to do?"

Fred grinned. "I'm going to make friends with Luce, and we're going for a little stroll around the grounds a few times. He makes me feel safe out here in this vast wilderness. He also knows the property inside and out. Have a good night's sleep, and don't worry about us. I spent a lot of time in the jungles while I was in the service."

We enjoyed a couple days and nights of peace after I spoke with Dom and Pete.

Dom had been insistent I keep the truck. He told me he discussed it with Pete, who informed him how much I loved my Sport Trac. It seemed they'd gone online to find another just like it. Much to their chagrin, there were none to be found, anywhere. What they found were either too old, beat, or with excessive mileage. During their search, Dom spotted the Lincoln Mark LT. It was red, with all the bells and whistles, and very low mileage. He and Pete arranged the purchase and delivery to the Bangor dealership timed for our arrival. The first time we were there earlier in day, it hadn't arrived, thus requiring the return trip.

It seemed both Dom and Pete enjoyed shopping for the vehicle more than I would've imagined. Dom told me if I didn't keep it, both he and Pete would be hurt. Boy, did he know how to sling the bull. I appreciated all their efforts, and truth be told, I did like the truck although I felt it was pretentious for my lifestyle.

Twenty-nine

We had several days of heavy rain and wind. I was watching the gradual rise of the river. I knew several lakes and larger streams in our area emptied into the river. I didn't feel it would impact us, although I moved the kayak up higher on the banking, just in case.

I knew Pete's canoe was in a small stream upriver from my beach. I wasn't sure if he had secured it before he left, due to the suddenness of his decision to go with Dom. I decided to pull on my boots and rain slicker to go see if the boat was safe. I told Fred I was going out and would be back shortly. Fred had been out off and on most of the day finding nothing amiss, so I figured he could rest. I left Miss Joy in the house where she was warm and dry.

I walked down to the shoreline and followed the riverbank, being careful not to get too close to the rapidly rising water. It was slow going as I picked my way through the thick alders that grew right to the water's edge.

My stamina wasn't what it had been prior to the accident. I always forgot about it until I was too far into a project to stop. I should pay more attention, or I would get myself in over my head.

By my thinking, I should be almost to the mouth of the stream. I could see a discoloration in the edge of the river indicating it would be from the muddy base of the stream. I saw the outlet, but needed to backtrack in order to get up into the area due to flooding. I walked back to where I thought I could make a turn and connect with the stream. Success, I was on solid ground with the stream right ahead of me. I followed along the bank on a much easier path because there were fewer alders. I plodded on. I hadn't been on this part of the property. It was pretty and, other than the soft patter of the rain on the trees overhead, very quiet. I wouldn't have been surprised to see a deer step out.

I was so busy watching my footing with the roots and hummocks I almost didn't see the canoe. It was dark green and camo so it blended into the tree pattern. Pete did a great job of hiding such a large canoe. The fast rising water had lifted it almost onto the bank of the stream. It was a good thing I had come to check or the canoe would have sunk or drifted downstream into the river.

It took all my effort to get it pulled up higher into the woods, and tied to a large tree. There was substantial water in the bottom. I secured the oars and flipped it over to prevent any damage more rain would do. Once I finished the task, I just sat on the bottom to catch my breath. I was *really* out of shape. I still needed to hike back to the house.

I was smart enough to realize I wasn't familiar with the area enough to try to walk back through the woods to the house. I would be lost, and it was beginning to get dusk early with all the clouds. The wind was also picking back up.

Retracing my steps to the river was not as easy as I remembered. *I must be to either the left or the right of where I came in.* I needed to stay calm and keep walking; I knew I would reach the river in due time.

As I tromped along, I noticed the quiet woods sounds had changed. I could hear the snapping of branches clashing against one another as if a moose were traveling through. Not a comforting sound, but I was content I'd saved Pete's canoe.

I was almost to the river and could clearly hear the water rushing by the shore when I heard a distinctly different sound behind me.

Having spent a great deal of time in the woods throughout my lifetime, I was very aware of sounds and smells.

There was a large clump of alders on my right. I cautiously stepped around them and crouched down. It was foolish of me to leave the house without either Luce or my revolver, or Fred. To make the situation even worse, my rain slicker was orange. I quickly shrugged out of it and held it down onto the wet ground out of sight.

I stayed low and slowed my breathing, which sharpened my hearing. What, or whomever, I heard had halted as well. God gifted me with patience to spare. I've hunted for years, so I would wait. Then I heard the sound again.

This time it was much closer. Whoever it was did not have good woodsman skills. I was thanking God for that fact when I saw a man come into sight. He was soaked to the skin with no rain gear and only a soft flat felt hat. His raindrop-covered glasses were hindering his vision. He passed by me close enough I could smell cigarette smoke and stale booze on his body. I froze, not even breathing. He was carrying an automatic pistol in one hand, and his other hand carelessly wrapped with a bandage. I could see where blood had seeped through the wrapping from either his bumping it on bushes or moisture from the rain.

I prayed Fred wouldn't come looking for me. I didn't have any way of letting him know the man was armed, and most likely ready to shoot at anything or anyone.

I watched as he attempted to pick his way through the alders. I wasn't going to move out of my hiding spot until I was certain he was a long way ahead of me, but still within my sight line. This man was crazy and very unpredictable. I liked only sane and secure folks.

I was paying close attention to the track he was taking and knew, from having been there a short time ago, he would have to backtrack in order to get to the riverbank.

Something soft touched my soaking wet shoulder. My heart stopped beating. He must not have been alone. I hadn't even considered that possibility. It could be my undoing. I turned my head and looked. It was like seeing an accident, and you couldn't look away. I slowly moved my head enough so my eyes could make out the dim form behind me. I almost spoke aloud. Luce was sitting directly behind me, not making a sound. I breathed a deep sigh of relief.

Luce seemed to understand the situation better than I did, perhaps because of all the years of hiding out in these woods with Pete. Luce stood up with a look that begged me to follow him. I trusted the big old guy. He knew the woods better than I did. He also could smell and hear better. I stayed bent over and followed him, being careful to walk silently.

The wind was really blowing so it muffled any missteps I might make. Luce was going away from the river, and it was almost dark in the woods. I always enjoyed good night vision. I could still see enough to follow him.

A few minutes into the walk, Luce took us onto what appeared to be an old logging tote road. The footing was great. After a few more minutes, Luce stopped and waited until I was abreast of him; still he waited. Then, off in the distance, I heard a car start and drive off. Luce looked up at me and stepped out of the woods by the side of my barn. He had brought me home. I hugged him so tight I scared him. A quick wet ear scratch was all it required to reinstate our friendship.

When I opened the door to the house, I found a really angry and upset Fred. "Where in hell have you been, and why didn't you tell me where you were going? Why didn't you take me with you? Luce was on the porch when you left, and he was making such a fuss, I let him out and he disappeared. I don't know where he is. What in hell were you thinking?"

He had every right to be upset and, when I told him where I went and what I'd seen, he was beyond angry. I was angry with myself for being so careless. Once I explained this lack of intelligence to him, he calmed down a little, very little.

Fred called Detective Jones to report the encounter. I was appreciative Fred didn't throw me under the bus because of my lack of common sense.

As soon as Fred finished his conversation on the phone, he looked at me and laughed. "You need to go get a warm shower and clean up. You look like a kid who went out into the rain and played in mud puddles. After you get presentable, we need to put together a serious game plan. Marty's getting too bold and because of his mental state, we need to have a solid plan to be ready for his return. He's desperate and has nothing left to lose.

"I spoke with Dom while you were out on your excursion. He told me Pete was able to trace one of the money sources Marty used to an offshore account. The Feds froze that one. Once Marty finds he can no longer access any of his stolen funds, he'll go for broke. We need to be prepared."

Fred was right; the warm shower and fresh clothing recharged my energy. I hadn't a clue how, or what, we would or could do to capture Marty.

After dinner, Fred cautioned me about expecting too much, if any, assistance from the state police or sheriff's department. They were just too undermanned to take on the task of an all out hunt for one man, even a dangerous one. Fred felt he could garner some support from the game wardens in the area, so he placed the call and waited for a response from them.

We spent the next couple of days in relative peace. We walked the perimeter lines looking for weak spots; there were many. It would be impossible to cover all the areas we had identified as suspect. We would have to be extra diligent in our everyday routine. Going to the city was too risky so we opted instead to have things delivered.

Fred ordered more monitors and installed them along the property line by the road with wireless capabilities and listening devices. I ordered groceries from the local market. They thought it odd, but complied just the same. When Fred went to the gate to get the deliveries from the locals, I think they thought Fred and I were hiding out for nefarious reasons. That piece of gossip would be all over the county in a heartbeat. *If only they knew the real reason.*

It was fun to chat with Pete on an almost daily basis. He looked great and was very excited to be back working with his professional skills. They would get his CPA certificate reinstated. Pete also told me Adam managed to get the funds Janet had stolen from him returned. Our best fun on these calls was to have Luce see Pete on the screen and hear his voice. Luce would look for Pete then return to stare at the screen as if to tell Pete to get out of the box and touch him.

Late one night, I awoke to smell gasoline. I bolted out of bed, and yelled for Fred. Just as I exited the kitchen door, I heard Luce bound by me chasing after someone fleeing. They were running hard. I hit the floodlights for the yard as I grabbed my shotgun while stuffing my feet into boots. I went out through the door just as Fred pushed past me. He was in hot pursuit with his gun in his hand. Luce, and whomever he was chasing, with me bringing up the rear must have been a scary sight to the intruder.

I rounded the end of the house to see flames just beginning to lick up the log wall toward the kitchen window. Pete had installed hoses at points all around the house and barn because of the ever-present danger of forest fires. I grabbed the closest one and began spraying the flames. I managed to extinguish the fire with minimal damage to the structure. Thank God, I was a light sleeper.

Fred returned with a defeated look on his face. He had been unable to catch the intruder. Pete's strict training of Luce to stay on the property, under any circumstances, meant he had stopped at the edge of the road. Fred saw the car drive away, but couldn't identify anything about it because of the darkness.

We checked the barn, making certain it wasn't doused with gasoline, like the house. We found a full gas can sitting against the building. We had interrupted Marty before he could use it. The situation was serious.

Fred checked the monitors to see where he entered the property. Nothing showed. In the morning, I checked the riverbank. I could clearly see where he walked along the bank then up onto the edge of my field, staying to the back and side of the barn, then across the back yard to the house.

Fred called Dom and told him he needed some manpower because we were under siege.

As always, Dom delivered. Later the same day a large black truck arrived with a bunch of men who looked like the militia from hell. I was terrified of how they looked while being grateful for their assistance.

I wasn't sure how Luce would respond to them. I took him out with me and asked him to sit beside me while we made introductions. I think they were more afraid of Luce than he was of them. He sniffed each of them in turn, as they introduced themselves. Then Luce, Miss Joy, and I returned to the house.

Later Fred explained his plan to me. The men deployed into the surrounding area. I wouldn't see them again. When I inquired of him how I would feed this new gang, he chuckled. "They feed themselves and will billet in the woods. These men are professionals, and would be resentful of any babysitting attempts from you. Also, if you want to go to the city, church or anywhere one of them will be with you with nobody being aware of their presence."

Great, now I had my own army to protect my kingdom. I was impressed.

I'd been captive in the house for way too long. I told Fred I was going to go for a grocery run and get a change of scenery. He said okay, but he was sending someone with me. He made his arrangements and, a few minutes later, a man appeared at the kitchen door.

The fellow was interesting to say the least. He was close to six feet tall, seemed rather stout for his line of work. He had white hair, a well-trimmed white beard. His completion wasn't ruddy; however, he was a person who was used to being outdoors. The most startling feature about him was his eyes; they were a deep blue. He had a pleasant looking face with laugh lines around his eyes. At some point in time, his nose had been broken more than once.

I was to learn later from Fred the reason Sach looked fat wasn't because he was out of shape physically, but he was wearing a full body brace under his Kevlar vest. He was recovering from a serious horseback riding accident.

When he spoke, his voice was a deep rich and soothing baritone. "Hi, I'm Sach. Fred told me I was needed to escort you on a drive."

"Come in while I get my things together. Meet Miss Joy…she'll be going with us. Do you like dogs?"

His reply was instant, "I like all animals. Your big dog is an interesting guy. He watches me all the time, but won't come to me. He doesn't seem to be afraid of me, just keeps his distance."

I said good-bye to Fred, who looked worried about my leaving, even with Sach. "You'll find him an interesting character, and I would trust my mother to his care. Have a safe trip and enjoy a little freedom."

I got the new truck out of the barn and headed down the driveway. Sach said, "I want you to open the gate; with the privacy screen being so dark on the windows, if anyone is watching they'll think you're alone."

When I got out onto our road with the truck, I drove to the right until I came to a small crossroad and took another right. I drove to the end of the road where it T'd into another road and went right again. If my calculations were close, my parcel of land should be inside that square with the river being the other line. I'd never been over here, so I didn't have any idea what I was looking for. I was aware Marty was staying close by, and couldn't understand why nobody had found him.

We were cruising along the road when I spotted a sign nailed to a tree. The sign was advertising a deer camp for rent. It was a simple homemade sign painted a faded white with black free-hand lettering.

I pulled into the yard of the slightly run-down property with old cars out back and an old pickup truck parked by the door. I told Sach to stay in the truck and taking one of the flyers Fred printed with Marty's picture on it went up the lopsided steps to the door. I knocked on the storm door and heard a dog begin to bark inside. I could hear someone walking toward the door.

An older man with thinning white hair, an unshaven face, and the worse fitting dentures I'd ever seen opened the inside door while trying to quiet the dog. In order to hear me, he stepped out onto the platform that served as the top step. "Can I help you? Are you lost?" he inquired.

"No. I stopped because I saw your sign for the camp rental. I wondered if you'd rented it."

He nodded his head. "Yup, just the other day. I rented it for a month. I have a couple of them so I could still rent you one."

"I'm not looking to rent a camp. I was wondering if you've seen this fellow, I think he was looking for a place in the area."

The man glanced at the photo and nodded. "Yup, he's the guy who came by and rented the camp. Funny he didn't look like a sport. I remember he was wearing dress shoes covered with mud, but it wasn't any of my business. I just rent the camps."

"Can you give me directions to the camp he rented?"

"It's easy enough to find. Go back the way you came, and you'll see a small white square wooden sign, on a tree with a number 'ten' on it. You can drive in on the tote road almost to the camp. Your truck's high enough to clear the ruts. I ain't sure if his car was or not, and he didn't come back. I hope that helps you out. Am I in trouble for renting it to him?"

I smiled my best smile and assured him he was fine and not in any trouble. I thanked him and returned to the truck. As I was backing around in the driveway, I filled Sach in with the information I'd gotten. He was busy on the phone with Fred.

Sach looked over at me and said, "Fred told me to make sure you're not going to the camp… period. They're on the way now. He wants us to meet him on the road before where the camp road is, and then he wants us out of there. He also said he won't take *no* for an answer, he said he knows you too well."

I snickered. What else could I do? It was true… Fred did know me; however, I doubted he understood me. I would respect his wishes. I wanted this to be finished as much as he did. I was certain all the men would like to return to their real lives. I knew I did.

I spotted Fred in the large black truck. He flew past us and up into the rutted camp road. I looked over at Sach and could see by the look on his face he wanted to join the others. "Sach, why don't you hop out and join them? I'll be fine. I'll drive down the road and park, and pick you up when it's over."

I watched his look waver for an instant, then he shook his head. "I'll stay right here with you; as instructed. Let's go down the road out of sight and wait."

I drove forward slowly with my eyes on the rearview mirror until I was about three-quarters of a mile away. I turned the truck around while Sach dug out a pair of field glasses.

We sat quietly in the truck; waited, and waited while nothing seemed to be happening. I hoped Marty hadn't moved out of the camp already. I was about to voice this thought to Sach, when a movement caught my attention in the rearview mirror. I saw a figure start out of the woods then dart back into the cover of the bushes at the edge of the road. I grabbed Sach's arm… he jumped, "What?"

"I just saw him behind the truck at the edge of the woods. He started to run out onto the road, then darted back to cover. Do you have your pistol with you? I have my revolver… let's go. We can get him."

I opened the truck door, grabbed the keys while drawing my weapon out of my shoulder holster. Sach was wide-eyed, but he was moving. As soon as he cleared the truck, I locked it shoving the keys deep into my pocket. There was no point telling Miss Joy not to bark. Marty already knew we were on his tail.

The woods were thick and wet. I could clearly see the footprints in the mossy ground where Marty fled. I was like a hound on the trail of a coon. I wanted him badly. I was done with this bullshit. I was ready to end it one way or another. I could feel Sach close behind me. He touched my shoulder and signaled for me to get behind him. I shook my head and indicated we should stay side by side if anything. He didn't like the idea. He pointed to his Kevlar vest trying to tell me he would give it to me. I shook my head. I wanted to move on quickly and not waste any more time.

We came to a brook, which was quite wide. I was all for crossing it. Sach was not. I couldn't see any footprints leading into the brook. Where had Marty gone? I didn't want him behind us; it would be too dangerous.

We hunkered down in a large clump of alders, watched and waited. I listened, but heard nothing moving. Still we waited. We must have been in the thicket waiting for close to an hour when I heard a twig snap. I was on hyper alert. So was Sach. We scanned the area very carefully without moving. We heard the sound of a footstep not far from where we were crouched. Sach looked at me and indicated he was ready. I nodded… so was I.

Sach twitched, and then pulled out his phone. It appeared he had a text message. I almost snorted... hell of a time for phone play. *This was serious business.*

Sach passed me his phone so I could read the screen. The message read, "I told you two to stay in the truck. I am right behind you. Don't shoot me."

Damn, Marty had gotten away from all of us. I was discouraged; we had been so close.

Sach focused on spotting Fred. I continued watching for Marty. I knew he was close by and probably having a good laugh at our expense.

Fred came into view through the bushes. He had been careful to stay low and quiet. When he got beside us, we told him what the story was and how we had tracked Marty to the brook. He'd fanned his crew out from the camp heading in this direction. He was planning on meeting them on the road when he spotted my truck and knew we were in the woods.

We withdrew to avoid being in a cross fire with the others. I couldn't believe we were all outsmarted.

When we reached the truck, Fred told us they had surprised Marty just as he was returning from the outhouse. He fled into the woods while they took up the chase. He was carrying an automatic handgun, didn't have a jacket, and his car was still parked at the camp. They'd disabled the car.

Fred called the game warden in the area for assistance to see if they had a dog or extra men. They were on their way.

"Fred, this means nobody's at my place, so if he circles around through the woods he can get there easily with no resistance. Did you lock your car parked in the driveway? Do you have the keys? He can break into the cottage to steal clothes and guns. I'm going back to the house. We know he tried to burn it down, now he'll be free to do whatever he wants."

I strode to my truck and was already inside with the key in the ignition when Sach jumped in. I drove off as if my pants were on fire. I knew what kind of mayhem Marty could create if he were there. I also worried if he would hurt Luce. He'd already hurt Marty, so I knew he would be laying for the dog.

When I got to the end of the driveway, Sach hopped out and opened the gate. We spotted a cruiser coming down the road fast so we waited.

The cruiser pulled into the drive behind me and told Sach he would be staying here with us. Gate locked, Sach got in, and we rolled toward the cottage. I didn't see anything out of the way; yet. When I stepped down out of the truck, I didn't see Luce. Not a good sign, although with the cruiser here he might not come out until he was certain it was okay.

I checked the cottage. It seemed all right. I went across to the barn where I could clearly see someone had jimmied the lock on the side door, tearing it from the jam. *Son of a bitch* I thought, some people just have to bust other folk's property up. Sach moved me aside and pushed open the door with his foot. The trooper was right behind him with his weapon drawn. They swung through the door on the ready. I hit the switch and flooded the area with bright light.

We knew he'd been in there, but now where had he gone? I walked over to look at where Pete's old truck sat. It was evident Marty planned to steal the vehicle. Joke was on him. Even though the keys were in the ignition, I had removed the battery and stored it in another part of the barn.

Was he still in here? He could be up in the loft where the water tank was. I made a silent gesture to Sach and the trooper to go up the stairs and check the tank room. I motioned where the light switch was on the outside of the room. They nodded and mounted the stairs.

He wasn't in there. I still hadn't seen Luce. I checked the pump house but still, no trace of Luce. I prayed Marty hadn't shot him or otherwise harmed the big dog.

We were outside standing by the vehicles when I heard a scream. It was blood curdling, making the hair on my neck stand up straight. The men reacted with drawn guns. The three of us started in the direction the scream came from. We pushed into the underbrush, listening. We finally heard a whimper, then another.

As we moved into a small clearing, we could clearly see what happened. I would guess Marty had stopped to relieve himself and Luce, being a smart and patient animal, had bided his time then struck; and held on with his jaws locked over both Marty's hand and what it held. In the heat of the action, Marty dropped his handgun. He was smart enough, even in his compromised state, not to move or remove the dog from his genitals.

One look at Luce's face said it all...*please get this out of my mouth.*

Marty was glaring with hatred at all of us, me in particular. When he spoke, he was venomous. "Are you idiots going to just stand there or are you going to get this mutt off me? I can't see what Dom possibly saw in you that he wanted to keep paying you off. You're nothing but an old, worn out, douche bag."

It always amazed me what people who are under pressure would say. What in hell was he ranting about and against whom was he railing? I figured I would never see him in a more compromising position, so I was going to have some answers. I motioned for Sach and the trooper to back off, and let Luce just 'hang on' for a few more minutes.

"Marty, just what do you think Dom is paying me off for?"

He snarled, "Do you think I don't understand affairs when I see one? Dom is a married man with a family and, ever since you showed up on the scene, he has chased your sorry wrinkled old ass all over hell's half acre. He should've taken care of the people who worked for him instead of spending money on a slut."

"Well Marty, I wondered what your bitch with me was. It's too bad you really didn't know the facts about any of this. I'm not going to enlighten you. I could tell you this...I am not, nor would I ever, have an affair with Dom or anyone else. Did you think if you killed me it would secure a position for you with him?"

Marty looked confused. "I don't need that cheap son of a bitch or his lousy job. I can take care of myself."

Just as he uttered those last words with a bit too much bravado for a man in his position, Luce applied a bit more pressure, resulting in another hair-raising screech from Marty.

"Get this thing off from me, NOW!"

I looked at the group of men standing there. Some had a grimace in their expressions, and some with a look of malicious humor. My only comment was, "You didn't say 'please'." I heard snickers from the men.

The trooper stepped forward, retrieved the gun from the ground, and read Marty his rights. He nodded to me to call Luce off so he could handcuff Marty.

As I was about to speak to Luce, Fred and his men arrived on the scene. Fred took the whole scenario in and began to bellow with laughter. When he caught his breath, he tried to speak. "Well Marty, it looks like you're in a bit of a dilemma here. Want to explain what happened?"

Marty's look of hatred said it all. "Go to hell, you bastard; you're still a piece of shit in my book."

Luce seemed to understand this was confrontational, so he applied more pressure, resulting in a howl of pain from his victim.

I spoke quietly to Luce. "Okay, big guy, you can spit him out now."

The expression on the dog's face was priceless. It went from *do I have to? To, yuk, I need mouthwash.* Luce released Marty, and ran to a standing mud puddle to wash his face and mouth. The dog was a constant source of amusement. Luce returned to me, and sat in front of my feet at the ready for whatever was going to happen next.

He didn't have long to wait. As the trooper waited, Marty quickly stowed his gear, zipped his fly, and then bolted for the woods. Even with all the men there, he thought he could still get away. His actions startled everyone, with one exception… Luce. The dog was off on a bound, quickly overtaking Marty and jumping on his back, pinning him to the ground. Luce just sat on his back while the trooper hurried to cuff him.

Fred made his report to Dom, then handed me the phone. Once I explained why Marty thought he was sending money to me, he laughed, then immediately became enraged to think anybody would ever see him as anyone but the honorable person who he was. I calmed Dom down to a steady roar, then gave the phone back to Fred.

The courts held Marty in Maine for trying to kill me when he blew up my truck, then sent him to Pennsylvania to stand trial for embezzling funds from Dom's company.

I was happy to see the whole mess over. All the men left the next day. Because they were all material witnesses, they would need to return for the court hearing.

When I spoke with Pete later during the day, he had a great laugh about what Luce had done. He missed the big beast, but knew Luce would not acclimate well to living in the city. He expressed his hope Luce could stay with Miss Joy and me.

He also told me he had been able to trace some of the money Marty had squirreled away in offshore accounts, and recovered a large portion of the stolen funds.

Dom wanted him to stay with the company as the chief financial officer. Pete said he was pleased at the offer, saying Dom was generous in the salary and benefit package he offered.

It surprised me when Pete asked for my opinion as to whether to accept the offer and stay, or if he should return home. I explained to him that his tree house was his, and he was always welcome to come and stay as he wished. I also expressed my thoughts about the fact he was a young man who needed to work at something he knew and enjoyed. He should also create a social life for himself, something he couldn't readily do here in the boondocks of Maine.

Thirty

I busied myself getting ready for winter. I needed to get the tractor out and get the snow blower attached. I knew I couldn't handle the job by myself. I enlisted the help of Nick, my road repairman. He told me he would send his man out to service the equipment and install the blower. He would come first thing in the morning.

True to his word, Nick's man arrived *first thing* in the morning. As I walked down to open the gate for him, I thought to myself I could leave the gate either open or unlocked; I was free from threats. It was an alien thought after all this time. I smiled to myself as the dogs and I walked the last few steps to the gate. It had not been a stress-free time by any means.

When the man pulled inside the gate, he stopped his pickup truck, got out, and offered his hand for a shake. He was a big man with a full head of curly iron-gray hair, an open smiling face, and dark eyes that seemed to twinkle with laughter. When he spoke, his voice was deep and sounded as if he were on the verge of laughter. "Hi there, I'm Nick's pseudo dad here to fix your tractor. My name's Curly…the name is really Curt, short for Curtis. Curly is easier for most folks to remember. I answer to either. Pleased to meet you, Nettie. Hop in, and we'll look at the piece of equipment. Bring the dogs with you." I scooped Miss Joy up in my arms and motioned for

Luce to come. Luce looked at me, shook his head, then jumped into the back of Curt's truck and sat. Okay, I guess it worked.

Curt said, "Nick told me you had a big strange looking dog out here. He didn't lie. I've never seen a dog so large. Is he friendly? Does he like people?"

I laughed. "He is big, and whether or not he likes people, I think he has only tasted one, and I don't think he liked the flavor because after he let go, he washed his mouth out in a mud puddle."

Curt roared with laughter, filling the truck with his mirth. I liked him.

We started the tractor, and brought it out of the barn. The equipment was in need of attention. Because the tractor had been idle and not serviced or started for a while, Curt changed the oil, greased it, checked all the belts, and then tested it by running it up and down the driveway. He drove it into the barn and attached the blower, took it outside to test it. When he returned it to the barn, he backed it in so I could just start it up and come out blowing snow.

He worked steadily for a couple of hours. I asked him if he would like a cup of coffee. He seemed pleased at the offer so I upped the ante with some homemade muffins. In between bites he uttered, "Don't feed me, or I'll never leave."

I smiled, because I'd lived alone for many, many years with no intention of changing any rules now.

A few days later, I was getting ready to chain saw some wood for my stoves, when I realized I couldn't use the tractor to haul out the cut wood with the blower mounted on the front. I didn't want to remove the blower. I needed a new plan.

When I had been at Nick's garage the other day, I noticed he had a side-by-side for sale. I wondered if it had a dump body on the back. I had always thought of them as more of a toy than anything else. It would work great in the woods, though. It was all-wheel drive, and most of them in this area of the state had winches on at least the front, so if you got stuck you could pull yourself out. This one even had a back seat so Luce could ride with me.

Miss Joy and I headed for town on a mission. When I pulled into Nick's yard, I stopped beside the four-wheeler and checked out the body and the winch. I was surprised it looked like new, had the hydraulic dump body along with a winch on both front and back. I was interested.

I was just walking toward the garage when Curt met me half way. "Hi there, don't tell me you broke the Kubota already? I noticed you were looking over the 'mule.' Can I help?"

"Thanks, Curt; I wondered what the history was on it, and how much Nick would be asking for it? Do you know anything about it? I want something to use in the woods while I'm cutting firewood. With the snow-blower on the tractor, I can't use the bucket to haul firewood."

Curt shook his massive head of curly hair and chuckled. "You do know we sell firewood cut to stove-length here, don't you?"

"I know you do, but I have plenty of wood on the property, and it needs some thinning out. I don't mind cutting and splitting, so that seemed like a reasonable solution. I just need something for moving the wood. I thought I would check this thing out. It's large enough for the dogs and me. It has double winches so I can get unstuck if I need to. Can you tell me about it? I assume it is used."

Curt gave me all the information he had; however, he told me he would have to check with Nick about the price. Nick would be away for the rest of the day doing a job. When he returned, Curt would have Nick call me.

We chatted for a few moments, and then I left for home to get on with my task. Winter would be here soon. I needed to have my firewood cut, drying, and stacked to keep me warm. I hadn't decided about putting central heat into the cabin. I had done some research, but wasn't ready to make a choice.

I was out in the woods behind the cabin cutting down trees with the chainsaw when Luce and Miss Joy alerted me someone was there. I laughed at Miss Joy; she never liked to be around the saws or equipment before she had Luce… now I couldn't get her to stay inside while I was working. Luce would either sit with her between his front legs or lie down with her curled inside his long legs.

I shut the saw off and took off my ear-protection so I could listen. Someone was driving up the driveway. I could see Nick's truck with a trailer behind carrying the four-wheeler.

Curt got out of the truck and began unloading the mule. He was efficient in his motions, and soon drove up to our location. "Nick sent this out for you to use for a few days to see if you really liked it before you purchased one. I filled it with gas and checked the oil. I also brought you a can filled with gas so you can run it for several days without having to go over town to get more fuel."

"Thanks, but I want to know the price of the toy before I fall in love with it."

He received my comment with a great laugh. "Are you always this careful about things?"

"Oh, you have no idea. I can get myself into all kinds of mischief without even trying. I think I have a sign on my back that says, 'trouble wanted here'."

We chatted back and forth for a few minutes, then Curt showed me how to run the toy. It was fun. I backed it up to the pile of wood I'd already cut into stove length, and loaded the back to see how much it would hold. Curt helped me stack the wood into the dump body. It held more than I thought. Once it was full, we got into the front seat and, without any coaching; the dogs helped themselves to the back seat. I was impressed with the amount of weight it carried without any effort.

I got to my woodpile, and Curt showed me the dump was hydraulic. How easy was that?

It was time for me to call it a day. I'd recovered well enough from the accident, and the scrape with crazy woman, but I was still lacking the endurance I used to have. Lord almighty, I prayed it had nothing to do with my advancing age. I was smiling to myself as I carried my saw and gas can into the barn. I would need to back up the tractor to make room for the space I needed for the mule to fit in the barn. I was just getting ready to hoist myself up onto the tractor when Curt surprised me by taking my arm and steering me out of the way so he could move it.

I was a little shocked. I think he saw it in my expression. He spoke kindly and with his big smile in place. "Why don't you make us a cup of coffee or tea, and I'll move this stuff around so you can get it out easily."

I couldn't tell if I'd been dismissed or assisted; I was really out of touch. I took the road less traveled and left to make coffee. Once inside, as I was taking off my heavy jacket and boots, I realized how tired I really was. *Damn, not good.* I had to get back into shape in a hurry, or I wouldn't get the chores necessary for winter survival here completed. I was mulling the thought over in my head when Curt came through the door.

"I appreciated your doing that for a cup of coffee. What happens if I add an oatmeal raisin cookie to the ante?"

"Madam, I would brush-hog the field, sweep the gravel drive, then I would rake the beach area. Better make it two cookies."

I enjoyed listening to him banter. He had a deep melodic voice that was very pleasant.

We talked about what I would do with the brush from cutting the trees. I knew I didn't want to leave it in piles on the ground, nor did I want to burn it. I inquired about having Nick come out and dig a hole with his backhoe so I could bury all of the brush. Curt's idea was to bury the brush, but pull the stumps and bury them also. It would give me a nice cleared area. In time, it would reseed and create new tree growth.

We talked at length about central heating for the house. It was always good for me to get different opinions and ideas when I was contemplating a project of that scope.

Thirty-one

"When you leave, would you please snap the lock on the gate for me?"

Curt looked troubled. "How come you're locking the gate again? Are you having problems out here?"

"I apparently have a couple of idiots who lost their village. They've come up into the driveway twice at night. I guess I should have the signs illuminated, perhaps with flashing neon?

"Although I carefully posted the property, for both trespassing and hunting, people still seemed to think it is okay to come inside the posted boundaries at will. The other night I went out and met them on the drive. I told them both if they returned, I would have them arrested for trespassing. They thought it was a hell of a laugh. I'm done with them. If they come again, and I encounter them on my property, it won't be pretty."

Curt laughed and said he would call before returning, so I wouldn't shoot him or have Luce chase him away.

I was resting after dinner listening to the radio and reading a new book when the gate alarm chimed. I got out of my chair and checked the screen. Same two damned fools who were here before. I was finished with this game.

I pulled on my jacket and boots, took my shotgun with extra shells, and put my .38 into the jacket pocket. I left Miss Joy in the house and whistled for Luce. I stopped by the garage for a coil of rope and some duct tape. I was ready.

Luce and I walked quietly across the field at the edge of the tree line. There was total darkness with no moon or stars. I have excellent night vision and by keeping the river as a backdrop, I would spot the jerks, but they wouldn't see me. I was so grateful Pete taught the dog to be silent. He knew there were people coming up the driveway, yet he walked along at my side without a sound. The dog was a great comfort to my well-being.

I was approaching the junction where the driveway came into the clearing of the field. I could smell cigarette smoke and hear them talking. They were certain I didn't know about their presence. They were discussing how they were going to scare me, then what they planned on doing to me along with my big stupid dog. *They were in for one hell of a surprise.*

One of them asked the other if he remembered to bring the spray cans of paint. The reply was crystal clear on the quiet night air. "Yeah, I got 'em, I want to write 'bitch' on the side of the fancy camper parked out back. Let's see how she likes that."

I was pissed. I stood at the edge of the clearing next to the low bushes and waited until they started to walk across the field at an angle toward the house. I let them get about ten feet ahead of me before I jacked a shell into the chamber of my .12 gauge. They stopped mid-step.

"Put your hands in the air and don't breathe. One move, and I'll shoot off both of your legs. Do it now. I'm using number six birdshot."

Slowly they put their hands up swearing like pirates. One of them began to turn slowly around.

"Stop moving, NOW!"

One of them began to whine. "I got a butt in my mouth. I need to take it out or get burned."

"Tuff shit. You move, and you'll be missing a leg or two. If you are smart enough to trespass, you should be smart enough to swallow the butt. You, with the cigarette, put your hands behind your back, and if your buddy doesn't want to watch you die, he'll stand *very* still."

I'd made a slipknot in the rope when I left the barn so I put it over one of his hands then made another loop over his other hand before securing it around his neck. I turned my attention to the other one and repeated the process.

"Okay smart alecks, let's take a slow walk back down the drive. One wrong move, and you'll both get shot." I walked them to the gate.

"Are you going to untie us before you go? We can't get into our truck like this."

What a whiney bunch these two jerks turned out to be. Some village would delight in getting rid of their idiots.

"Oh no, I don't intend to untie either of you. Stand next to that post." I looped the rope up over the main gatepost, bringing it down behind them then around them several times. I'd trussed them tightly, without any slack, so they had to remain standing. I then took the duct tape and secured their legs together. I didn't want to listen to them any longer. Their cussing and foul language was disgusting, so I duct taped their mouths.

"I'll call the state troopers and tell them were to find you. I'll press charges for your antics. I told you before to stay off my property. I meant it. Now, I'm finished with both of you. If you ever return here, for any reason, I won't say a word to you. I'll just shoot you dead. Do you understand me? Just nod your heads. Have a great time waiting for the law to come, if, and when they bother to respond."

I walked off up the drive with Luce while I called the troopers.

After we had the issue with Marty, the troopers were nice enough from time to time to call in and make sure I was doing all right. My call got immediate attention, and the dispatcher assured me somebody would be there shortly. I told them where to find the men and mentioned I would press charges. When I told the dispatcher I had hung them out to dry on the gatepost, he enjoyed a good laugh. He told me, "We'll pick up the dirty laundry shortly. Thanks for being so considerate as to package it for us."

Thirty-two

The next day, in the early afternoon, I was out on the woodlot cutting when Luce came and stood off to the side, but well within my range of vision. He did that when he wanted to alert me. I don't know if Pete taught him to do this or if it was instinct. I shut the saw off and took off my ear protectors. The gate alarm was sounding.

I put the dogs into the four-wheeler, checked my pocket to be certain I had my revolver with me, and we headed for the gate.

I found a very distraught Curt there. It seemed he had been there for several minutes waiting for me to let him in. "I could hear the saw running, but after what I just heard in the village, I didn't want to take a chance on getting 'hung out to dry' with the rest of the riff-raff."

"I'm sorry it took Luce a few minutes to get my attention. I can't hear the alarm when I have on ear protectors. Let me unlock the gate. What brings you out here so early in the day? Are you going to take my toy? I should have called Nick and told him I was going to purchase it."

The expression on Curt's face assured me that he had not come about the four-wheeler. "I'm not here about that thing. Can I come in and talk to you for a few minutes?"

I unlocked the gate and swung it open so he could drive through. Now, what do you suppose he wanted? I didn't know, but I would be polite and listen. As soon as his truck entered, I closed and locked the gate. I knew the idiots would return. They didn't look like *early learners*, and I was certain their noses would be out of joint. I wasn't going to take any chances. The authorities informed me if intruders were on my posted property; they would be trespassers, whether the gate was open or locked. I was finished with the local bullshit.

I got into the four-wheeler and headed for the house with Curt all but in my hip pocket. I noticed his usually cheerful facial features were totally absent today. I hoped there was nothing wrong at the garage.

I called over to him as he was exiting his truck. "Do you want a coffee?"

I did get a half smile and a head nod, so I started into the kitchen to set a pot to brew.

I poured the coffee and produced a fresh muffin, but Curt still looked troubled. "What's on your mind this morning? You don't seem to be yourself. Is there a problem at the garage? Or did you just get up on the wrong side of the bed?" I tried to keep it light because I knew nothing about Curt's personal life or his relationships. Nor did I want to know.

"Nettie, I know this is none of my business, but there's talk in town you had a scuffle with a couple of local guys last night out here. I heard you captured them at gunpoint and tied them to the gate then called the police to come get them. Was it true?"

"Yeah, I would say that was a fairly accurate account, I guess. The police must have collected them at some point because they weren't still there when you came. Is that what's bothering you?"

"Yes, and the fact you're out here alone using a chain saw and working without anyone here if you got hurt. By the way, as a disclaimer, Nick told me to mind my own business because you didn't cotton well to strangers. I'm sorry if I've offended you. I have never met a woman like you. You fascinate me and scare the living hell out of me at the same time."

Thirty-three

I contemplated my reply for a few minutes before answering. It was none of Curt's business who I was, or what I was, and I don't like people knowing my business. I wanted to be polite while expressing this to him. I thought he was probably a nice enough man, or person, for that matter. I liked him but wasn't ever looking for any kind of relationship beyond a casual friend. While I was still running my mental railroad, he shifted in his chair, and I knew he had something else on his mind.

"Why do you always carry a gun? Are you in trouble or something?"

I couldn't help it. I burst into laughter, shocking him. Then the expression on his face sent me into gales of laughter. There were tears running down my cheeks, and still I couldn't stop. I excused myself to grab a paper towel and try to rein myself in. I didn't want to come across as rude or crazy or maybe both. I took a deep breath and stabilized myself. Before my outburst of mirth, I could have just dismissed him and sent him on his way without any explanation. Now I felt duty bound to make an effort and try to explain, I am neither crazy nor delusional.

I refilled our cups then sat down to finish this business. "Curt, I'm sorry for the display. Now that I've proved I'm presenting as being unhinged, I need to clarify my position."

Strangely, when I made the statement I saw something flicker in his expression. I wondered what was going on in his mind. The change in his eyes set off a warning bell in my brain. I trust my instincts one-hundred percent. Perhaps I should ask him some background questions first. This was like playing poker with a total stranger, which in truth he was.

"Curt, why are you here? I don't mean here, at my house, I mean here in town. I know from your speech you're not a native of Maine. How do you know Nick? I think if you want to play question and answers, fair is fair on both sides of the situation. If that's uncomfortable for you, then just let yourself out of the gate, and we'll call it a draw."

I thought the waiting period was long and drawn out. I recognized he was having a personal wrestling match with his thoughts. I could wait because I was either going to have some answers, or I would personally escort him to the other side of the gate. I wasn't the one who started this silly standoff.

Finally, Curt made his decision. Now the question in my mind was whether he would, or could, be honest. I've been lied to so many times in my life, I couldn't begin to count them. Sometimes for big things and other times, because, increasingly, people would rather cheat and lie than be honest. I never figured that out. I, on the other hand, am honest to a fault, even when it costs me big time.

"You may want me to leave after I tell you. I knew Nick's father from years ago. We were both in the military and remained friends for a few years until he died in an accident. I used to visit with him and his wife and knew Nick as a toddler. Because of our friendship, I kept up with Nick and his mom over the years. Nick's mom remarried a few years ago, with Nick's blessings, and moved south. The boy and I continued to be buddies and, often, you'll hear him refer to me as either his dad or uncle.

"When I finished my time with the military, they gave me a job working with, but not for, the FBI as a profiler. I had taken courses during college in criminal justice and psychology. That, along with good people skills and an ability to listen and discern, worked well in the field.

I worked for several years with a good track record until the case where I blew it. I've often wondered if I had gotten either cocky or sloppy. Hindsight is a bitch. I still don't know which it was after all this time and mental anguish.

"Two people died because I didn't see what was obvious. First, I took a leave of absence, but I couldn't get over the error I'd made, so I quit. They were good to me and told me the position would be mine any time I wanted to return. I still don't want to go back.

"I came to Maine to visit with Nick and see if I could get my head back together."

Curt looked like he had been deflated. I could see and feel his pain. He could have told me it was none of my business and brushed it off. He hadn't, and I respected him for the effort.

Thirty-four

"Okay Nettie; that was my sad tale, now it's your turn. You can tell me it's none of my business, and tell me to take a hike. I would understand. I know some of the history about this property from Nick and the gossip in the village. I don't put too much stock in local folk lore."

It was indeed my turn. How much was I willing to share would be the question.

"If I told you the whole saga of why I'm here, why I lock the gate, carry a gun, and appear paranoid, it would take an inordinate amount of both your, and my, time. We would be old and gray, and most likely sick of each other in the process."

I received a hearty laugh as he rose and refilled our cups. "Lady, I have nothing but time, so go for it. Did they ever find the folks who lived here before you came? What happened to them? Isn't the big dog the same one the man had when he lived here?"

Suddenly, I was uncomfortable with the questions. I'd been through too much with too many bad, bad, memories to go down the rabbit-hole yet again.

Curt's expression became very guarded. He retained a pleasant exterior, but his eyes reflected something I couldn't read. Was he part of the shakedown scheme on Pete? I needed to buy myself some time to do a little background check on my guest. I was trying to figure out how when his phone rang. He answered it without hesitation, spoke with the party on the line, smiled, and passed the phone to me. What was going on here?

I took the phone and said a reserved "Hello" Then waited. .

"Hello Nettie, how are you doing?"

I was so shocked, I just stared at the instrument in my hand as if it were a snake. I instantly recognized the voice on the other end of the call. It was Adam. He was the FBI agent who had worked so hard for Pete. He also helped to save me from the crazy woman. Why would he be on Curt's phone? I needed to know.

"Hello Adam, how are you? You know me well enough to know I want answers to all kinds of questions. What are you going to share with me?"

In true Adam-fashion, he went straight to the point. "First I want you to know Curt is okay. I would trust him with my life, and I have. How he connected with you is pure coincidence. He spoke with me earlier today about something else entirely and mentioned he'd met a lady. When I was joshing with him about running off with a farmer's wife, he assured me Nettie was not in *that* category. When he said Nettie, because the name is not common, I needed more info. He told me he was concerned because you lived in a remote area away from town or neighbors and the fact you always carried a gun. In addition, there had been a problem with some local yokels. He knew you were not very trusting, so he asked if I would vouch for him. I do; he is a great man, and when he gets over being mad at himself because he isn't perfect, I want him back. Anything else I can help you with?"

"Not a thing. As always, you've completely covered all of the bases, and then some. Thanks for your help, yet again. I'll return you to Curt." I passed the phone across the table to a grinning man.

Curt thanked Adam and ended the call, then sat waiting.

"If you talked with Adam, then you know most of the story, so I don't need to bore you to death with details."

Curt shook his curly head. "Nope, that won't fly. You have to tell me because I never asked Adam how or why he knew you. Call it the 'Code of the West' in a manner of speaking. He simply told me you had good reason to carry a gun, and he was surprised you were only carrying one. He told me to behave because you could take me in a fair fight, and you never fought fairly, or to lose. I trust Adam. Now, I want to trust you to tell me what's going on."

"Nothing, I hope, other than the idiots from town. I know they'll be back looking for revenge."

"To answer your question about Pete, the man who built this house is alive, well, and working happily out of state. I expect he may come home for Thanksgiving. The woman, who the bank thought was his wife, wasn't. She's dead. No, I didn't kill her although it was touch and go if she would kill me, or I could manage to kill her. It is a long story of no consequence.

"Right after I bought the property with all the issues, I had to make a trip to Virginia to my sister's home. On the way back, I had a horrific accident with a tractor-trailer. My old motor home was a total wreck, as anyone might surmise. Thankfully, I was not. During the process of recovery, I met a great gentleman, and he was a good friend of Adam's. While I was trying to recover from the injuries, the crazy woman attacked me several times. Finally, she died.

"I returned back here to try to reclaim my life and figure out what to do with the property. Shortly after my return on a trip to Bangor, a man blew my truck to hell and back. The fiasco involved several men and some time. They finally captured him. At present, things are good in the valley, with the exception of the idiots. End of the story."

Curt sat shaking his head. "I understand why you carry a gun. Do you need another?"

"Nope, I have several, thank you just the same. I have bored you to death, so if you can tolerate leftover beef stew with dumplings, I'll at least feed you."

"Nettie, do you want me to take the first watch for my dinner?"

I laughed. It was nice to kid with someone for a change. I wondered if my life would ever settle back into a normal, or as near normal, routine as my life ever gets.

We enjoyed dinner, and I even managed to find dessert for the man. He liked his food. I liked feeding folks, so it was great all around.

"Are you married Curt?" I didn't really care... it was just conversation.

My question clearly caught him off balance. The expressions on his face were a mixture of emotions all in one. Finally, he managed to answer. "No, Nettie, I'm not married. I have been. Twice in fact, I have also been divorced twice. Now, how about you while we are on the subject, what is your status? Married, or are you divorced or widowed?"

My turn to be stunned, as old as I am, you would think I'd know better than to open up a can of worms. I pondered the question for a second before responding. "All of the above. Presently single and have been for many, many years."

It always amazes me how difficult it is for me to discuss anything of a personal nature. "Curt, do you have children? I have three, two girls and a son, and three grandchildren. Again, I have two granddaughters and a grandson."

His face showed sadness. "I do have grown children. A son and one daughter, but we're not close. I was gone too much when they were little. They hardly knew who I was. When their mothers and I divorced, the children were young and my ex-wives remarried very quickly so the kids saw the new husbands as their fathers. It was just as well. I think I wouldn't have been a very good father. I enjoyed my work, liked making good money to support them, but was never home.

"Are you close with your kids? How about your grandkids? Do you see them often?"

"I am close with my kids. I was a single mom, and we grew up together. I worked hard, and so did they. Thankfully, they are all great people and very productive. I'm proud of them and the grandkids."

"I have to ask, Nettie, what do they think of what's been happening to you?"

I replied in a clipped manner I instantly regretted after the fact. "They don't know any of it, and I'll *never* share it with them. I'm sorry that sounded so brash, but I don't ever want anything in my life to touch my family. It's hard enough for folks to just live their work-a-day lives without having to worry about a parent."

We sat and drank the last of our coffee and chatted about easy things. When it was time for Curt go, he seemed reluctant. I knew he enjoyed the afternoon and evening, but it was time for him to leave.

"Would you please lock the gate on your way out? Doing so would save me a trip down the driveway. I would appreciate it."

We said our goodbyes and Curt left. I watched on the monitor while he locked the gate and drove off.

Thirty-five

It had been a busy day and a pleasant evening, but I was tired and ready for bed. I wanted to be rested and ready for tomorrow. I planned to cut down the remaining trees on that patch of ground. After I finished the cutting, I would have Nick come and clean up the area with his heavy equipment.

The next day dawned with clear skies and comfortable temps for the time of year. I love fall, so I looked forward to my tasks for the day. If I hurried, I would have time for a paddle in the kayak later.

After breakfast and dog feeding, I put Miss Joy in the house because she really hated the noise the chainsaw made, and I couldn't watch where she might be while trees and brush were flying.

I gathered up the tools, putting them into the four-wheeler with Luce sitting on the seat beside me. He was so funny. He never let me out of his sight. He also made me feel very secure. I wouldn't tell him because I didn't want him to get a swelled head. After all, he was big enough already.

I had been working for an hour or so and making good progress when I smelled something odd…it was a combination of stagnant cigarette smoke and bad body odor. At first, I thought it was my imagination. My sense of smell is so acute, I sometimes wonder if I'm part bloodhound. Then the scent was stronger.

I was ready to shut off the saw and check it out when a hand grabbed my jacket collar. I froze. What the hell was going on? My fright meter went out of sight. I still had the saw in my hand, and it was running. I could feel the tension on my collar tightening. I stepped back two quick steps, which surprised whoever was there. I swung around as far as I could with the saw chain engaged. My move stunned the village idiot, and he let go of my coat. Now, I was pissed to the nines. I wanted to saw the jerk in half.

I knew I couldn't get my hand onto my revolver. I think he must have read my expression because he grabbed the long branch of wood I'd just limbed off the downed tree and began to swing it at me like a club. He was too far from me to get him with the saw blade. As I ducked and stepped back, I lost my balance and began to fall. I released the trigger on the saw as I tumbled. It stopped, but then I was on the ground in a pile of brush and very vulnerable. I had to get up, get my gun, and stop this damn fool. He jumped onto me and pushed me back hard into the brush pile.

"Now who's the smart one? I'm going to make you sorrier than you have ever been in your whole, damn, old life, bitch. Then I am going to bury you where they'll never find you."

I was kicking and fighting as hard as I could with the horrible disadvantage of being pinned in a brush pile.

Where was Luce? Had this son of bitch killed him? That thought made me madder still. I managed to get my hand on a short piece of wood, grabbed it with all my might, and swung it hard into his face. I hit him across the bridge of his nose, stunning him for a nano second. I managed to roll away from him with the stick still in my grasp. I hit him again on the side of his head at the temple. His eyes glazed over, then reopened.

Now, he was mad and ready to kill me. We were even. I was ready and willing to kill him. I hate being touched roughly, or manhandled; it set all of my PTSD into high gear. I think he read it in my eyes, and knew he had to finish me off quickly.

He charged me like a mad bull, knocking me off my feet back onto the ground. I had held onto the stick so I clubbed him again. I was rapidly running out of energy.

My other hand felt a large stone. He was so fixated on the hand with the stick, he didn't see what I had. I hit him as hard as I could muster on the side of his head with the rock.

He was out cold but he was still lying on top of me. I squirmed out from under him and drew my revolver from my shoulder holster. I was ready when he opened his eyes and rolled over. No conversation; I was just going to shoot him dead. He knew he was a goner.

My mind was wild with enough adrenaline to power a California grid. I was just beginning to squeeze the trigger when I heard Curt holler. I never took my eyes of the idiot as Curt ran up beside me. He was carrying a .45 auto. He was ready to use it. From the look on his face, he really wanted to finish my first thought and just pull the trigger.

"Nettie, get your phone and call the law; now. This scum isn't worth either of us being arrested, or convicted for his death. Where is Luce?"

I called the police and received an instant response. They were in the area and headed my way.

"I don't know, but if this asshole harmed him, I'm going to do the same thing to him. Where is he?"

"I tied him to a tree; he ain't dead."

I knew he lied because Luce would have eaten him. He'd harmed the dog. I needed to go find him.

Curt grabbed the scumbag by the front of his shirt and stood him up with the gun pointed at his head. "Start walking and find the dog. If you so much as breathe, I *will* finish you with no regrets. This piece has a hair trigger with hollow point ammo, and I'm a very nervous man. Do you understand?"

The jerk grunted, but he began to lead the way into the woods. Curt had a death-grip on the back of his neck. We walked about thirty feet into the woods on the trail when I spotted Luce lying on the ground.

The jerk had thrown a large camo-net over the dog, and then hit him on the head with something. I pulled the net free. Luce was just beginning to come around. I spoke to him, and his tail made a feeble wag. He rolled onto his stomach and tried to get up. He was still too groggy to make it. I told him to stay, hoping he would get his bearings.

Just then, the jerk decided to try to break free and make a run for it; big stupid mistake!

The minute he moved, Luce came off the ground like a tiger, and lunged for his throat. I screamed. Curt let go of the jerk. Luce had him pinned to the ground with his whole body on top of him.

For the first time I could ever remember, I didn't know what to do. Should I call the dog off? Would he even come? The hair on Luce's back was standing up like a wire brush, and he was growling so loudly he scared me.

I didn't want Luce to get into trouble. I had to try to coax him off. To make matters worse, the jerk was screaming like a girl. He not only peed himself; he'd lost all control of his bowels.

Somehow, Luce knew he had won. He turned his big head toward me with a look of *see what happens when someone messes with us*.

"Luce, good boy, now come." To my surprise, he stood and walked over to me and sat in front of my feet.

We heard the sirens of the cruiser coming. "Curt, you keep him; I'll go unlock the gate. Where is your truck?"

"I left it in front of the gate; the keys are in it. I'll guard stupid, and pray he tries to get away again."

I hurried to the gate through the woods while calling to the officers letting them know I was coming. I didn't want them to break down my gate. I reached the drive, unlocked the gate, and opened it. One of the men in the cruiser moved Curt's truck inside the fence.

"Are you okay? You look like hell, are you hurt? Should I call an ambulance? Where is the offender?"

"I'm fine, just roughed up. Your prisoner is in the woods, and you'll need a garbage bag to sit him on. It seems he had an accident in his undies. Something scared him."

I led them to the site. To say they were yucked-out by what they needed to transport in their car would have been a total understatement.

I quickly explained what had transpired, and told them I would press charges, not just for me, but also for the abuse to Luce.

The officers cuffed their prisoner and headed to the river. They told him they were going to strip search him while they read him his rights.

Curt and I stood back, away from the river, but we could see the show. They made him undress completely, even down to his boots and socks. Smart move on their part, because he had two knives stashed in his boots. Then they pushed him into the cold river water to clean him up. He yelled and screamed all to no avail. When they let him come out of the water, they gave him his shirt and jacket. He was still cussing.

Thirty-six

I was done with the whole mess. I turned and thanked Curt for his assistance and began to wobble toward the house. For some reason or other, it appeared to me the house was moving away from me. I knew I had to get inside quickly. I was going to be sick to my stomach. I was also suddenly freezing. Never a good thing for me, because stress does this, then I become hypothermic and lapse into shock.

I don't remember walking to the house. When I woke up, it was dusk. I was lying on the sofa wrapped in blankets with a hot fire burning in the Franklin stove.

I was trying to get my mind to process how I got there and why when Curt spoke. He was sitting in the chair across the room. I hadn't seen him. "How do you feel? Are you okay or should I take you to the hospital?"

I turned my head so I could see him better. "I'm fine, thank you. I hope you didn't waste your whole day sitting there watching me snooze."

Curt moved the large leather hassock over so he could sit in front of me. "I watched him leaving the village this morning, so as a precaution I followed him. He must have spotted me because he made a couple of stops and turns. I had a hunch, after hearing he bragged around town he had a score to settle, I knew just where he was going… to find you. When I swung by your gate, I saw his truck tucked in on the woods road across the way. When Luce didn't come, I knew something was wrong."

I tried to sit up without any success. This was not good. I didn't want to embarrass myself in front of Curt, so I pretended to be repositioning; he wasn't that easily fooled.

"If I make you some tea, could you drink it? Are you hungry?"

"Please don't fuss over me. You wasted your day here. I need to get up and go take care of my tools I left outdoors. In a few minutes, I'll be fine. I appreciate your concern along with your assistance. Had you not arrived when you did, I would have killed him then and there. How dare he come here and think he could just pound on me, and I wouldn't retaliate? He must be dumber than he looks, if possible."

Curt stood. I was glad he was going to leave so I could assess my condition and see if I could, in fact, get up and navigate.

He walked slowly to the door, then looked back and told me to stay put… he would tend to the tools and lock the barn. He assured me he would be right back, whether I liked it or not.

While he was absent, I made a stab at getting up. I could sit up. I just couldn't manage to stand. I would wait for a few minutes then try again. I knew what was wrong. The massive surge of adrenalin knocked my brain out of kilter. It had happened before. I just needed to get calmed down. I'd be okay. At least I hoped I could, or I would be in deep trouble.

When Curt returned, he noted my efforts with a nod then busied himself in the kitchen. What, I wondered, was he doing in there?

He walked into the room carrying a bowl of soup he'd found in the fridge and warmed up. "Can you hold this on your lap or do you need me to bring a small table over? I want you to eat this and drink the tea."

"Where's yours? I'm certain you're hungry; it's been a long day. There was plenty for both of us."

He smiled, and then walked into the kitchen, returning with a bowl for himself. He sat the bowl on the hearth and stoked the stove, adding more wood to the fire. He retrieved his bowl and came to sit beside me on the sofa.

My cell phone was still in my shirt pocket where I carry it when I'm working outside. When it rang, I almost tossed my soup into the air. My nerves were raw. I needed to get a grip and quickly. The call was from the police detective wanting to know if I was doing all right. He also wanted to inform me the idiot would not be getting a bail hearing, so he would not be pestering me anytime soon. It was good news, but I knew how the system worked… he would get out again, and would return to prove a point, whatever it was.

Curt listened to the conversation, but he also saw my look of resignation and knew I was upset. So much so, I couldn't hide it. "What did he say to disturb you so much?"

I pondered what I was going to tell him. I was also at a place I needed to stop kidding myself. This revelation was painful. I couldn't do it anymore. I had to be honest with myself. It hurt to stare truth in the eye. I'd always prided myself on being able to do, withstand, recover, etcetera from anything. For the first time in my life, I knew I really couldn't, and I was discouraged. I hated liars. My dad had always told me, 'you can watch a thief, but not a liar.' When folks lie to themselves, it becomes a no-win situation, especially if they believe it is true. It was time to stop kidding myself.

"Curt, would you please get me a drink of the brandy from the cupboard under the sink? Help yourself if you want."

Praise God he never said a word, picked up our soup bowls and walked into the kitchen. He returned with the bottle and two small glasses. He placed everything on the hassock then poured us both a shot, handing me my glass. I'm not a drinker other than a glass of wine in the afternoon when my day is done. I knew wine would not help, not this time.

I took a sip, bracing for the burn. I seldom ever drank hard liquor.

Curt slid the big leather chair closer to the sofa and sat quietly watching me. I liked his demeanor. He didn't look challenging or bored, just companionable. He gave the impression he could sit and wait for at least one hundred years, if necessary.

"When I came here, I was running from what I thought was a world gone mad because people no longer had any restraints or a moral compass guiding them. I thought this would be rural, quiet, and peaceful. I was so wrong.

"I liked the property, understood the bank was in a bind, and looking for a quick sale. I knew it was a good buy. When my house sold the day I listed it, and closed in five days for cash, I was elated. I didn't have a clue I had a problem here until I was moving my belongings into the barn.

"I met Pete that day and heard his sad tale of woe. I've always looked out and fought for the underdog. I'd been around long enough to know things can go crazy with government programs. I was also certain, because I'm logical and have worked with different government programs, I could assist him to get it straightened out quickly.

"Then I met the *crazy woman*. On the second meeting with her, we had a physical altercation, which shocked even me. I didn't have any idea I was so angry inside. I should've quit then and walked away. I couldn't and didn't. The problem was, at that point, I didn't own the property, regardless of what the deed said. I was, in fact, homeless unless I could straighten out the chain of title. I shudder when I think about the angst the next person who searches the property's chain of title will go through to get a viable title.

"When I left for Virginia, I didn't have any clearer idea of how to resolve the mess. There was no choice but to go take care of my sister's dilemma, so I went with my old camper. Sometimes, when I'm trying to puzzle things out, a road trip helps. I call it a geographical cure.

"On the way home, as I told you before, I had an accident with a tractor trailer which could have been fatal. I sustained some injuries; however, the camper was a total loss… thankfully, Miss Joy was not hurt.

"As a result of the accident, I met the owner of the trucking company involved. His younger son was the driver. Thank God, he recovered with only minor injuries. He was high on drugs with a substantial habit unknown to his father.

"Dom, his father, was very generous to me with an immediate settlement, after care, camper replacement, and then his connections the Feds were beyond compare.

"I was so worried about Pete and this nut-job woman I was a mental wreck. In the end, I told Wade, the man who was taking care of my sorry self, on the first night in his care. He called Dom and explained as much of the situation as he knew. Dom was good friends and college buddies with Adam, the person you know at the FBI who could help.

"Before I was even able to travel again, the crazy woman showed up in Pennsylvania and began raising hell with me. She was a spook, and it seemed no one could catch her. Long story short, her and I had another physical conflict while I was still wearing a cast. I got the short end of the scrap with another broken arm and a head injury.

"It took a small army and more casualties to end her reign of terror before she died. Not, however, before the agency found she had terrorized others in the resettled whistle blowers program. There were fatalities related to her shakedowns that came to light from the investigations. There was another agent involved as well. This became evident because of my involvement and immediate distrust of him. Even though she'd left the agency, this man fed her information so she could continue to track those folks. That was how she kept finding Pete.

"With the help of Dom and the agency, we managed to clear the title for the property which legally Pete still owned. He then deeded it to me.

"I came home still recovering from the injuries of the accident and the subsequent battering with a shit-load more PTSD to try and put myself back together.

"I thought I was doing great until the day I drove to Bangor to get my computer fixed. When I left the computer store and stopped in the parking lot out back to relieve Miss Joy, my truck got blown to smithereens. I had walked a short distance away from the vehicle to take care of her needs. The explosion knocked me to the ground. I wasn't injured, but I was pissed. Certain of the source, I immediately called the only person who I was still costing money and unloaded on Dom.

"I was dead wrong with my reasoning. Dom arrived in Bangor as fast as his company plane could deliver him, along with Fred, his main security man, in tow. In the past, Wade had told me to avoid Dom when he was angry at any cost. I found out why in a hell of a hurry. He was great to me while achieving quick results with the person who did the bombing.

"We spent another couple of weeks routing out the culprit who had a real vendetta against me without ever knowing any of the facts.

"I was just beginning to settle in here and feel like it could become home when the village idiots decided to come calling. It was strange, because before I bought the property, you couldn't pay anyone enough money to come out here.

"Somehow they knew Pete wasn't here anymore. He had returned with Dom to take a position in his company and loved it.

"I have a target painted on my back or something. All I wanted was peace and quiet. I'm not certain in this new world if that's even possible. I know I can't go another round. I think, after all is said and done, I'll need to concede.

"My problem is I don't know what to do now. I've never quit anything in my life. I have no basis on how to proceed.

"You know as well as I do, they'll let the jerk out of custody with some bleeding-heart theory, and he'll be back for another round. Most certainly, he'll bring his posse with him the next time. I won't do another round. I should have just shot him and been done with it.

"I don't want to live the rest of my time on hyper-alert status, carrying a gun and being angry. It was never the intent for my *'golden years'*."

Curt sat quietly throughout my lengthy diatribe. Then he spoke calmly. "I'm surprised you're still sane and physically able to do what you can. If the last few months have been like this, I would hate to ask what the preceding years were like. This is not the first rough patch you've weathered, or you wouldn't have retained the strength and courage to make it this far. Would you like me to pour you another sip of brandy?"

I laughed. "Nope, as you can see, I don't hold my booze very well and am a talkative drinker. Besides, I still have all but the first sip in my glass."

It was his turn to chuckle.

We visited for a short while, and Curt left to go home. I knew he was reluctant to go. I was not going to set a new precedent about anyone staying. I mostly enjoyed my single life and didn't want to complicate it because of a scuffle with anyone.

I was thinking that thought as I drifted off to sleep. My nightmares during the night were horrible until they finally woke me as daylight was dawning. It was a shock to find I'd fallen asleep, still on the sofa fully clothed, and without even brushing my teeth. I was beyond disgusted with myself.

Thirty-seven

I put a pot of coffee on to brew while I showered and dressed. Once I got the dogs fed and cared for, I turned my attention to the coffee while trying to assimilate a new game plan for my life. I knew it was time to make a change. I wasn't quite sure where to start.

I needed to finish getting the wood gathered and stored in the woodshed on the side of the barn, and in the small shelter at the end of the screened porch.

I was working on my second cup of coffee when my cell phone rang. It was Pete calling. I was surprised because he seldom called during the day, and never this early in the morning. "Hello stranger, how are you doing? Is everything okay?"

"I just wanted to call and see how you were doing. I knew you were thinking about cutting wood for the winter, and it occurred to me I'd neglected to tell you something. I have plenty of wood all cut and split for this winter. It's out in the woods stacked between trees with brush up against it. If you're walking along, it looks like a brush pile. Move the brush away from the pile, and you'll find about a cord under each pile. I did it so nobody would know I was cutting it to use. Take the tractor out there with the bucket, and bring it back to the shed. It'll keep you warm for more than all winter."

"Are you a mind reader or something? I started to harvest wood, but now I need to stack what I've cut, and use your wood because it's seasoned and ready to burn. Do you still like your job? Have you found a place to live? "

"Nettie, I love the work I'm doing, and Dom is great to work with. We have made some great changes that have helped his business here and other venues he has. I have even done some work for Wade at his motel and restaurant. He's a great guy, and an even better chef. He wanted me to be say 'hello' to you. He wants you and Miss Joy to come back for a visit. He told me since you left, he's bored. I have to run, or I'll be late getting to the office. I'll call later in the week. Is Luce behaving himself?"

"Luce is doing fine; he keeps me in line. I'll talk to you soon, and thanks for the tip about the wood. Bye for now, stay well."

Problem number one solved, thanks to Pete. I would get dressed, round up the dogs, and go find the hidden treasure. After I got the wood moved, I would work on the rest of my 'new life' plan.

We all piled into the four-wheeler to go exploring. I hadn't spent a lot of time out in that particular section of woods because I assumed it was where Pete's tree house was. As I was picking my way along what appeared to be a path of sorts, I noticed a large brush pile. If I'd spotted it earlier, I would have been planning on getting Nick to bury the brush so it wouldn't be a fire hazard. I pulled the stacked branches away from the front of the pile and saw the neatly stacked wood. There was at least one cord all split and sized for my stoves. We hauled wood until I had it neatly placed in the woodshed.

I stopped to get lunch when the gate alarm sounded. It was Curt, so we drove down to let him in. He told me he was delivering fresh Italian sandwiches so he stopped to see if he could sell me one. I laughed at his silliness.

We ate the sandwiches in silence. What a treat!

He seemed relieved I wasn't either still on the couch, or perhaps under it sucking my thumb.

I was glad he came because I wanted to bounce some ideas off him. When you are going to change something, or yourself, it is always good to have second opinions. I was contemplating bringing in power to the property. I knew how I wanted it done, but was unsure if my idea was practical, given the distance I would need to go with the line work.

We discussed the idea then walked out through the woods to where I would need to pick it up at the road. I wanted to buy the line and run everything underground without making a big swath through the existing wooded area. I really didn't want outsiders knowing I had power back here. I knew I couldn't do solar because I would have to place the panels out in the open field, and they would be an eyesore to me.

In the end, we decided to call an expert…Nick. When he arrived, we showed him the direction we'd discussed. He agreed with us and added his expertise. It would be expensive to bring in power the way I wanted to, but in the end, it wasn't too much more than stringing poles all the way in and much more reliable as far as storm damages. Nick told me he could run it with minimal change to the woods because he would dig it with a ditch-witch. He would install the conduit with line for cable, phone, and electric, which would take care of high-speed internet. While he was there, Nick would also pull stumps and bury the brush.

Thirty-eight

I thanked the guys and sent them off. I needed to go to the lumberyard. I had a project in mind that I wanted to start at once. When Pete built the cabin, although it had log siding on the exterior over plywood on the interior, he had sheet rocked the walls. His taping was very professional. He had done a great job of making the walls smooth. He then painted them in a mid-range color, making it too dark for my liking. I was going to repaint the interior and brighten it up, making it homier. I would then hang some of my art when I finished. I was always better mentally if my hands were busy.

I wanted to see if I could get Luce to ride in the truck with Miss Joy and me. I was certain if anybody saw us, everyone would think I was certifiable. I would be driving an elegant Lincoln truck with leather seats with a moose of a dog riding on the back seat. At least I hoped I would be able to convince him to ride back there.

I dug out some nice clean old quilts and went out to prepare the truck for my planned dog excursion. Both dogs came out and watched my efforts to cover the nice seats. I didn't have to be concerned about Miss Joy; she weighed so little her claws wouldn't harm the leather. However, Luce was a big heavy dog, and I had never tried to clip his nails, and I knew he could puncture the seats.

Once the covering was in place, I grabbed my purse, called the dogs, told them to load, and then watched to see just what would happen. Miss Joy, as always, sat and lifted her front foot for me to lift her onto the seat. Then she would get onto the console to ride. I should have named her GPS because she thought she knew more than I did about where and how we should travel. I lifted her onto the front passenger seat. I had the back door open for Luce. He sat on the ground, looked at me, lifted his front paw the same as Miss Joy, and I burst into laughter. He looked confused. I patted the back seat and told him to come. He stood, looked at me then Miss Joy, and climbed carefully onto the front passenger seat filling it to the max with his head so close to the ceiling he had to duck to see out of the windshield or the side window. I closed the doors, walked around to the driver's side, and stepped in. I couldn't see past Luce to look out of the side window and see in the mirror. I thought for a minute, then got out walked around, opened his door and put his seat back with the electric seat controls. Now I could see at least some of what I needed.

I drove to town with my buddies without any problems and on to the lumber store. When I parked in front of the showroom window, I saw Brad Cory do a double take when he saw Luce sitting in the front seat. I dropped the window so he would have air and could stick his head out if he wanted to. I wasn't sure what he would do when I got out, and Miss Joy began barking as she always does when I leave the vehicle. I told her to be quiet, knowing it wouldn't make any difference. She had barked whenever I left since she was a puppy, and I could never break her of the bad habit. I stepped out of the truck… no need to lock the doors with Luce in there. He would stop most folks by just being there. I walked away from the truck and, for the first time ever, she didn't make a sound. *Praise the Lord, a solution at last!*

Brad came over with a big grin on his face, and I knew he wanted to rib me, but wasn't too sure if he should. I thought I would put him out of his misery. "Hi Brad, I had to take the kids for a drive so I thought this would be productive. I need some paint and supplies. Do you want me to give you a list and come back for them or do you want me to help you put the order together?"

"Nettie, it is good to see you looking so well. Are you enjoying the property? I see you have an addition to your family." Brad delivered the last statement with a great deal of humor in his eyes.

"Oh, you mean Luce? He lives with me; he's been a great comfort. It saved me buying a horse, and he eats less. He also saves me time and effort… I never have to lock the truck."

Once we had the supplies loaded, I stopped by the bank to check on some business I needed to do with Jeff Smart. As he walked me out to the truck, he nearly fainted when Luce stuck his big head out of the window as Jeff walked by. I would have loved to have a photo of his expression. I said my goodbyes, and we arrived home just as Nick and Curt arrived with a bunch of equipment.

Thirty-nine

I began my claiming of the house. Miss Joy understood the process, having witnessed it many times before. Luce was not too sure, so he sat at the tree line, and watched the men work, glancing over his shoulder from time to time, checking on the house.

Later in the afternoon, when Nick and Curt were finished for the day, Nick took the time to invite me to come to the small church in the village. He explained that there was a local group of folks with a great young minister, who was developing a productive youth program. He and Curt both belonged. I had been thinking about checking it out. I have always belonged to a church and missed it during all the upheaval since coming here to live. It was time to get back to having a normal life.

Luce came to the kitchen door and began to bang his paw against it. He had never done that before. I was concerned about what was wrong. When I opened the door, he took my hand in his mouth almost pulling me through the doorway. What was wrong with him? He walked quickly down almost to the riverbank then along to the tree line, stopped and sat in front of my feet looking out toward the water. I scanned the area, but saw nothing out of the ordinary. Luce cocked his head to one side and lifted his ear on that side as if he were listening intently for something to happen. I heard nothing. I trusted his instincts so I stood waiting and watching.

I heard the first sound coming from way off in the distance. The sky darkened with Canadian geese flying in formations, circling over the river with thunderous noise between their honking and the wing sounds. They just kept coming, filling the river. I was in awe at the sight. Luce looked up at me as if to say, 'what do you think of that?' I patted his big head and gave him an ear scratch for his efforts.

Once I began working on the interior of the house Luce changed. I began to notice it when we would walk down to the river or go check on Nick's progress. Luce was reverting to puppy-like behavior. He would run ahead, turn, dash back, and jump in the air. He had always been stoic, resembling an old man. I didn't know what to make of his antics.

Any time I would be going to the store, he wanted to go, so I took him. When we got our first snowstorm of the year with enough snow to require me to get the snow blower out, I was amazed when he decided he had to ride on the tractor with me. There wasn't enough room on the seat for both of us so I didn't know where I was going to put him. He took matters onto himself and climbed on the fender then sat behind me on the skirt over the fuel tank. What a clown. I didn't know if he had done this with Pete in the past or not. I also didn't know if he would sit there while I ran the equipment.

I made a pass down the drive to the gate, opened it, and blew out to the road. After I got the end of the drive cleared, I started back up for a couple more passes.

I was on my last run from the road to the house when Curt arrived with a plow truck. He got out, shook his head, and laughed his way to the side of my tractor. "What a sight. I wish I had a camera. How did you get him to do that?"

"I didn't. He put himself up there and seems to be enjoying his perch. I'm sorry Nick sent you out with the truck. He must have forgotten you mounted my blower and serviced the tractor."

Curt's smile lit up his whole face. "He didn't send me. I came because I wanted to. I wasn't certain if you were up to the task of snow removal on your own right now. I should have known better. It's great to see you're feeling better." As soon as the words left his mouth, he looked embarrassed he'd uttered them.

"Curt, thank you for your concern, I appreciate it. I don't tend to wallow for long and working on the house is always a great energizer for me. Thanks for coming… I owe you dinner for your effort." I waved and began my last pass as a way of allowing him to get back to his work.

We had a mild winter with adequate snow, but no large storms. Each time I went to blow snow, I had my co-pilot.

Forty

The winter sped by and I could see signs of spring beginning. I was excited for kayaking, swimming, fishing and gardening.

I brought the kayak down to the spot on the shore where I kept it handy to the river for quick use. The first time I began to put it into the water, Luce looked puzzled. I realized he wanted to go with Miss Joy and me, but it was only a one-person boat. I thought it over then took the dogs and went to the place where I had stored Pete's big canoe.

I have never canoed much, so I was hesitant to try to paddle all three of us down to the shore. I knew the water close to the shoreline wasn't too deep, and I could get us ashore if I tipped it over. As I waited to think this through, Luce jumped into the canoe. I have no idea how he managed to get in while positioning his body in the area just behind the middle seat. He sat, without even moving the boat. I guess he made up my mind for me. I gently lifted Miss Joy onto the seat in the stern. Oh, what the hell, I needed to step out of my comfort zone. I got in, placed the oarlocks into the holes, and started to row.

Our trip out of the creek and around to my beach went without incident. I needed to figure out how to land the canoe on the beach so we could all get out carefully. I slid the canoe up onto the sand as far as I could. Miss Joy sat quietly as she would have in the kayak and waited. Luce stood, and then hopped out of the boat onto the sand. For a large dog, he was so graceful in his movements he amazed me.

With Luce out of the canoe, I could urge it farther up onto the sand so dismounting was a piece of cake. I took Miss Joy from the seat and placed her on the ground. As I looked at the two dogs, I had to laugh out loud. Luce looked like he had won the lottery, and Miss Joy was sitting in between his front paws. What a sight.

I went online in the evening and found where I could get the floatation devices to attach to the sides of the canoe to make it more stable. I fully understood wherever I went, Luce planned on going too. I ordered a life jacket for Miss Joy just to be on the safe side. They didn't stock lifejackets for horse-sized dogs. I would never take us out far from shore, and I knew Luce was a great swimmer. We often swam together, with him towing me around in the water. Miss Joy would do a short dip to get wet up to her belly, then sit on the bank to dry and watch us play in the water.

Forty-one

Pete came back for a short vacation in the late spring. He brought a very nice lady with him. Luce was glad to see him like an old friend; however, it was plain he had adopted Miss Joy and me as his people.

Pete was pleased at the changes I'd made, including new gardens for both flowers and food. We now had a real lawn area. We enjoyed a cookout in the back yard. I teased Pete about the fact he wanted to stay in his tree house instead of the guest room in the house. His lady opted for the guest room so he was on his own out in the woods. She seemed nice and her intentions were clear... she liked Pete a lot. I was happy for both of them. I wanted nothing, but a good life, for Pete and whomever he wanted in his life.

When Pete got ready to go, I could see he missed Luce, but understood this was where the dog should stay. Luce made it even clearer when they began to walk toward the car. The big lug came and sat on my feet leaning against my legs, almost upending me. He was mine, and I was thrilled. During the visit, I had considered how I would handle it if Pete wanted to take him. Pete assured me he wouldn't disrupt the household for anything.

Except for a short visit, he told me he most likely would not return. He was intent on rebuilding his life and was content with where he was. He also told me I could dismantle his tree house. I grinned. "Then where would I hide?" He laughed and they drove away.

Forty-two

It was the beginning of a great and productive summer. I loved to hike in the foothills and mountains, but now it was too strenuous for Miss Joy at her age. She wanted to go, and I ended up carrying her in my backpack. I was also getting too old to go for any distance with her on my back.

I had an idea that would maybe work if I could do it. I bought some heavy material resembling light canvas. I fashioned a pack for Luce so he could carry Miss Joy on one side with water, treats, and lunch on the other. I wasn't sure how he would like being a mule, but as always, he was happy with the task. He would do anything to have us all together on an adventure. He had great stamina and enjoyed the exercise.

Both the dogs and I enjoyed the river: fishing, paddling, and swimming. Luce surprised me one day when I got my fishing rod out. I wanted some fresh fish for supper. When I started down to the canoe, he took my hand and began to lead me out back behind the house. I thought he'd gone totally bonkers. I knew he understood fishing because we'd gone out a couple of times, but I only caught sunfish.

I remembered Pete brought me some beautiful trout when I first arrived. That was what I wanted to catch. Luce walked on along the trail where I'd gotten the firewood, and then turned off the path into the woods. I knew he had a destination in mind, and I didn't want to leave my fishing gear on the ground to follow him, so I continued to follow and carry it. Luce made a quick turn into an alder thicket I was certain I wouldn't get through. I was a step behind him when I turned the corner… low and behold; there was a clear pathway to walk on. After about ten steps or so, he stopped and looked back at me with a smirky look on his face.

As I came abreast of him, there was a perfect trout-fishing hole in the creek. I could see the fish swimming. I caught two nice big ones and left the others to grow for another time. Luce all but pranced back to the house.

We often had visits from Curt and sometimes he would join us for a hike or a swim. He seemed to be getting restless in an odd way. One day when he stopped to see us, he said he was thinking of opening an office in the Bangor area and going back into counseling. I encouraged him. He was too young not to be productive, and it would be good for him socially as well.

Forty-three

I was longing for the coast. The river was okay, but I am a coastal person, and missed the rocky shore and smells of the ocean. I hadn't used the new camper since I drove it home after the accident and the dustup with the crazy woman. It was time. I had no idea how Luce would adjust to traveling in it, but it was time to find out. I had worked with him about wearing a collar with his dog tag on it.

As a funny aside, when I had stopped at the town office to get the dogs registered, I inquired if I needed to bring them in. I knew Luce was never registered. I didn't know if they needed to see him. The clerk looked out through the window and allowed she had seen enough. I needed to see if he would walk on a leash with me. When I got home, I attached the leash to his collar and began to walk with Miss Joy on her leash on the other side. Luce checked out how she was doing, and then just followed suit. He acted as if we did this every day. I then taught him to carry his own leash in his mouth. After a couple of tries, he understood the process.

I pulled the camper over to the house so I could load things for our trip. Luce didn't like what I was doing, and launched his protest by sitting in front of the steps leading into the coach. He wouldn't move. I tried to bribe him away to no avail. On my next trip into the house, I was carrying my duffel and Miss Joy was with me. She sat with her paw up for me to lift her into the camper. As soon as I sat her onto the floor, Luce leapt over me in one bound and sat next to her. I think he thought I was packing and moving away.

Miss Joy always rides on a small hassock between the driver's and passenger seats so she can see out through the windshield. I had already put the old quilt over the passenger seat for Luce. He understood it was his seat. I didn't know how he would react to other dogs in the campground, or how he would like staying in the camper with us. The ocean would be new to him, too. We would soon see.

I haven't camped with a large dog since my small Rottweiler passed away years ago. Most parks restrict the dog's size to around forty pounds, so Luce would qualify as three dogs. I decided I would go to the wilderness camping area in a Federal park in the eastern area of the state.

When I checked in, I noticed the park had fewer campers than I expected, and I requested a more remote lot. I didn't need any services because I had a generator for power, and the stove and fridge worked off propane.

I parked the rig and began to set up the campsite. First, I set out the large mat on the ground and Luce promptly sat on the corner as if to anchor it. I put the awning out, and then set my chairs and small table up. Wanting to sit for a minute before taking the dogs for a walk, I brought out a drink of soda and the dog' water bowls. They drank and took their treats. Miss Joy had camped with me since she was a puppy; this was not new to her. Luce kept looking at me as if to ask, 'what next, why are we here?'

I got his pack out, loaded Miss Joy and some water. He was ready to work. I put his leash on him and, after I locked the camper, we started for a walk. We followed a footpath down to the shore. The coming tide was about half way in when we arrived. Luce stopped, looked it over, put his nose in the air, and began to sniff. He looked at me to see if we should be there.

I took Joy out of the pack and removed it so if the big goof went swimming, I wouldn't have to dry it out. After placing the pack on a rock, I checked to be certain there wasn't anyone else on that stretch of the shoreline, and I let both dogs free. Miss Joy wanted to run and play on the beach. Luce looked at me to make sure it was okay and joined her. He went to the waterline and watched as the small waves came ashore. He tasted it then shook his head and came back to me. We wandered along the shore then back to get his pack so we could explore the rest of the park.

As we were walking across a big open field, I saw the ranger coming on his four-wheeler. This could be interesting. He came to within twenty feet of me and called, "Is that a dog? Is it friendly?"

He was an older man with a pleasant manner, and I hoped he was dog friendly. Luce was sitting by my foot with Miss Joy in the backpack. He began to dismount from his machine when he lost his balance and nearly fell. Once he righted himself, he grinned and spoke kiddingly, "Rented leg. I neglected to inform it that it was supposed to hold me up." I could see he had a slight disability when walking.

As he came closer to me, Luce stood. I gave him a pat on the top of his massive head, and told him it was all right. He sat back down, but never took his eyes off the ranger. The man was savvy and stopped to chat outside of what I consider my private space.

"How much does he weigh? What breed is he? I've never in all my years seen a dog like that."

"He weighs about one hundred and fifty pounds, I would guess. I never tried to put him on a scale. I'm not sure of his lineage; he came to me as an adult. He's quite funny and wonderful company. I hope you are not going to evict us because of his size."

The ranger chuckled. "Nope, I don't think you'll be annoyed by anybody. I also won't set any campers down in this area. Most folks want to be close to the bathrooms. Is he friendly to kids, other dogs, wildlife, and etcetera?"

"We live in a rural area on a river so he is used to wildlife, and I don't know about kids or other dogs. This is our first camping trip together. He is very gentle, and he travels with me everywhere without issue. I don't expect he'll be any different here than at home. He never leaves my side, nor would he leave the little one. I'll be sure we stay away from the main part of the campground, just to ease your mind."

"I don't want you to do that. I came down to let you know there's a concert here tonight up in the big field by the gazebo, and everyone is welcome to attend. The band is great; I think you might enjoy it. Everyone brings their dogs and kids, and we get locals who come just for the entertainment. It starts at six… bring a chair or a blanket to sit on. It looks like a nice evening for the group. I look forward to seeing *all* of you there."

When dinner was over and the dishes taken care of, I thought perhaps I would take the dogs and walk up to see how they would do with a crowd. I packed Miss Joy into the pack with a blanket and some water and soda, and off we went. My part in this was to stay calm and not let the dogs know I had any concerns. We arrived just as the band was tuning up and getting ready to start. I spread the big beach towel on the grass at the back of the crowd, sat Miss Joy on the pad, and loosened Luce's pack.

As soon as I sat down, he sat right behind me the same as he does on the tractor or in the canoe. I don't block his vision because he can look over my head.

I watched as people came with their children and dogs. Other than some strange glances, nobody bothered us. We enjoyed the concert, then packed up and returned to the camper for the night. It was a great evening.

We wandered the coast for another couple of days on our way home. Even with his size, none of the campgrounds seemed to mind Luce being with me. He had become a 'companion dog to a dog.' How funny was that?

We stopped at Moose Point State Park for lunch and a stroll on some of our old territory. It was refreshing to visit familiar places again and smell the wonderful ocean smells mingled with the scent of fir trees.

I headed back north on the interstate, but wanted to make one more stop on our circuit. I headed for a campground in Newport where I had often stayed. It is small, friendly, and right on the lake. It was fun to visit again with the owners. I explained I had two dogs with me, and one was large. They already knew Miss Joy from our previous stays. The owner cautioned me they'd been having a problem with a marauding stray dog. It attacked two of the camper's dogs in the last couple of days. The wardens or the police couldn't catch it. They were not sure if it was rabid.

Later in the afternoon, I took my dogs out for a long walk up the drive and along the railroad bed. Miss Joy and I had walked it many times so I took her out of Luce's pack and was letting her stroll along beside me. Luce, being an old man, would never do his business where anyone could see; however, as a boy-dog, he would lift his leg on a blade of grass. He had walked off into the wooded area beside the tracks to take care of his needs. I heard the bushes rustle and thinking it was Luce, I wasn't concerned and walked on. The next thing I saw was an animal streaking for Miss Joy. It was a large black German shepherd-type dog with his teeth bared and drool foaming from his mouth. I leaned over to snatch Miss Joy from the ground when Luce head butted the dog at a dead run. He rammed the stray dog so hard he flipped up and over the railroad tracks, landing on the other side with a thump that shook the ground. Luce was standing over him with teeth bared, snarling, and every hair on his back standing straight up.

I was horrified. If they began to fight, I knew I couldn't separate them. I had my phone, so I called the campground for help. The dogs had not moved, and the growling had not lessened from Luce. I could hear the campground owner's mule coming. He arrived in a cloud of dust. He looked at the two dogs, and admitted he didn't know what to do. He did have rope in the mule. Perhaps we could tie the stray to hold him until the police came. The owner had called them as soon as I contacted him.

I was never the bravest person around ugly dogs, but I didn't want it to get away or bite Luce. I took the rope, made a noose, and walked slowly toward the dogs. I knew Luce could see me by the tilt of his head. The other dog was not snarling any longer and almost looked like it had surrendered…I didn't trust him. I got closer and threw the loop over his nose and down onto his neck. I prayed that if he jumped up, I could hold him. I knew Luce wouldn't allow him to bite me. Once the rope was in place, Luce changed his growl for more of a savage bark, and then he backed up a step. I don't begin to understand dog-talk, but the stray must have because he cautiously rolled over onto his stomach. Luce stood guard. I held the rope and waited for the police. I could hear the siren coming.

Talk about a comedy of errors! When the officer finally arrived on the scene with his gun drawn, he thought Luce was the stray, and the reason I had a rope on the other dog was because he was mine. I straightened him out in short order by handing him the rope and calling Luce to me. The officer looked more afraid of Luce than the stray. His problem not mine. I was going back to the camper to reward my protector with treats and myself with a glass of wine.

Later in the evening, while we were sitting outside watching the sunset, the campground owner came down and chatted about the whole mess. He was grateful to be free of the problem with the stray. He invited us to stay as long as we wanted, *gratis*. I thanked him and told him we would come back; however, we needed to be going home in the morning.

Forty-four

Our summer was peaceful and enjoyable. Our lives had settled into a pattern of contentment, finally.

Pete was getting married in the fall. He wanted us to attend and visit with Wade.

Curt opened his office in Bangor and dealt mostly with children, enjoying every minute. On weekends, he sometimes called in to visit. I prayed he would find a lady to complete his life. He was a good man.

On one of his weekend visits, he shared an idea with me. He wanted to start a club of sorts for children with no, or marginal father figures in their lives. He wanted to make it partly an outdoor camp and partly a study group of sorts. Most of the children he was seeing in his practice lacked any sort of male or sometime any, parental guidance. Because of my years of working with foster care programs, I understood.

While we were discussing this, I had an idea. Why couldn't we use my property for outings? We already had the beach, and we could turn the large field into a site for tenting. We could build a fire-pit, and temporarily use porta-potties. We could rig an outdoor shower. We both liked the idea.

I began in earnest to enlist the locals for donations of kayaks, life jackets, a float for diving and the fire-pit.

Within a two-week period, I had the float donated and installed by Brad Cory, the fire-pit from Nick was completed, Jeff Small donated two kayaks, paddles, and jackets and our church would assist with volunteers to help with the children. Our local store would provide food and drinks along with delivery. I loved it when a plan came together!

As I watched this all come to fruition, I was happy and content. We would make use of this property for a good cause. At first, the kids would come in small groups for a weekend.

At the end of the first three weeks, Curt and I began to see how we could make this a summer-long venture for children.

When I spoke with Pete, I told him what we were doing and plans for the next stage. He wanted us to use his tree house in the program, and said he would be sending some funds for more supplies. He told Dom about our plan. Dom called to tell me he was going to contribute to the project. Did he ever! He sent a check for twenty thousand dollars.

All in all, things seem to be working well for everyone, including me. It was time to pour a glass of wine and sit down on the beach to watch the sunset with my dogs before campers arrived the next day. God had been good to all of us.

Curt's camp adventure was a great success. When he came with the next group of campers, he had an assistant with him. The new group of children consisted of girls and boys between the ages of twelve and sixteen. Curt's assistant was June, a pretty lady with the nice fresh appearance of an outdoors person. She was soft spoken, but with authority, in a pleasant manner. The kids respected her and Curt. Later in the evening, when we were all sitting around the campfire, I noticed that perhaps she and Curt were developing a relationship. I liked her and approved of their choices.

As the summer was passing, we had a camp almost every weekend. In August, Curt and June told me they were thinking about getting married. I was thrilled for both of them.

With the days of summer flying by, I became more and more restless. I missed the ocean and the coast. After returning from our camping trip in the late spring, I knew I wanted to be back at the coast. The river was good, but the restlessness of the ocean's tides fit my personality better. I always felt at home on the shore by the ocean. I began to check out real estate listings on the computer.

Forty-five

Before I could alter anything, I had unfinished business here to take care of. I called an attorney for some solid advice before initiating the changes.

My next call was to Dom because I wanted to discuss some business with him. His first question was always the same. "What do you need and how can I help?" This time I wanted to change something with him. I hoped he'd understand my reasoning. I asked if he could make a trip to Maine so we could talk face to face, and requested he bring Wade if possible.

He arrived the next morning in true 'Dom' fashion. He always looked like he was ready to save the world. Truth be known; he probably could, and would, if given a chance. We all sat on the screened porch with coffee and pastries Wade brought along for me.

I was aware I needed to be very careful in my approach with Dom, because I knew he would never agree with me.

"Dom, the reason I requested you to bring Wade, other than the fact I wanted to see him again, was the fact he was in on our original conversation after the accident." I watched carefully as the coffee cups stopped in midair at the mention of the accident. I could almost read their thinking. They were so wrong. I would let them have their moment of thinking I wanted something more before I continued.

"First, I want you to know I've appreciated all the support you gave me both morally and financially. However, I want to change some things." I could tell they were both waiting for the other shoe to drop.

I didn't want to drag out the conversation so I came directly to my point. "I want you to stop sending me the monthly funds. I've been extremely prudent with the monies you provided, and can live comfortably without draining you on an ongoing basis.

"I'm going to give this property to Curt and June for their camp program. I hope in time they'll come here to live and perhaps bring foster children here to live with them.

"My plan is to purchase a place on the coast somewhere, and go there with my dogs to live on or near the shore.

"I've already discussed the possibility of Pete's interest in returning here, and he assures me he has none. He's settled and very happy where he is. Thanks again to you."

Dom sat stoically, not even blinking. Wade looked like he didn't know if he should stay, hide, or go. I sipped my coffee and waited for a response.

When Dom spoke, he was very hesitant, which I believed was a first for him. "Nettie, I've listened very carefully while you were speaking; now I want you to listen to me. I *do not* intend to honor your request. I think it's wonderful you are thinking of going to another area of this state that's perhaps a better fit for you, without any bad memories.

"What you decide to do with the monies I send you will be your business, but I'll continue to send them. I made a deal with you after the accident, and I won't change it. With your varied interests, you'll do more good with the money than anything I could ever imagine. You somehow have the ability to see causes and support them.

"I hope in the future, you'll continue to include me in those actions. I'm not very philanthropic; I see day-to-day problems. You have the ability to see the long-term benefits. I think it's your gift, and I want to support it.

"When are you planning on making a move?"

"I'll be leaving soon. I want to be in and settled before fall. I haven't found where I want to go yet, but I'm not concerned.

"I really would be more comfortable if you would consider what I requested of you. I can live very comfortably with monies I have in savings, thanks to you, and I'm certain you could do without the drain on your finances. I want this to be comfortable for both of us. Please consider my request."

Dom sat quietly without speaking for several minutes, and then a slight smile crossed his lips extending up into his eyes. I'd witnessed this expression with him before. He always looked like this when he felt he'd won. What was going on in his mind I had not a clue. When he reached into his pocket and produced a small cigar, I knew I was correct. He only smoked when he was very angry or when he was very happy. Wade and I waited.

"Nettie, I'll make a deal with you. I'll consider reducing the monthly amount of the settlement, but I want to pay for the new property you purchase. The property has to meet certain requirements. It must be on the water, a year-around residence configured so you can live there for as long as you desire, and it must have an in-law suite either attached or detached. The property has got have a three-car attached garage. There also must be an easy access to the shore."

I was gaping at his request. On the shore in Maine, even in remote areas he was talking a million-dollar property. I was thinking of a small cottage-like home with perhaps a two-car garage in the five-hundred-thousand-dollar range. I would never comply with his standards. First, it would be too much house for me to maintain or pay the taxes on.

As always, Dom figured he had won the battle, hands down. He was wrong this time. I would need to refigure how I could get him to do what I wanted.

Once he thought he'd settled the deal, he was ready to fly off and wait for me to show him what I wanted. I smirked. I already knew what I would do. It wouldn't be what he thought, but I would let him think he'd won for now.

Forty-six

When Curt and June arrived on Friday to set up for the weekend camp, I called a meeting and presented them with the paperwork I had the lawyer prepare. I was pleased they were both sitting down when it happened, or I would've had two folks on the floor. They looked at me then at each other and back to me. I had deeded the property to them jointly because they were married. I'd added a check for them to use for the continuation and growth of the camp project.

My work here was completed. I would take the camper, my dogs, the truck and some personal things, and we would go off to seek a new adventure on the coast.

I've believed for all of my life, you need to leave any situation better than when you found it, or in this case, it found me. I knew when I drove out of the yard, the view I would see in my mirror would be satisfying.

Forty-seven

I was excited and anxious to begin our new quest.

I knew what I wanted, and where I wanted it to be located. I could see it in my mind. I wanted a small home nestled on either the shoreline, or the rocks overlooking the ocean. I wanted it to be shingled, preferably soft gray with white trim, Cape Cod blue shutters, and a bright yellow door. I wanted a two-car garage, and I needed garden space for flowers. I would like it to be on a nice long driveway that wound through fir trees and perhaps with some wild low bush blueberries growing close by. Nice to know what you wanted; the next thing was to find it. I love a good challenge.

I'd also decided when I found what I wanted, I would simply purchase it without a discussion with Dom. I didn't want anything extravagant. I felt a little like a naughty child. It made me very happy!

I had watched the real estate listings on the computer, but nothing had attracted my attention. We parked the camper in a nice quiet campground on the coast where I often stayed before moving to the cabin. They enjoy the best sunsets I'd ever seen. I removed the truck from the tow bar and we began to check out the areas for my dream.

On the second day of my excursion, I spotted a for sale sign on a road that ran alongside a rocky shoreline. I drove down the driveway and there it was… my dream cottage.

It was medium sized with a nice porch overlooking a small lawn with a few raised beds for gardening. It had a nice two-car garage with storage overhead. It had weathered gray cedar shingles, no shutters, white trim, and cranberry colored doors. I liked the cranberry doors, and I would add either white or black shutters.

The cottage was empty, so I did my usual window peeking. The interior looked homey. There was a stove in the living room that was either wood or gas fired. I noticed there were all brand, new windows with full screens.

I wanted to see more. I called the number on the sign. An elderly voice answered. I introduced myself and explained why I called, and inquired how I could see the property. The person who answered the phone asked if I could stay on the line while he tried to call someone in my area to do a showing.

I was taking advantage of the view and a chance to wander around the edge of the lawn. When he returned to our conversation, and informed me a person would come to meet with me in fifteen minutes or so, if I wanted to wait. I thanked him, ended the call, and continued my stroll to see if I could get down onto the beach easily.

I heard a vehicle driving down the driveway. A man of about fifty stepped out and came toward me. He was of medium height with the muscle tone and complexion of an active, outdoor person. His sandy hair was long and secured into a ponytail. His facial expression was pleasant; he had almost-green eyes. He reminded me of a large, tawny, mischievous cat. He had his hand extended for a shake as he introduced himself. "Hi, I'm Jason and your name is…"

"Hello, I'm Nettie Small, and I would like to view the property and know of any history you might give me. Thank you for coming on such short notice."

Jason explained he was the grandson of the owner. The elderly grandfather lived out of state, and Jason lived on the adjacent property.

He explained his grandparents owned the cottage for many years and always summered there. He wanted me to understand it was his gram's pet project. About ten years previously, they decided to winterize the cottage so they could stay later into autumn and come earlier in the spring. They found they enjoyed being on the coast longer, only returning to their permanent home for about three months of the year. His grandmother passed away this last winter, and his grandfather said he would no longer use the property. He wanted to sell it.

We walked to the door I assumed would lead into the kitchen area. He unlocked the door and ushered me into the room; a small space with coat hooks on the wall and a boot mat under them. We walked to another door and entered a small, but well-appointed kitchen. It was neat and clean. The appliances appeared to be brand new. There was an abundance of white, glass-fronted cupboards along with open shelving. The counter top was a dark, gray slate or soapstone.

We continued into the main room. This space served as a dining and living room combined. There were windows on three sides of the room with views of the water. The windows on the back wall looked out on a small lawn.

Jason told me the stove was gas fired.

The floors were wood with large braided rugs covering them. All of the furniture was in good condition and appropriate for this type of property.

He directed me to the large bedroom with an attached bath. The bath was complete, with a large walk-in shower and a stacked washer and dryer set. Again, the bedrooms windows afforded a great view of the water.

He showed me the stairway to the second floor. There was a small powder room tucked in under the staircase.

On the second story, there were two large bedrooms and a full bath. The rooms were nicely furnished and cozy in the cottage style I enjoyed.

We went outside and checked the exterior of the building. It was weathered, but in good condition.

He unlocked the entrance to the basement and we made our way down the stairs. The owners had installed a hot air furnace, and there was an electric water heater. He told me that, although they stayed later and came earlier they had commissioned the plumber to put in a manifold system for the water, making the cottage easily winterized, without any fuss.

The basement was dry with no musty smell and showed no apparent signs of leaking or standing water.

We went on to inspect the garage. I was impressed with the construction of the building; it was more than adequate for my needs.

We returned to the interior and stood in the kitchen where we discussed price and terms, and if the sale included the furnishings. I was interested. The price was right; the property was perfect for my needs. It would not require any immediate renovations in order to live there.

As I was expressing my interest to him, he grinned and looked like a twelve-year-old. He smiled at me and explained he lived next door. The lot this cottage sat on had been one of four lots when his grandparents had purchased it years ago. They retained three of the lots, building in the middle with a full lot on either side. They gave Jason, their only grandchild, a lot for him to build on.

I soon found out the reason for his grin… he told me he was a musician, a sailor, and an artist who loved his solitude. He kind of hung his head and told me often times in the afternoons, he would sit on his porch and play either his flute or his trumpet. He didn't want his 'racket,' as he called it, to be a shock to me.

When I asked him about how easy it was to access the shore, he was quick to lead the way. Once outside, he showed me the stairs that led down to the water. There was a small shed down there at the tree line where I could store my kayak or whatever I had for a boat. The beach was a combination of sand and small pebbles washed smooth by the tides.

He'd noticed my dogs in the truck when he arrived. Jason told me that, although he was noisy, he didn't have pets. He was often away when he would have gigs where he played for an extended period, or he would go sailing for a couple of weeks at a time.

I loved the property and hoped we could come to an agreement, so I could purchase it.

I asked Jason how long the property had been on the market and how anxious his granddad was to sell.

His demeanor changed abruptly. He stood looking at me and shook his head slightly before replying. "My grandpa wants it sold. He decided last year to market the property, and we engaged a local realtor to sell it. Several people came to look at it, but then wanted to break the property up and sell the lots on either side to someone else. Neither my gramp nor I wanted that, so we took the listing away from the broker. We wanted to keep those lots in place as a buffer."

"I would not want to change anything. I think it was smart planning on his part to protect the integrity of the property. Do you know if he plans to sell it furnished?"

"I do. We'll sell it just as you are seeing it now. It will transfer by Warranty Deed, with a clean title. When did you want to move in? Are you certain my music will not disturb you?"

I chuckled. "One of my fondest memories was standing on the deck of my boat on a beautiful fall day with the colors all around, and the sun warm on my back while I listened to the most beautiful trumpet solo played by a man on a sailboat going down the reach. It was many years ago, and the memory is still so pleasant I recall it often."

"Nettie, what do you do for work? You seem to know quite a bit about construction. I hope I haven't offended you by asking."

"No harm, no foul. I'm retired, and I want to have a quiet place where I can write, paint, and play with a boat and my dogs. I love to garden on a small scale. I want to enjoy the rest of my life being able to smell the salt water and hear the waves on the shore."

Jason smiled. "Well if can agree on price and time, I think we have a deal. What do you think? Would you want all of the furnishings?"

"Yes, it is perfect. I would do a cash sale, instantly, if the price was right, and I would move in at once. Now, we are down to the basics. There isn't any broker involved, so that helps the bottom line on price unless you're going to take a cut."

We stood there on the stone ledge overlooking the water and made our deal. He was happy, and so was I.

I would search the title for issues, and he would engage the attorney to draw the deed. We could close in a couple of days. I was delighted.

Forty-eight

Moving day was a fun time. I reflected back to other moves I'd made in my lifetime where it took a flotilla of trucks and equipment trailers to get my stuff hauled from one place to another. The move to the cabin had required a small U-haul truck. The move in was easily accomplished, with just the totes I had in the camper and the back of my truck. I was done in a matter of a couple of hours.

The dogs and I spent the rest of the day exploring the small beach and the rocky shoreline, then sitting on the porch with a glass of wine, special dog treats, and munchies for me. We were sitting watching the day slowly become dusk listening to the sound of the waves softly brush the shore and rocks when I heard an almost magical sound. At first, the music seemed to float on the still air like soft spring rain, and then it increased in crescendo and tempo. I was enjoying the concert when I noticed the first of the stars had begun to fill the evening sky. How wonderful a welcome was that?

For the first time in what felt like forever, my soul, body, and mind felt at peace. I prayed it would last. I'd never discovered how or why I had that restless spirit. It lives inside of me and seemingly wants to push me to move on. It drives me to find new and different things that need fixing or replacing. Perhaps God had finally decided I was finished with what he sent me here to do, and would let me rest there on the coast for the rest of my time.

Other Works From The Pen Of

H. Wakefield

The Boat - The winds of evil are blowing strong while forecasting more disasters. How did a sunken, derelict sailboat washed ashore during a violent storm on my secluded cove in Downeast Maine create so much trouble?

Meet H. Wakefield

H. Wakefield resides in the beautiful state of Maine sharing her home with Miss Joy, a miniature Australian Shepherd. She has loved and enjoyed many dogs and horses throughout her lifetime. Her passion for the outdoors is evident in her many hobbies such as gardening, kayaking, hiking, and RVing. She also enjoys painting, writing, and renovating homes. In short, she enjoys life! Her first published book, *The Boat*, astonished her when folks of all ages and backgrounds expressed their genuine enjoyment of the storytelling.

VISIT OUR WEBSITE
FOR THE FULL INVENTORY
OF QUALITY BOOKS:

www.books-by-wings-epress.com

Quality trade paperbacks and downloads
in multiple formats,
in genres ranging from light romantic comedy to general
fiction and horror. Wings has something
for every reader's taste.
Visit the website, then bookmark it.
We add new titles each month!

www.ingramcontent.com/pod-product-compliance
Lightning Source LLC
Chambersburg PA
CBHW061027120726
47910CB00006B/2135